THE HITLER ERROR

Another title by the author:

The August Strangers

THE HITLER ERROR

A Novel

Mike Slosberg

For Hal —
Thanks for all the kind
words ... and the parking
Meter !!
Cheers
Mike

VANTAGE PRESS
New York

Cover design by VogtGoldstein

FIRST EDITION

Published by Vantage Press, Inc.
419 Park Ave. South, New York, NY 10016

Manufactured in the United States of America
ISBN: 0-533-15118-X

Library of Congress Catalog Card No.: 2004099923

0 9 8 7 6 5 4 3 2 1

For Janet

"Certainly there is no hunting like the hunting of man."
—Ernest Hemingway

ACKNOWLEDGMENTS

Once again, I must thank Richard Marek for beating a manuscript of mine into a readable novel. Grateful thanks to Google, for their blessed on-line gift to all writers. Thanks, too, to Arleen Shaw, a gem of a Gemologist who taught me about diamonds; Tony Schenk for information about carrier pigeons; Timothy Benford, author of *The Ultimate WWII Quiz Book, Vol. 1*, and Stephen R. Datz, author of *The 2001 Catalogue of Errors on U.S. Postage Stamps*.

THE HITLER ERROR

PROLOGUE

Berlin, 1944.

A wounded city bleeds rubble and takes a long time to die.

In the misty half-light of dawn two dusty military vehicles weave cautiously over and around the ruinous aftermath of another night's bombing.

SS Obersturmbannfuhrer Josef Hauptmann's large frame fills the passenger seat of the lead car and he hunkers down against the early morning cold, cocooned within the folds of his greatcoat, pulling hard on a Russian cigarette.

Hauptmann, recently withdrawn from fighting on the Western Front, still wears the effects of combat etched on his face and in his hooded eyes.

A well-worn dispatch case rests on the floorboard next to his feet. Every few minutes he reaches out with his boot to touch it, like a nervous man on a crowded streetcar checking to be sure his wallet hasn't been lifted.

1

Hauptmann snuffs out his cigarette between a calloused thumb and forefinger; places the butt behind his ear, wipes his hands across his coat, reaches down to unlatch the leather case and withdraws an envelope, one of many. He lets it rest on his broad palm, examining the graceful calligraphy of the address. The script is a personal touch, which Hauptmann feels is effeminate and at odds with the letter's serious content. The signature alone has the power to give the letter its authority.

He turns the envelope over and runs a thick finger across the hardened wax seal. It's deeply impressed with the official emblem of the Reichstag, a clear iconographic warning: *None save the addressee should dare to break it.*

The letter is short, a single page, and Hauptmann knows every word by heart.

He sighs deeply, almost reverently, then replaces the envelope with the others and secures the case, retrieves the cigarette from behind his ear and lights it.

There are twenty-four such letters, each addressed to a different Concentration Camp Commandant. Other than the address and salutation, their content is identical.

The letters direct each recipient to turn over to *SS Obersturmbannfuhrer* Hauptmann all the diamonds confiscated from arriving prisoners.

And to do so by order of Hermann Goering.

*   *   *

It takes Hauptmann three weeks to present the two-dozen letters.

The camp commandants ask no questions nor do they have any reason to object. Hauptmann's credentials are in order, the letters, signature and seals are recognizably authentic.

The order, written over the signature of Hermann

Goering, Commander & Chief of the Nazi Luftwaffe, is beyond question.

After leaving the last camp, Hauptmann has collected a total of 66,000 carats of diamonds, weighing 39 pounds. He carries them in a three-foot-long, cylindrical metal map case. Their value, depending on the appraisal of individual stones, is anywhere from $30 to $50 million dollars.

His mission completed, Hauptmann directs his driver to head back toward Berlin. They ride in a Wehrmacht *Schwimmwagen,* a modification of the 1938 Volkswagen design, which can operate on water as well as land. The second car, carrying two soldiers, is a *Kubelwagen,* another military version of the Volkswagen design, this one shaped a bit like a *kubel,* a tub.

The *Kubelwagen* pulls a large, two-wheeled military trailer loaded with cans of spare petrol, equipment, and rations for the three soldiers. It also holds Hauptmann's BMW motorcycle.

The boot of each vehicle is filled with assorted gear, including several hundred-pound bags of a dry sand and cement mixture.

The metal map case is never out of Haupmann's sight.

On the outskirts of Potsdam, the two-car caravan halts for the evening.

Potsdam, like nearby Berlin, nestles in an intricate network of rivers and canals that criss-cross the Northern German plain, extending from the Baltic Sea to the Danube and Rhine rivers.

The next morning the soldiers locate a farm where they exchange a bottle of Cognac and a portion of their rations for a number of rusted tools, some wooden boards, twenty meters of rope and a broken tractor wheel, items Hauptmann had not bothered to bring from Berlin.

The SS officer consults a detailed military field map of the area, makes a choice, and directs his driver to one of the many lakes in the area. They motor along its perimeter until they come upon a grove of evergreen trees on its north shore, a site Hauptmann feels is suitable to make camp.

While the men organize the campsite, Hauptmann takes the *Schwimmwagen* and, using the field map, locates another lake, larger, about five miles from the campsite. He picks his way along the rutted cart path that traces its perimeter. The area is deserted. Most of the shore is covered with large trees and undergrowth growing right up to the water's edge. It takes some time but he finally locates a suitable space between the trees and launches the *Schwimmwagen* into the water.

He adjusts the levers that engage the propeller at the rear of the amphibian and cruises slowly on the water to a spot in the center of the lake that seems deep enough.

Using powerful binoculars, he carefully scans the shoreline looking for life, but sees no one. Then he ties rope to the steel wheel, which he lowers into the water until he feels it hit the lake bottom. He hauls the wheel back into the amphibian, measuring the rope by his arm-lengths; and calculates the depth to be fifteen meters, approximately fifty feet from the surface.

Referring to the field map, he memorizes the coordinates for his location. He also notes his distance from several trees and rocks on the shore so that he can find the approximate spot when he returns. Those details attended to, he lights a cigarette, surrenders to the bright sun and enjoys the first solitude he's experienced in a long time.

An hour later he's back at the clearing with the others. He explains to the soldiers what he needs, scratching sketches in the dirt with a stick, to help them understand. They construct a wooden box, fifty-inches long by twenty-four inches square, closed at one end, open at the other.

Once the box is completed, the men dig a pit in the earth and use the hole to mix lake water with the bags of cement and sand they've carried from Berlin.

Then, under Hauptmann's supervision, the soldiers shovel the mixture slowly into the box so that the cement surrounds the metal map case.

The men have no idea of what might be inside the tube but there are plenty of rumors, none of which is close to the truth.

Once the map tube is encased in the wet cement, a steel post ring salvaged from Berlin rubble is imbedded halfway into the cement on the open end of the box. With the cement dry, the exposed half-ring will function as a handle someday, when it's safe to haul the cement block to the surface.

It takes almost two days for the cement to set and harden. And for two days the soldiers sleep, eat the food they rustle up in the nearby village, smoke cigarettes and work their way through many bottles of wine, purchased from a tavern in a nearby town.

There is a case of Cognac—a gift from the commandant at Dachau—but other than the bottle used for barter with the farmer, Hauptmann is saving the rest for a farewell party.

When the cement is rock-hard, the men lift the box into the *Schwimmwagen*. Hauptmann leaves the men and drives back to the lake he had visited several days before, enters the water and, using his visual benchmarks, motors out to the approximate spot where he measured the lake's depth.

It takes all his strength to struggle the box into the water. It sinks rapidly out of sight.

Satisfied, he returns to the campsite, distributes the rest of the Cognac and tells his men to build a bonfire.

He drives off for a short time and returns with two chickens. One of the men fashions a spit from green tree branches and cooks them.

Hours later, drunk and under extra blankets to ward off the night's chill, the soldiers fall asleep in the warmth of the campfire.

The surface of the lake is the color of pewter and the cold air smells of pending rain. Hauptmann, wrapped in his greatcoat, hunches by the fading fire and studies the sky. A meteor scribes an arc across the heavens. The taste of the chicken is still in his mouth and, like his sleeping men, he's drunk from Cognac, exhaustion and a sense of accomplishment.

He takes a deep breath, lets out a sigh of resignation, and stands. He removes a five-inch-long metal cylinder from a small pocket sewn to the inside of his right boot top, which he screws onto the barrel of his Luger. The attachment, precision made by Maxims Arms Company, claims to muffle the sound of a Luger to something not much louder than the pop of a soap bubble.

He soon discovers that their claim is greatly exaggerated.

*   *   *

Hauptmann is a powerful man but he still has to struggle to load the three dead soldiers' bodies into the vehicles, two in the *Kubelwagen* and one in the *Schwimmwagen*. He tosses the tools and all the other gear into the two-wheeled trailer.

Using wire from the roll he'd packed in the boot, he secures the soldiers in sitting positions in the car seats. They will eventually be discovered but, given the tens of thousands of war casualties, he's certain that no one will make much of a few more dead bodies.

The *Kubelwagen* and the trailer take almost ten minutes to sink.

The amphibious car, its interior valves opened to the lake water, sinks more quickly. Hauptmann sits on his motorcycle, a blanket wound tightly around his shoulders, smoking a cigarette and watching as the car, with his dead driver securely wired upright behind the steering wheel, disappears beneath the black water.

He clears the campsite of all traces of their presence. Two remaining bottles of Cognac, too valuable to waste, go into the saddlebags on the back of his motorcycle, along with his gear.

It's raining lightly by the time he accelerates away from the campsite and barely dawn when he rides into Berlin. Fires from the night's bombing blaze all over the city.

Now it's time for Hauptmann to put the Jew back to work.

That is, if the poor bastard is still alive.

CHAPTER 1

(Florida. The present)

A SMILING MOE GREEN, LEANING LIGHTLY ON HIS ALUMINUM WALKER, stood in the small local branch of the Grand Western Bank.

He was telling a joke to the manager, a blonde young enough to be his granddaughter. Moe delivered the punch line, which detonated a little explosion of laughter from both of them.

Moe Green was a sprightly looking eighty-six, short, slightly overweight and dressed in his signature outfit: a polyester jump suit, this one a lemon-yellow number, tan Mephisto walking shoes and a New York Yankee's baseball cap worn at a rakish angle. Wisps of white hair flew out from the sides of the cap and covered the back of his neck.

Turning, he pushed his walker toward the front door, glancing up at the wall clock.

Good. I've at least twenty-minutes before the shuttle bus gets here. Enough time for that chat I've been meaning to have.

Moe maneuvered his walker along the sidewalk of the strip-mall.

It was already turning dark but the air remained mid-day hot and sticky. Night insects had plastered themselves to the storefront windows, drawn to the glass by the bright interior lights. Moving slowly, Moe passed by the establishments he'd become familiar with over the years: a laundromat, drugstore, dry-cleaner, coffee shop, the chiropractor with a dusty, larger-than-life plastic spinal column in the window and finally, the stamp and coin store.

Moe paused for a moment to catch his breath, then pushed open the door. The conditioned air felt good. A faint odor of lilac was not unpleasant. An old overhead neon fixture emitted a comfortable hum; Moe watched, fascinated, as a swarm of flying insects attempted to mate with the bulb.

He leaned against the glass top of a display case that did double duty as a counter, and examined the merchandise. There were dozens of stamps, each in its own plastic sleeve, tagged with relevant descriptions and prices. Coins were similarly displayed. He wasn't particularly interested in stamps or coins but he did have a question he wanted answered.

A huge man materialized through a curtain from the rear of the store and seeing Moe, took a step back.

"Hello! You startled me," the fat man said, breathing hard from the simple exertion of walking. "I could have sworn I locked the front door. I was just getting ready to leave. Unless it's urgent, maybe you could stop in sometime next week?"

The man wasn't just heavy he was obese, with thinning red hair pulled back into six inches of ponytail, exposing a florid face screwed into an expression of confusion and surprise. Rimless, bottle-thick glasses exaggerated rheumy, red-rimmed eyes.

"I must have passed this place a million times," Moe said. "Always been meaning to stop in. Never saw anyone in here before." As the man got closer, the scent of lilac became stronger.

"Yes, well, truth be told, I don't get many walk-in customers," the proprietor said. "Most of my business is done by phone and over the Internet. How can I help you?"

"I've got a question about a stamp. I use the bank at the corner," Moe said, flicking his head toward the bank in an attempt to establish some level of bona fides. "The Palm Village shuttle bus drops me and picks me up just outside."

"Right, I've noticed the bus. Why don't you ask me your question?" Moe could see the dealer was anxious to leave.

"The stamp question. Right. Got it in the war. I'm hoping it has some value."

"May I take a look?"

Moe reached into his back pocket and pulled out a well-worn wallet. He rummaged through, methodically littering the counter top with a collection of credit cards, AARP and Medicare insurance cards, Lottery stubs, a bus pass, pictures, and an odd assortment of notes and numbers jotted on miscellaneous scraps of paper.

"*Damn,* I'd sworn I had it with me. Must have left it on my desk at home."

"Okay," the fat man said, trying not to show his impatience. "Maybe you can describe it? Tell me what it looks like?"

"What does it look like?" Moe shrugged. "It looks like a stamp. No, seriously, let's see . . . well, it's *German,* a German stamp." Moe closed his eyes for a moment. "There's a circle in the center. Inside the circle it has the head, a profile, of Hitler—*may he rot in hell.* On one side of the circle it got like a sort of torch and on the other side I think there's a . . ."

"And on the other side there's a sword, right?"

"Yeah, a sword," Moe said, impressed.

"And it's a horizontal shape stamp."

"Right again."

"And under the circle it says, *'Deutsches Reich'* "?

"I think so. You're good at this."

"It's my business. Actually, the stamp you've got is a fairly common commemorative that was minted in the early 1940s to celebrate Hitler's fifty-fourth birthday."

"Really? His birthday? They should have one to celebrate his death day, the bastard."

"You're right. Anyway, there were six versions that were all alike except that each had its own postage price and each was a different color. Do you happen to recall the denomination or color of your stamp?

"It's sort of redish. With some numbers on the top. A twelve and a thirty-eight, I think. I guess that's the price."

"Correct. The numbers indicate the amount of postage in Reichmarks. Was the stamp ever franked? Used for postage? I mean, is it cancelled? You know, with little black lines stamped across it?"

Moe thought for a moment. "I don't think so."

"I see. Well, Mr. . . . ?"

"Green," he said, extending his hand. "Moe Green."

"Well, Mr. Green, glad to meet you. My name is Carl Kunze. If your stamp is in really good condition and not cancelled, you might be able to sell it at retail—like, for example, if you ran an ad in one of the stamp magazines or put it onto the Internet—you'd maybe get about five or ten dollars for it. Since I'd have to eventually sell it at a profit, I couldn't give you much more than half of that, contingent, of course, on being able to actually examine it. I've seen ads for the whole set of six for under thirty dollars."

"That's not very much, is it," Moe said, more as a statement than a question. He had hoped the stamp was valuable, something to leave to his son, Jake or his granddaughter, Adrian. Over time the stamp's worth had grown exponentially in his imagination.

He turned away from the fat man and started his slow shuffle toward the door. "I got that stamp a long time ago," he said wistfully, over his shoulder. "It's always had sentimental value. But I figured it was worth something. Anyway, thanks for the information. I may bring it in for a look-see. Have a nice weekend. Sorry to have kept you."

Kunze lumbered around the counter and with one hand held the door open for Moe so he could navigate through with his walker.

"Thanks again," Moe paused, "There is one other question I have about the stamp, Mr. Katz,"

"*Kunze*. What's that?"

"Yes, Kunze. Sorry. The head inside the circle. Hitler's head. Were all six versions like mine—with his head upside down?"

CHAPTER 2

(Paris. Several days later)

A BUTLER PICKED UP THE PHONE ON THE FIRST RING.

Moments later he approached intricately carved floor-to-ceiling doors, knocked once, and entered. The room was a spacious, sun-filled study; part of a large apartment situated on the Seine's Rive Gauche, and, for a few hours each day, under the shadow of the Musée D'Orsay.

The butler approached his employer. "Pardon me, General. There is a Herr Kessler from Berlin for you on line one."

The General nodded, and waited for the butler to leave.

Not everyone referred to him by his former military rank, but most did; some, without ever making the connection. The sobriquet was fitting for he possessed the requisites of a successful commander. He was brilliant and ruthless.

14

The General was a fit looking seventy-seven-year-old; tall and ramrod straight, well over six feet and tanned to a deep shade of mahogany. His white hair was trimmed to little more than a short bristle. He was casually dressed in a black, long sleeve silk shirt, open at the neck, revealing a knotted paisley scarf; tan doeskin slacks and black Gucci loafers.

Even the puckered scar on the left side of his face—the result of an explosion—seemed fitting, adding a bit more threat, a bit more mystery to his appearance. Even so, he'd had plastic surgery to remove as much of it as possible. What no surgeon could change were his eyes. They looked out at the world, devoid of feeling; frightening. The eyes of a predator. Women, as well as men, were drawn to him, as lemmings are attracted to cliffs.

Alone now, the General walked quickly across the room to a cabinet in the bookcase, which held a small piece of electronic equipment with a cradle and a portable phone receiver. The mechanism was designed to scramble all his calls, not an unreasonable precaution for an active businessman in an age of such advanced technology.

He fingered the appropriate buttons. "Herr Kessler? Good morning. How are you?" the General's English was tinged with a hint of the Teutonic.

"Very well, thank you." Kessler's voice boomed out of the speaker and the General dialed down the volume. "A bit of a cold but you know how damp Berlin can be this time of year," Kessler cleared his throat. "Sorry to bother you this early in the morning but something exciting has come up that I thought you would want to know about."

"And what would that be?"

"You've asked me to keep a sharp eye for any German inverts. One has surfaced."

The General drew a quick breath and after a few moments of silence realized he had neglected to breathe. "I'm sorry," he finally said. "We have a bad connection. Repeat what you just said."

"A German invert may . . . just *may* have come onto the market. I thought I should call."

The General reached for a chair from behind the desk nearby, pulling it close to lean on it, afraid he might faint.

"Tell me about the stamp."

"It's from that Hitler set—you know the horizontal commemorative series they minted for his fifty-fourth birthday. The red 12.38 RM."

"And you say the error is an *invert,* Herr Kessler?"

"Correct. The head of Hitler . . . it's upside down."

The General's heart was pounding so hard he could feel the blood pulsing in his neck and temples. "Interesting," he barely managed. "Tell me, how did such a stamp come to your attention?"

"I had a message from an American I know. Carl Kunze, a dealer from America. Florida. His e-mail referred me to his website where the information, along with a little sketch of the stamp, was posted. I've done business with Kunze before. A reputable man."

"You say there was a drawing on his website? Why a drawing and not a photo of the stamp?"

"I don't know, but I'd be happy to make further inquiries. Would you like me to do that?"

"Please, no. I'll take it from here. If a sale results, you will of course get your commission. You say it was posted on the website belonging to Carl Kunze?"

"Correct.

"Was any price mentioned?"

"No, but at this point I wouldn't expect it. Obviously, Kunze would like to get a sense of how much the market feels it's worth."

"Of course. Now if you'd be kind enough to give me that web address, please." He jotted down the information. "Good. Good. Thank you. I very much appreciate your call."

"The pleasure is mine, *Mein General.*"

The General replaced the receiver and walked slowly to the window where he stood staring down at the river, blotting sweat from his palms, face and forehead with a linen handkerchief.

Was it possible? Could it have actually appeared after more than fifty years? Just the idea, the slightest sliver of a hint that it might actually be true; that the stamp could still exist after this much time was . . . intoxicating.

He considered taking a sedative and dismissed it. He had to remain in full control. Important decisions would have to be made.

How he wished the others were here!

He walked to his computer, booted it, then pulled up the Florida dealer's website. There it was—the posting for the German invert. He read it over, then sat, deep in thought.

Finally, a decision made, he poured a finger of Talisker, downed it, and strode back to the phone and dialed the person known to him only as Joshua.

Joshua was the best of an elite group of skilled professionals who worked almost exclusively for ODESSA, a loose organization quickly thrown together at the end of World War II by a group of SS officers. Its sole purpose at the time was to provide the forged documents and money needed to escape from Germany ahead of the Allied Armies. The rumors of its present existence and far-reaching influence were true.

The General had just been presented with a problem. Joshua made problems go away.

A machine answered. The message was short and spoken in a voice not Joshua's. *"Talk to me"* was all it said.

The General did. Five minutes later Joshua called.

"I must see you. It's important," the General said.

"Very well. When?"

"Tomorrow morning. The boat."

"Impossible. I'm not even on your continent."

"Charter a plane. Dammit!"

For a full thirty seconds the General heard nothing but Joshua's breathing.

Finally, "I can make it, but not until afternoon."

"Excellent. You'll be met and flown out." The General broke the connection.

CHAPTER 3

(The following day)

THE *SIGFRIED IV* ROSE AND FELL AT ANCHOR IN THE MEDITERRANEAN waters off the French coast, about a mile west of Monaco.

The General had arrived on board the night before, slept fitfully, and was up at first light. His morning exercise was particularly strenuous, including an hour spent swimming laps around the boat.

The exertion succeeded in calming him. Now he lay naked in the sun, on the blue cushions of a lounger. A tiny patch of blue terrycloth was draped just below his hard stomach to cover his groin; opaque plastic shields, the size of two teaspoons, protected his eyes.

The *Sigfried IV* was forty meters long with wooden hull, teak bright-work, and solid brass fittings. When the U.S. stock market crashed in 1929 the boat's owners were

19

forced to sell it. The German Navy picked it up; during the war years it was used as a floating hospital, but later fell into disrepair.

In 1990 the General bought the near-wreck for little more than salvage value. He had it towed to a shipyard where a half-dozen craftsmen scooped it out like a melon, down to the bare hull, then meticulously and lovingly restored it. No expense was spared for its interior, its furnishings, its electronics.

The boat's helipad normally hosted a highly efficient Hughes Model 369, lashed down like some captured prehistoric bird. At the moment, however, the copter was in the air.

He heard the rhythmic THWAP-n-THWAP-n-THWAP of the returning craft while it was still a mile off his port side. Soon it swooped in over the boat, pulled its nose up at a sharp angle, hovered in place for a few moments, and then slowly corkscrewed itself onto the landing pad.

As soon as the rotors shut down Joshua emerged, descended the short ladder leading to the main deck and walked aft. "Good afternoon." As always, Joshua spoke to the General in English.

"How was your flight?"

"To be honest, I prefer a larger craft. Something with wings, several engines and a decent movie."

The General's mouth twitched. "That's strange. Whenever I fly her, I feel quite secure."

"That's because you're piloting the damned thing. I'm just the hapless passenger."

Rising, the General removed the protective discs and examined his guest. "You look tired. A little pale, perhaps. Sit and relax. By the way, where were you when we spoke yesterday?"

"Chicago. In the lounge at O'Hare, getting ready to fly to New York. I was able to rearrange my schedule and get onto a Paris flight. It saved you a fortune in charter fees. As for my pallor, I've been indoors a lot lately," Joshua settled into an adjacent lounger. "Business has been unusually busy."

"Yes, well I'm about to add to your workload. A light lunch is coming, then I'll tell you about it."

"Good. I'm famished."

A waiter arrived with an assortment of finger sand-wiches, a bowl of fresh melon and tall glasses of iced tea.

"Something important has come up," the General said when the waiter left.

"How I can help?" Joshua asked, reaching for one of the sandwiches.

The General considered Joshua to be one of those nec-essary evils in life and was reluctant to place his fate into an assassin's hands. But there was little choice. He had wondered how much to say. In the end he decided the most expedient thing to do would be to stick closely to the facts and trust Joshua to deliver.

"I need you to retrieve something for me."

"And that would be?"

"A stamp."

Joshua's brow creased, head tilted slightly to the side. "A stamp? What kind of stamp?"

"A postage stamp. A common, sixty-year-old German postage stamp."

Joshua snorted. "And its significance would be what?"

"The stamp itself is irrelevant. However, the informa-tion printed on it is of great value."

Joshua leaned forward. "Go on."

"Near the end of the war, it was 1945, a friend, actually my partner, was to deliver a stamp to me in Berlin. The night before our meeting, he was killed. Blown up when a bomb destroyed the building where he was staying."

"And the stamp along with him?"

"That's what I thought. Until now."

"So it survived?"

"Possibly. Yesterday I learned that one just like it had suddenly surfaced."

"*Jesus!* It's been, what . . . almost sixty years? You said it was a common stamp. How could you possibly know it's the one you're looking for?"

"I'll tell you how. The stamp he was bringing was a counterfeit. The information, visible only with magnification, had been carefully incorporated into the new engraving. It was a perfect duplication of the real stamp, which featured the head of Adolf Hitler."

"I still don't see how. . . ."

"The head of Hitler on our version . . . is upside down."

"Amazing," Joshua said, clearly impressed. "How did you learn it had suddenly appeared?"

"For years I've had a dealer alerted to my interest in such a stamp. Its uniqueness all but guaranteed that it would attract his attention. He called after seeing a posting made by an American dealer on the Internet."

"Obviously he doesn't know it's a fake."

"Of course not. He has no reason to think it's anything but a potentially valuable collectible. A unique specimen that philatelists call, an error."

"And you want me to get it for you."

"Correct."

"Why can't you just pick up the phone, call whoever advertised it and buy the damned thing?"

The General walked to the railing, tearing off pieces of sandwich bread and throwing them onto the water. This was the tricky part, he thought. He needed Joshua to believe that the stamp had no value without his input.

"I can't do that, you see. If I offer to buy the stamp, the seller will begin to shop it around. No matter what I offer, my bid will simply become the floor price."

"But you could outbid anyone. It can't be that expensive."

The General shook his head. "That's not the point.

More interest in the stamp means more people examining it. Look, Joshua, I won't lie to you. I need to get that stamp before too many people have the opportunity to study it closely. The information on it is worth a great deal, enough to raise questions."

Joshua's eyes narrowed. "You don't mean questions about ODESSA, do you?"

The General took a moment to digest the question. *Why not let Joshua believe the information concerns ODESSA? It might improve the odds against Joshua running off with the stamp.*

"Yes. It could jeopardize ODESSA. And I'd hate to see you loose such a lucrative source of income. Don't you agree?"

"Excellent point. But hasn't whoever posted the stamp on the Internet already examined it?"

"Apparently not closely enough. If they had, it might never have been advertised."

Joshua joined the General at the railing, "Let me see if I understand. You want me to get the stamp quickly, before more people can scrutinize it. And we must operate under the assumption that anyone who's already seen it, or sees it before I can lay my hands on it, has discovered what's on the stamp and therefore, has to be . . ."

"That's what I like most about you. You get right to the heart of a situation."

"What if it's a coincidence?" Joshua asked. "The right stamp, but not *your* stamp?"

"Not possible. It's the same issue that we had counterfeited—the right value and color. The head of Hitler is upside down. One copy was printed and the plate was destroyed. The odds that it's not my stamp are impossible to calculate."

"Why put the information on a stamp, in the first place?"

"Security. The war was ending and my friend and I

were preparing to get out of Germany. The American and Russians were advancing. There was a chance we would be caught, put into prison. If that happened and we were searched, a stamp was innocuous enough not to be confiscated. When the stamp was destroyed, along with my friend, it was a monumental loss."

"I'd say you've done well for yourself—even without the stamp—don't you agree?"

"Looks can be deceiving," the General snapped. "I need the stamp. That's all you have to know."

Joshua smiled. "As I see it, there's only one possible explanation for . . . how can I put it . . . this miraculous resurrection?"

"Which is?"

"Occam's razor."

"The simplest answer."

"Exactly. If you're correct and the stamp was blown up along with your partner, then there had to be a second copy, lying dormant ever since. God only knows where."

The General went back to the table; Joshua followed. "Yes, I've considered that. You're right. It's the only explanation that makes sense."

"Why would your friend have made another copy?"

"I don't know and, frankly, I don't care. What really puzzles me is why the stamp suddenly surfaced, now . . . all these years later?"

"Does it really make any difference?"

The General pondered for a moment. "No, you're right—it doesn't."

Joshua sipped some tea. "As I mentioned before, I'm under a staggering workload. . . ."

"Entirely your problem."

". . . however, I believe I can rearrange my calendar. It won't be easy."

"You *believe* or you will? I must know now."

Joshua only hesitated for a moment. "I will make time."

"Good."

The General told Joshua about the Internet posting. "You'll see, the notice on Kunze's website will tell you enough to get started. I want that stamp. And I want it quickly. Do whatever's necessary but when you're finished, I don't want anyone left behind who can cause problems. Is that clear?"

"Yes, very," Joshua said. "But first, a necessary question."

The General grimaced. "Don't worry . . . you'll be well paid."

"I'm sure . . . but let's talk specifics."

"By the time you get back to shore, $75,000 will have been wired to your account. That money is yours, regardless. Think of it as an advance on expenses. Once you bring me the stamp, and it has the information I want, I will give you . . . an additional $2 million."

The size of the fee begged two questions, which Joshua pondered as the helicopter rose above the *Sigfried IV*: Why was it so generous? And could he be trusted?

CHAPTER 4

(New York City. Two weeks later)

JAKE GREEN, NAKED AND FILTHY, STOOD ON BLEEDING FEET IN THE center of a tiny concrete room in the middle of the jungle. His arms extended out from his sides. A fragment grenade was taped into each hand.

Just another Jew on a cross.

Taut wires from the ceiling were affixed to the detonation pins so when either arm dropped the grenade would explode.

Jake faced a window-size opening in the concrete wall. He could hear his captors laughing and babbling in Vietnamese on the far side of the wall.

Sweat poured down Jake's body and his arms were shaking from the pain. He knew it was only seconds before his arms would fall. He knew he was going to die and had stopped caring. His bloody bits would feed the jungle.

When he blew up, they would be protected.

At that moment he decided: Fuck it! I'll take the bastards with me.

He took a breath and yanked down with both arms. The grenade pins danced free on the ends of the wires. He hobbled on broken feet to the window, poked both arms into the opening and waited for the blast that would kill them all.

Nothing happened.

The soldiers dragged him back to the center of the room and beat him. Their laughter was deafening.

Jake came out of his nightmare as he always did: fast, gulping for air and fighting that split second of panic before the realization that he wasn't still in Vietnam.

Early morning light bled around the edges of the window blinds throwing a dull yellow glow across the darkened room. Jake swung his legs over the side of the bed and sat on the edge, head down, waiting for his pulse to stop racing.

He glanced back at the soft mound under the covers. A pillow partially hid a woman's long blonde hair; poking out from under the linen, five red toenails punctuated the end of a graceful foot.

In the fourteen years since his wife's death, Jake hadn't suffered from lack of female companionship. He was, as the personals would put it: *Straight, healthy, successful.* An eligible bachelor whose friends never stopped trying to marry off. So he'd had his pick.

But it amazed Jake that, even after all the years, he still felt moments of guilt when he was with a woman. As if he were being unfaithful to his dead wife. It started on Jake's first official anniversary as a widower. The woman had been nice enough. The newly divorced best friend of a friend. They both soldiered through a nightmarish dinner and never saw each other again.

Jake learned to live with the guilt feelings, eventually looking on them as Norma's wise council, delivered from

The Other Side. A loving admonition that whispered in his head, *"Don't be a schmuck, darling. This one's not good enough for you. Keep looking."*

Jake shuffled quietly into the bathroom, considerate enough to close the door before flipping on the lights.

The sudden illumination triggered a slight throb in his temples. Bloodshot eyes stared back at him from the mirror over the sink. Jake cursed the second bottle of Shiraz he'd ordered at dinner and swallowed three Advil with a full glass of tap water.

A hot shower coaxed him closer to the land of the living and a brisk towel-down got his blood circulating.

Jake Green was a youthful forty-nine. Several work-outs a week kept him reasonably fit. His hair, worn moderately long, was a rich shade of brown, gone gray at the sides. He stood just shy of six-foot tall.

His looks, though pleasant enough, wouldn't have drawn much attention, but for his nose, which had been once broken and never fixed. It lent him a kind of ruggedness that attracted women and sent men the erroneous signal that he'd been a fighter and just might be dangerous.

This particular morning, the woman under Jake's duvet was Helen Faye. He'd met her more than a dozen years before when she was an oncology resident at the hospital where Norma Green was being treated. She'd been attentive and caring to the dying woman, especially during the difficult final days of Norma's fight with cancer. A godsend at a time when Jake needed one.

After Norma's funeral, Jake lost touch with the young doctor. Years later, she called him. She was moving to a larger office, remembered Jake and hired his firm to design and supervise the build-out of her new Central Park South office space.

From that innocent beginning, a friendship developed, which on occasion led to the bedroom. But as comfortable as the arrangement was, both agreed that what they had didn't add up to anything strong enough for marriage.

At first Jake didn't hear the phone through the thick bathroom door. When he finally did, he rushed to answer, hoping it hadn't woken Helen.

It had. Helen was sprawled across his side of the bed, looking sleep-tousled and clutching the receiver. "For you," she murmured sleepily.

He sat, kissed her lightly and took the phone. "Hello."

"Sorry to be calling so early," a man's voice said. "Is this Mister Jack Green?"

The voice had a bureaucratic ring. Jake was instantly alert. His first concern was for Adrian, his grown daughter who lived in London. "Yes. Is something wrong?"

"Sir, this is Detective Sam Stein of the Palm Beach Police Department. Is Morris Green . . ."

Oh Christ! Moe is dead!

". . . of Palm Village, apartment 244 in West Palm Beach, Florida your father?"

"Yes . . . Is he?"

"Mister Green, I'm sorry to inform you that your father passed away."

Jake's body sagged beneath the news. *"Shit!"* he whispered, uttering the word reflexively, in a tone that made the curse into a prayer.

Jake sipped water from a glass on his nightstand. He was aware of Helen's hand on his back. "When? What happened?" he said into the phone.

"A heart attack. The housekeeper found him late yesterday afternoon when she came to work. I'm sorry it's taken us so long to track you down. Will you be coming here soon? It would be helpful if you could, if only to identify the body."

"Yes, of course."

"Good. Do you have any idea of when you might be arriving?"

The question was infuriating! How could he be expected to know that now? "Look, I'll take the first flight I can get on. What was your name again?"

The detective either didn't hear or didn't care about Jake's angry reaction. "Detective Stein. I'd appreciate if you'd call me when you get in. To go over some of the details of the case." The Detective gave Jake his cell number, said goodbye and broke the connection.

"What is it, Jake? You okay?" Helen asked, her hand continuing to stroke Jake's back.

He turned toward her. "My . . . father," was all he could manage.

It took a few moments for the full impact of the call to hit. Jake sat in a tangle of bedclothes, clutching the mute receiver, encircled by Helen's arms, sobbing.

Some time later, clad in his pajama bottoms, Jake padded into the kitchen. Helen had made a pot of coffee before she left for her rounds at the hospital and Jake sat, hands around a steaming mug, trying to come to grips with the inevitable.

It wasn't as if his father's death had been a complete surprise. After all, eighty-six years wasn't exactly the prime of life. On the other hand, Moe Green had been in reasonably good shape, except for a few instances of disorientation and, more recently the need for walker. He had been looking forward to reaching a hundred, what he called, *My Willard Scott Moment.*

He wished Adrian could be with him. He picked up the phone, auto-dialed his daughter's number and was confronted with the sound of a busy signal.

Jake finished his coffee, found the folder of information he'd put together a dozen years before when his mother died; called the funeral home he'd used in Florida, alerted them to the situation, gave the necessary details and arranged to come in when he arrived.

His mother had also died in Florida. Her body had been

flown to New York for the funeral. There had been flowers, a rabbi, a memorial service and a week of sitting *shivah,* the traditional mourning period.

That was twelve years ago. In the interim, the small circle of his parents' friends and the few remaining relatives had died off, so there was no reason for traditional funeral embellishments. He would have Moe cremated in Florida, then bring the ashes back to New York to be buried.

Jake booked the first available flight to West Palm Beach. The detective said he needed to identify the body and he wanted to see his father one last time before the cremation. He'd have to clear out Moe's apartment. The old man was a packrat. There would be a ton of stuff to be thrown away.

These thoughts were on Jake's mind several hours later as he sat waiting for the car service that would take him to the airport. He tried once again to reach Adrian but hung up when he got the answering machine. A grandfather's death was not the kind of message a twenty-seven-year-old should hear on a recording. He would just have to keep trying.

Something the detective had said kept gnawing at Jake. He dug out the number and called.

"Stein here."

"Detective Stein, this is Jake Green. You called me earlier . . ."

"Right."

"You said you wanted to go over the details of the case with me."

"Right."

"You used the word case. Since when is an eighty-six-year-old man dying of a heart attack considered a case?"

There was pause. From the ambient sounds Jake concluded the detective was seated at the counter of a coffee shop.

"There's something more going on here, isn't there?"

"Honestly, Mister Green, I think this would be best discussed in person."

Jake was surprised by his own anger. "No. Let's talk about it now. He's my father and I have the right to know what the hell's going on."

The Detective sighed. "I know this is hard, Mister Green, but I gotta ask you to wait until we can speak in person. Call me when you land."

"Why can't you tell me now?" Jake shouted before he realized the connection had been broken.

CHAPTER 5

IT WAS LATE AFTERNOON BY THE TIME JAKE'S PLANE TOUCHED DOWN AT the West Palm Beach Airport.

He phoned Stein immediately and arranged to meet him at Palm Village the following morning.

Then he picked up a rental car and drove to his hotel, The Boca Raton Resort. It was where he always stayed when he visited his father. He unpacked, showered and dozed off for an hour. Later that evening Jake went down to The Monkey Bar for a much needed drink.

The bar, so named for the original owner's passion for pet monkeys, was a five-stool, six-table space tucked into the far end of the hotel's lobby. Jake had always loved the quiet atmosphere of the place and so had his father.

Moe Green's appreciation of good food seemed to grow in proportion to his age and Jake would search out restaurants for them to try. Invariably, Moe would want to preface dinner with a martini at the Monkey Bar.

Jake thought about those evenings as he rode the elevator down to the lobby. He wished there had been more of them.

He hoped Harry would be there. Jake had gotten into the habit of having long talks with the bartender, and this evening he was especially in need of unloading.

He slid onto one of the padded stools. The trauma of the last few days had caught up with him; he felt drained.

Harry wasn't there. His replacement was a young woman he'd not seen before.

"Good evening, Sir. What'll it be?"

"Where's Harry?"

"Vacation. I'm filling in until he gets back. It's my first night."

"Two Stoli Martinis. Straight up with a twist."

Minutes later she poured both drinks. "Do you want me to keep this one iced 'til your guest gets here?"

"Trust me, you don't have enough ice."

"I don't understand."

"One's for my father. He passed away a few days ago."

"Wow. Now I'm really confused."

"I used to bring him here. We'd have a Martini before dinner. This is where he'd sit," Jake said, patting the stool to his right. "He always loved coming here."

Jake reached over and touched his glass to the one designated for his father, then took a generous sip of his drink. It was hard to believe that only a month before he'd been on the same spot. Only then his father was holding the glass, alive and well and happy. Moe was always happy when he was with Jake.

"That's a nice memory. Sounds like you two had a lot going. How about I buy you both these drinks? On the house."

"I'd appreciate that," he said, smiling. "I'm Jake Green."

"Pleased to meet you Mr. Green. Name's Toby. Toby Benjamin." She extended her hand.

It was cool and dry. Jake focused on her for the first time. Toby Benjamin had incredibly white teeth framed by full, red lips. Deep auburn hair was pulled back tightly, in a long ponytail. She had a square, athletic jaw and large, wide-set green eyes. And even in her shapeless bartender's black jacket and slacks, Jake could see she was slim and shapely.

He released her hand but she held on for a fraction longer. Her eyes never left his.

The place wasn't having a busy night. Jake, anxious to avoid thinking about tomorrow, gladly escaped into conversation with Toby. She spoke with, what sounded to Jake, like a slight English accent and he enjoyed listening to her.

He decided he didn't have the energy or desire to leave the hotel for dinner, and instead, ordered a cheeseburger from the bar menu, along with another martini.

It was midnight when he asked for his bill. He thanked Toby again, signed the tab and penned in a more than generous tip.

Then Jake stood unsteadily, saluted the empty bar stool, and staggered toward the elevators.

CHAPTER 6

JAKE SPOTTED SAM STEIN AS SOON AS HE
ENTERED THE PALM VILLAGE reception area. Beside a
few employees, the detective was the only person standing
without the help of a cane or walker. Jake figured Stein to
be in his late forties, short and stocky, with a dour expression, which seemed to be permanently plastered under a
shaved head.

"Okay, I'm here," Jake said, a bit louder than he intended, as he approached Stein. "Now tell me what happened to my father?"

Stein didn't answer immediately, just took Jake's arm
and steered him toward the section of the building where
Moe's apartment was located.

"As I told you," Stein began, "the housekeeper found
him three days ago."

36

"That would be Lilly Missirian. She's been coming in once a week for years."

"She saw your father when she opened the front door to the apartment. He was in the living room, sitting in his chair. She thought he was asleep." Stein shed his jacket and slung it over his shoulder. They passed a knot of old people who went wide-eyed, as they spotted the detective's holstered weapon. "Before the woman got beyond the front door, she fainted. When she came to she ran screaming to the front desk."

Jake fished for his keys, unlocked the apartment door but before swinging it open, paused.

"If Lilly thought my father was asleep, why would she pass out?"

The detective placed his palm on the door. "I think you'll understand when you see the apartment. Brace yourself, Mister Green. It isn't pretty."

CHAPTER 7

JAKE STOOD FROZEN ON THE THRESHOLD. Everything within his field of vision looked as if it had been ground up in a giant blender.

The living room furniture was overturned and the upholstery ripped open. A grotesque, black swastika was sloppily sprayed across one wall. Fingers of excess paint had run and pooled onto the carpet. Scrawled across a large smashed mirror were the words Jew Pig! Smaller swastikas appeared on overturned chairs, on the open refrigerator door and on the smashed floral print that had hung over the sofa.

It was a full minute before Jake was able to move. Then he walked, slowly, unsteadily, through the rest of the wrecked apartment. Drawers had been pulled out and emptied, mattress and clothing shredded, pillows sliced open, pictures yanked from their frames, ice dumped out of the freezer trays.

Each room was in the same desecrated state. Jake's reaction whipsawed from blinding rage to gagging nausea. The thought of what his father must have endured was unbearable.

When he'd been through every room, he picked his way back over the mess, headed toward the front door. "I need some air," he said, without looking back at Stein.

*   *   *

Fifteen minutes later Jake sat across from the detective in a local delicatessen.

It was mid-morning, several hours before the lunch rush, so they had the place to themselves.

"Can you explain what I just saw?" Jake fidgeted nervously with his coffee spoon and fought the urge to buy a pack of cigarettes.

The detective shrugged his frustration. "All I know is, I took the call when it came in from Palm Village. When I got there I found it just as you saw it. All the same, except that your father was still in his chair. As soon as I took one look at the mess, I called it in as a homicide."

"You said he died of a heart attack, why a homicide?"

"The Felony Murder Statute. It says that any death that occurs during the commission of a crime is a homicide. Even before I knew the cause of death, it was clear there had been a crime, and the situation was going to fit that statute."

"Do you have any idea what happened?"

"What happened?" Stein paused, sipped coffee, taking time to organize an answer. "Here's what I know: According to the Medical Examiner, your father died of a myocardial infarction, a massive heart attack. Based on the temperature of the body, the ME calculated he'd been dead for about 8-hours."

Jake winced at hearing his father referred to as *the*

body and hesitated before asking the next question. It pained him to think about the possible answer. "Was my father . . . you know, had he been hurt . . . in any way?"

"No." Stein shook his head. "He looked peaceful. I doubt he was touched at all. Hadn't been tied up or gagged, nothing like that. The coroner's examination didn't reveal any signs of fresh bruises or cuts. Just a few older black and blue marks. Maybe from a fall. It's common with older folks."

"Yes, he'd told me about falling."

"Best guess is that he just passed away sitting in his chair. His heart simply gave out. I like to believe the rest of it happened afterwards."

"About him looking peaceful. That's a comforting thought. Thanks."

The two men sat in silence.

"What about robbery?" Jake finally asked. "Maybe all that vandalism was just smoke to cover one up? In all that mess I couldn't tell what was or wasn't still there. I'd have to examine the apartment more carefully."

"No way a robbery." Stein shook his head. "We've got plenty of experience in that area. Lots of rich retired people down here and they get ripped off on a regular basis."

"So, the crooks go where the money is. Like Willy Sutton?"

Jake saw Stein smile for the first time. "You got it. No self-respecting thief would have left so much good stuff lying around. Two televisions, a VCR and a wallet with cash and a few credit cards, not to mention a nice Rolex, still on your dad's wrist."

"Are his things in the apartment?"

"Impounded. Soon as you make the I.D. you'll get his effects." The detective motioned to the waitress for more coffee. "Was there any life insurance?"

"He didn't believe in it."

"Enemies?"

"Maybe the old guy he used to always beat playing pool. He'd take him for at least a dollar a week."

"I assume he was Jewish. Did he belong to a temple or synagogue?"

"My father was an orthodox agnostic."

Stein sugared his coffee.

"So, detective, what's your best guess?"

Stein pulled a napkin out of its holder. "Sorry, allergies." He blew his nose. "Probably some whacked-out skin-heads on a rampage. Although I admit it doesn't make much sense."

"It doesn't," Jake agreed. "In that whole complex only one apartment broken into. And how could some weirdo skinheads walk into a place like Palm Village and not cause a small riot? And why my father?"

"Truth is, we don't dwell much on why this stuff happens. Motives are for prosecutors to worry about. All we can do is deal with what, not why, and hope that the crazy bastards who pull crap like this are dumber than we are. That's the cop's edge. Most of the time we catch the bad guys because, eventually, they make stupid mistakes."

"So you think it was just a run-of-the-mill hate crime?"

The detective glared at him. "Mister Green, all crimes are based on some kind of hate. I hate my boss. I hate my spouse. Hate being poor. Hate your color, nationality, religion. Hate your guts, hate you making eye contact. Hate you cutting me off at the intersection. You get the idea?"

"Indeed," Jake said. He was quiet for a moment, then asked the detective, "Listen, when can I, you know, see my father?"

"If you're up to it, we can go to the coroner's right now. Once you make the identification I can release your father's effects. You'll see, it won't be so bad. Only takes a second. It's all done by television now."

His father's words came back to him: *Always do the things you fear the most.*

Jake pushed himself up from the table, took the check and headed for the cashier.

"Okay, let's get it over with."

CHAPTER 8

JAKE TAILED SAM STEIN'S CAR TO THE CORONER'S OFFICE AND identified his father's body, which looked at peace, a good way to remember him.

After the viewing, Stein handed Jake a small plastic bag containing his father's effects. Jake thanked the detective who promised to call if there were any new developments on the case.

"Nothing will develop, will it?" Jake said.

Stein's eyes locked on Jake's. "Look, Mr. Green, I won't shit you. This kind of case, you know, not a real homicide, not a theft, it don't have a lot going for it. Put it this way, it's not at the top of our To Do list. We're understaffed like you wouldn't believe. Will it get our utmost attention? I wish I could promise that. I can assure you the file will stay open. We can hope the assholes who did it get sloppy, maybe get picked up doing something else. It could happen."

Jake knew there was no use in arguing. He shook the detective's hand, left and drove to the funeral home, signed the necessary papers to authorize the cremation, and headed back to Palm Village. Now that the initial shock was over, he felt his second visit to the apartment could be more objective.

*   *   *

When he opened the front door Jake was, as always, hit with the apartment's familiar smell, a mix of medicine, tropical mildew, and boiled chicken.

In the past the smell had always bothered him. Now it triggered bittersweet memories and it took him a few minutes to get his emotions under control.

At one point his foot trod on a smashed picture frame, beside it a photograph of his daughter, Adrian. Jake picked it up and brushed away the glass shards. It was a picture Jake had snapped at Adrian's college graduation; the expression he'd captured shouted his daughter's happiness and optimism. Jake wondered, as he had so many times over the years, if Adrian would have turned out much differently had her mother not been felled by cancer.

Well, I didn't do a half-bad job raising her, Jake thought.

The kitchen phone was still working and Jake dug into his wallet for Adrian's number and punched in the fifteen digits necessary for the London call.

He let the phone ring for some time and was about to break the connection when a breathless voice answered. "Hello! Don't hang up! Sorry . . . was just running in."

"It's me. I've been trying to reach you since yesterday," Jake said.

"In . . . Paris," Adrian panted, trying to catch her breath. "Daddy, what's wrong?"

"It's . . . grandpa." Jake had trouble getting the words out.

A long pause then in a shaky voice, "What happened?"

"His heart. It was over in an instant. He didn't suffer."

Adrian choked back tears. "Let me call you back. I need a few minutes to let this sink in. Okay?"

"Sure. I'm in Florida, at the apartment. I'll be here for a while, then I'll be back at the hotel." He gave her the number for the Boca Resort.

The call reminded Jake of the nightmare of breaking the news to Adrian when Norma died. She was only seven at the time and couldn't fully comprehend the concept of death. She cried of course, and Jake consoled her. Finally Adrian had looked up at him and, in the most serious, tearful, lip-quivering way, asked, "But who's going to make dinner?" Jake could do little more than hug her tightly and laugh until he, too was weeping.

Adrian called back in an hour. Jake related the story, every detail, from detective Stein's first call, to the present.

They agreed on the funeral arrangements.

By the time Jake hung up, he was in no mood to begin cleaning out his father's apartment.

*   *   *

Back at the hotel, he fell across the bed, fully clothed, and gave in to the emotional exhaustion. Later he showered, dressed and decided to go out for dinner.

The lobby was mobbed with a large wedding party, all wanting their cars.

The frazzled valet attendants were doing their best but it was clear that Jake wasn't going anywhere for quite a while.

Rather than stand around, he headed for the Monkey Bar.

"Evening, Mr. Green," Toby said. "That's a Stoli martini, straight up with a twist, right?"

"I barely remember where I was last night," he joked, "and you've got my name and my drink down pat. That's quite a gift."

"Remembering customers and what they drink is what we bartenders do best. Besides, I wasn't drinking last night, *you* were."

Jake smiled. "I certainly was."

"Will it be just the one martini tonight or do we want one for your dad, too?"

"Just the one should do it."

Jake ended up spending the rest of the evening at the bar. He had a steak for dinner and talked with Toby, filling the long pauses between customers. He told her a little about the strange and disturbing events surrounding his father's death. Toby was an excellent listener.

"Tomorrow you start cleaning out his place?" Toby asked.

"Yeah."

"Could you use some help? I take pride in my ability to throw things out."

"No, really. It's nice of you to offer."

"Think about it. Believe me, the extra money would come in handy."

Jake considered. "Okay. When can you start?"

"I can do noon to six tomorrow. Fifty bucks. And I'll work hard."

*   *   *

Moe's body was cremated early the next day, and Jake, wishing he wasn't alone, went to the funeral home and collected the ashes. It was a strange sensation having the urn containing his father sitting next to him on the passenger seat. He would take the ashes back to New York and, when

Adrian returned to America, they would bury Moe's remains in the family plot next to his wife.

At Palm Village Jake left Toby's name with the receptionist so she wouldn't have trouble getting in, and went to Moe's apartment prepared to work. He righted the overturned coffee table in the living room and placed Moe's ashes on its top, then sat in the middle of the living room on what was left of Moe's sliced-open recliner and looked at the metal urn.

"*What the hell happened, Pop?*" he said aloud then settled into the task of sifting through and cleaning out the contents of the apartment.

He started in the kitchen, then continued with the rest of the rooms, working them one at a time. Given that the place had been pulled to pieces, it was a difficult, slow and depressing job.

At ten minutes before noon Toby arrived at the front door.

"Reporting for duty. With lunch," she said, smiling, her arms wrapped around a grocery bag. A Boca Resort baseball cap protected her auburn hair; her ponytail poked out from the opening in its back. A GAP tee and baggy shorts showed off her excellent figure nicely, without flaunting it. Pink flip-flops rounded out the look.

"Hardly recognized you without your bar."

Toby walked in and stopped. Her smile morphed into shock as she surveyed the room. "Oh, my God, Jake, this is incredible. You told me but I never imagined . . ."

It took a few minutes for Toby to digest the scene and get down to work. They filled bags and boxes with clothing, dishes, pots, pans; all the usable things—which he planned on giving, along with the furniture and small appliances, to Lilly Missirian, the housekeeper, or to Good Will. Everything else went into large, heavy-duty trash bags, which Jake hauled down to the dumpster behind the building.

He would keep the personal stuff—photographs, letters, and his father's few pieces of jewelry.

After two hours, Toby retrieved the bag she'd brought with her and they sat on the floor for lunch, which she'd spread out on the coffee table. The Chablis, refrigerated when she arrived, was crisp and cold. A small wheel of Brie was correctly ripe, as were the tomatoes. Hard-boiled eggs, chicken salad, and a two-foot long baguette of French bread rounded out the meal. Jake was hungry.

"Great catering," he said, biting into a hard-boiled egg. "Of course I insist on reimbursing you."

"I figured you would. The receipts are on the counter."

They ate in silence for some time.

"Who's that in the picture over there?" Toby asked, pointing to a photo near her, ripped out of its silver frame.

"Me. I must have been about thirteen or fourteen."

Toby held it up and glanced back and forth between it and Jake. "I'd never have guessed."

Jake laughed. "My mother called it, Jake BBN."

Toby looked puzzled. "Okay, I give up."

" 'Before Broken Nose.' It's a stupid story."

"I like your nose. Tell me the stupid story. Please."

It took a few moments for Jake to organize his montage of old memories.

"When I started high school I looked like what kids today would call a nerd. Skinny. Thick glasses. And to make things worse, good grades."

"So you had to put up with lots of crap from your classmates."

"Actually, putting up with crap would have been a blessing. It was worse. They just ignored me. I felt invisible. One day, about a month into the term, everything changed. I got on the wrong side of a swinging door just as some guy came crashing out of the lunchroom."

"And broke your nose?"

"Did a good job, too. My face was a rainbow for weeks.

Of course my folks were upset. My mom begged me to have it straightened but I pleaded terror at the thought of an operation."

"Don't blame you."

"Truthfully, the surgery didn't have a damn thing to do with it."

"Wait. Don't tell me." Toby leaned back on her elbows. "You liked the way it made you look."

"You got it. I looked in the mirror and the nerd was gone. No way I wanted to change that. My dad understood and calmed down my mom. He even sprang for contact lenses."

"Overnight you went from nerd to stud."

"Damned near. I started working out, put on some weight. Kids in school began to react differently. Guys started saying hello."

"And girls?"

"Sophomore year I earned a letter for track and dated one of the cheerleaders. And, I'll have you know, she wasn't the only one who thought I looked like Marlon Brando."

"I'll bet your grades went all to hell."

"You'd lose. I was accepted by Yale."

"So, with a smack in the face, Jake Green was given a hard, outer shell that covered a sensitive intellectual core. An interesting combination."

"I guess, in a manner of speaking."

"I'll admit, with that boxer's nose you certainly look tough. Are you?"

Jake pondered Toby's question. "I don't know. I went to Vietnam and fought in a war. But I've never been in an actual fist fight."

Toby took the last of her wine in one long sip, stood and stretched. "Okay, Mr. Brando, let's get this show back on the road."

"Please, call me Marlon."

* * *

The more cleaning they did the more it became obvious to Jake that the place hadn't been pulled apart randomly, but for some reason. But why would anyone trashing the apartment be so compulsive in the way they went about it? Why would the destruction—seemingly arbitrary—actually be so methodical?

Clearly, someone had been searching the place. But for what? As far as Jake could tell, nothing seemed to be missing.

Nothing that he could see.

And why the hate graffiti?

CHAPTER 9

THE NEXT MORNING JAKE WAS BACK AT THE
APARTMENT BY NINE. TOBY joined him an hour later.

They toiled side by side and by lunchtime had worked
their way through all the rooms except for the spare bedroom, the one that Moe used as his office.

"You ready for a break?" Toby asked. "I can run out and
get some food."

"Actually, why don't you wrap it up for the day? I want
to work on this room alone. Lots of personal stuff. You can
understand?"

Toby seemed hurt. "You're sure?"

"Really. It's going to be the hardest part for me and I
want to be alone. With his stuff, you know?" Jake paid her
and walked her to the front door.

She kissed him on the cheek. "Promise me you'll come
by the bar tonight, okay?"

"Of course," Jake said.

He went back and contemplated the room; one his father had laughingly referred to as his Worldwide Headquarters.

An ancient hide-a-bed, neatly disemboweled, its synthetic batting exploded over the carpet. A small desk, once positioned under the room's large window, overturned, the contents spread across the floor. A desk chair, a TV on a rolling stand, a coffee table and a bookcase—all, from the looks of it, carefully picked apart and examined.

A collection of family photographs, which had hung across one wall, had been torn from their frames and now lay scattered on the floor like landlocked flotsam.

Jake picked through the mess, examining his father's ancient and mostly outdated files; years of cancelled checks, Medicare statements and lapsed car insurance policies, items that should have been trashed when he was alive, now made irrelevant by death.

Mixed in with the mess Jake found and salvaged yellowing, tissue-thin V-Mail letters written during the Second World War to his mother from the then thirty-two year old Staff Sgt. Morris Green. The outside borders of little red, white and blue airmail stripes had faded long ago.

Each one had been opened. Jake read bits here and there as he arranged them into chronological order and added them to his "keeper" box. Things to explore back in New York.

He found stacks of Moe's crossword and cryptology magazines and tied them into bundles for the trash. Moe loved crosswords, brain-twisters—just about anything having to do with cryptology and ciphers. There must have been more than a hundred publications in the stacks.

His father had introduced Jake, early on, to the fun of codes; he couldn't have been more than six or seven years old.

In recent years Moe had confessed to Jake his feelings

of guilt about working away from home so much; how concerned he'd been that the relationship with his young son would suffer by his absence.

"That's why," Moe had explained, "when you were growing up, the weekends were reserved just for you."

Jake remembered their times together. Model planes, games of catch, Monopoly, ball games, movies—anything Moe could think of to keep them close.

But Moe wanted something that would keep him in touch with his son during the week as well. So when Jake was six, Moe showed him how to construct a special code, one which they alone could use to mail "secret" messages to one another when Moe was away.

Moe began with a horizontal strip of cardboard about a foot long. Then, using one of Jake's big black crayons, he printed out each letter of the alphabet, left to right, A to Z on the strip. Underneath each letter he printed the numbers one to twenty-six. So that under *A* was number 1, under *B* was number 2, and so on.

Jake never forgot the first coded message Moe gave him to decifer. 9-12-15-22-5-25-15-21: *I love you.*

The messages between them continued. Even when Jake grew older he and his father would occasionally use it. Sometimes, just for a note on the bottom of a birthday or holiday card or, when Jake was away at college, a postscript on a letter.

One time Jake used the code in a letter home from Vietnam. Military Intelligence had been all over him until he was able to explain what the numbers meant.

Warm memories.

Later, walking back from the kitchen with a cold beer, Jake noticed the bag he'd brought back from the coroner's with Moe's effects and spread the contents on the floor in Moe's office. There was the Rolex. A set of keys. A wallet and its contents, Moe's Army dog tag, attached to a thin, gold chain.

Jake picked up the dog tag. As a surprise for his father's seventieth birthday, he'd had it cast in gold. His delighted father always wore it around his neck.

Jake placed it around his own neck and shuddered. He remembered one of his mother's many superstitions, the one about shivering: *It means someone you love is thinking about you.*

He hoped she was right.

CHAPTER 10

JAKE WALKED THROUGH THE APARTMENT ONE
LAST TIME.

The housekeeper's husband would remove the furniture and truck it out that evening. The painters would come in a few days and Jake could return to New York knowing the place would be turned over to the next occupant as spotless as it was when he moved his father in a decade before.

Lilly, the housekeeper, arrived as he was leaving, He hugged her and thanked her, got into his rented car and drove out of the apartment complex for the last time.

The sun was sinking behind the horizon, a shimmering half-orange.

Another door closed. Jake wondered what might be on the other side of the next one to open.

*   *   *

Jake's stomach growled just as he took the Boca Raton exit ramp, a rude reminder that he'd forgotten to have lunch. He stopped at a Japanese restaurant near his hotel and devoured a plate of sushi, washed down with an ice-cold bottle of Sapporo.

A few hours later Jake was freshly shaved and showered. He would leave the following morning, but before he did, he wanted to see if his father had a safety deposit box and, somewhat to his own surprise, he had a strong desire to see Toby again.

He made eye contact with her when he was still a good thirty yards from the bar. They both broke into broad smiles.

He slid onto his usual stool. She placed a frosted martini glass in front of him.

"Did you finish?"

"Yep. Done. Wrestled with lots of ghosts after you left."

"Did the ghosts reveal anything interesting?"

"Other than a few hundred thousand in small bills I found inside a pillow, there was nothing worthwhile."

"In your dreams," Toby said as she filled the martini glass exactly to its rim; the rounded, liquid surface quivered and caught the light.

"See how the fluid rises a little bit above the rim of the glass?" Jake asked. "The thing that keeps it from spilling over is called surface tension, which is the cohesive force between the liquid molecules." He leaned forward and took a first sip without touching the glass.

Toby rolled her eyes and went to a nearby table to take an order.

"So, tell me, are you enjoying working here?" Jake asked, when she returned.

"Most bars are pretty much the same. What changes are the stories. Like this thing with your dad."

Jake nodded.

"It must have been tough. Going through everything of his."

"It sucked."

"Some twisted folks in this world."

"Tell me about it."

"They say you're not a man until your father dies."

"That's one hell of a way to grow up. Well, anyway, I'm off to New York tomorrow. Looking forward to being back and getting on with my life."

The bar phone rang. Toby answered, listened for a moment, covered the mouthpiece with her hand and motioned to Jake with a tilt of her head. "Someone on the house phone in the lobby asking me to page Mr. Green. Are you here?"

"Female?"

Toby made a sour face. "A man. Sounds weird, like he has asthma."

CHAPTER 11

HE WAS ONE OF THE FATTEST MEN JAKE HAD EVER SEEN —Jake guessed he was in his late forties but it was impossible to tell.

He was dressed in a massive flower-patterned short-sleeve shirt and white linen trousers with a girth-accommodating elastic waistband and he wore his long, thinning red hair pulled back into the short tuft of a ponytail. He smelled of lilac water.

Sweating from the effort of walking to the bar, the huge man introduced himself.

"Mr. Green . . . I'm Carl Kunze." He struggled onto the bar stool and handed Jake his business card.

Jake read the card. *Stamps?* "What can I do for you, Mr. Kunze?" Jake said, puzzled.

"I met your father a few weeks back. I just heard that . . . well, I'm so sorry about your loss. Just terrible."

"Thank you." Where is this going? Jake wondered, distracted by the man's size.

"He came into my store."

"Your store? Why? Rare stamps and coins weren't exactly my father's thing. About the only thing he collected were losing sweepstakes entries." Jake paused, confused. "How did you know where to find me?"

"Oh, yes—well you see, yesterday I called the number your father had given me but nobody answered. So I, uh, looked up his address and this evening after I closed my store I drove out to Palm Village to see if I might catch him there. A nice couple—your father's housekeeper and her husband, I believe—were loading a truck with furniture. She was kind enough to tell me that Mr. Green had passed away. She explained that you were in town and staying at this hotel so I, uh . . . took a chance."

"And you say my father frequented your store?"

"Far from it. He only came in that one time. Just walked in when I was closing up. I'm located in the same mall as the bank your father uses . . . *used*. He wanted information about a stamp that he, uh, claimed he had. A German stamp. He was interested in learning how much it might be worth."

Jake had heard stories of confidence men who preyed on grieving relatives of the recently deceased and wondered if this behemoth could be one of them. "I've got to tell you, that seems really strange. I'm not aware my father had any stamps or any interest in stamps."

Kunze shrugged. "That may well be. He certainly didn't display any knowledge of stamp collecting. He said he came in to my store that particular night because his bus was late and the bugs were bothering him. He didn't even have the stamp with him. I just assumed he had it tucked away in a drawer at home. So I asked him to tell me what the stamp looked like and he was able to do that in some detail—enough so that I recognized the issue."

Carl Kunze removed a piece of notebook paper from his breast pocket and smoothed it out on the table.

"From his description I was able to make this sketch," Kunze pushed the paper toward Jake.

The sketch looked like something the mother of a five-year-old would Scotch Tape to the refrigerator door. "Could anyone actually tell anything about the stamp from this drawing?"

"Absolutely. Without question. Even though, as you infer, I'm no Norman Rockwell, you'd be surprised that the drawing—even though it's primitive—is quite explicit. To any dealer familiar with German stamps this drawing would be instantly identifiable—as recognizable to them as, say, a child-like drawing of the Eiffel Tower would be to you."

"Intriguing. Please go on."

"A stamp like your father described was printed in large quantities in the Third Reich in 1943 to commemorate Hitler's fifty-fourth birthday—so it's well known." Kunze removed his glasses and cleaned them with a handkerchief. "In fact, it was printed in six similar versions in six different colors and denominations. You see, Hitler collected royalties on every stamp bearing his image and, not surprisingly, all six versions of the stamp featured his likeness in profile."

"Not a bad deal . . . but if this stamp was so common . . ." Jake didn't need to finish the obvious question.

"Yes, uh, well, one would think that it would be virtually worthless. But it does have *some* small value as a collectable simply because so few unused examples survived. The British and Americans pounded the hell out of Berlin. I'd imagine that any surviving stockpiles warehoused in and around that city—that's where they printed most of Germany's stamps—uh, would probably have been destroyed by the Russian bombing, which followed."

Jake wondered just where this philatelic history lesson

was leading. "So what is the stamp worth?" For just a fleeting moment he pictured himself handing Adrian a check to buy a flat in London.

"A single stamp, regardless of which version; not cancelled, in excellent condition and with its intended image, might bring five or ten dollars from a collector; possibly a bit more on the Internet."

Jake's fantasy collapsed. "Hell, that amount of money is hardly worth your driving out here, is it?"

Kunze lowered his voice. "That was certainly my initial thought. But then, as your father was leaving my store, he mentioned that the stamp had something unusual about it. What he went on to describe was what we, in the trade, call a *find*."

"A find?"

"Yes. A version of a stamp that has never before been known to exist."

Jake frowned. The story was sounding more and more bizarre. Was it possible Kunze was setting him up to ask for money?

"Understand, Mr. Green, this stamp was issued sixty years ago. It was never again officially printed. It's a safe guess that the plates themselves were destroyed. And in all of those six decades—until your father walked into my store—no error of this particular stamp—in any of its six versions—has ever surfaced or, for that matter, has ever been known to exist."

For a moment Jake was tempted to let the fat man continue, even if he didn't understand the jargon. The moment passed. "Hold on, you lost me again. What do you mean by error?"

"Sorry, a collector's term meaning a mistake—a version of a known stamp that, because of some sort of production problem is, in fact, a variation of the normal print run. There are dozens of ways a stamp can be considered an error or an EFO."

"EFO?"

"Error, Freak, or Oddity."

"Could you give me an example?"

"I'll give you several. One type of error is what's called an albino—a stamp that is nothing more than the impression made by an un-inked printing plate. Or an error might result from accidental double strike of the printing plate—that is, a stamp printed twice, which produces a ghost image. Or it might be one that's trimmed in the wrong place, which could result, say, in perforations on the face of the stamp rather than in the proper place along the border. Things like that are considered errors and, since they're rare, they understandably command a higher value than the stamp in its intended form."

"It sounds like an arcane area of stamp collecting."

"Not really. Most collectors I've ever met, if and when presented with the opportunity, will include errors as part of their collection. In fact, there are some enthusiasts who collect nothing but. Believe me, such stamps can be extremely valuable. The most commonly known error is one you may be familiar with. A stamp where some portion, the center image, for example, is printed upside down. In the trade it's called an invert."

"I've seen pictures of one . . . with an airplane."

"Exactly. The famous Inverted Jenny. It's a 24-cent United States stamp from 1918 with an upside down biplane on the face. Most everyone has seen a picture of it at one time or another. That stamp—actually, an entire plate of 100 was printed before the error was discovered—is worth a great deal."

"Like, how much?"

Kunze paused for a moment, "A stamp from the original sheet of 100—one in very fine condition—sold at auction in October of 1998 for $192,500!"

Jake's head snapped up in surprise. *"Are you serious!"*

He examined Carl Kunze's child-like sketch again, this time more carefully and with greater respect.

"What is the error supposed to be here?" Jake asked, squinting at the drawing.

"According to your father, his stamp has the central image—the head of Hitler—inverted."

"You mean like the Jenny stamp?"

"Yes."

"*Christ.*" Jake pulled the drawing toward him. The fat man had sketched a horizontal stamp with a circle in the center and what looked like a potato inside the circle. There were vertical elements to the right and left of the circle. One looked like a sword while the other part of the drawing could have been anything.

"Let me show you," Kunze began, a teacher explaining the obvious to a slow student, "Here, facing toward you, is the legend, *'Deutsches Reich'* under the center. On the left is a torch and on the right a sword. And, here, over the center circle, is the stamp's price—12 on the left and .38 on the right. However, within the center—see, here's the eye, the nose and mustache—is a profile of Adolf Hitler . . . and, as can you see . . . it's upside down." Now that the dealer pointed it out, Jake could see the inverted head in the center.

Errors, inverts, and UFOs. Jake was totally absorbed. If Kunze was a grifter, he was a damn good one. "This is really bizarre. I've never heard my father mention stamps of any kind. He wasn't a collector. Could he have been making up the story? He had a vivid imagination and could be quite the kidder."

"It's possible. But, uh, given the specifics he described, I think it's unlikely."

"So you believe he really had the stamp?"

"I can only report to you that which your father told me."

Jake felt excitement. Or maybe it was greed. "Let's say,

for the sake of argument, the stamp does exist, how much do you think it would be worth?"

"That's what your father wanted to know. But I had no way to give him an answer then, and I've no way of knowing now. You see, when a stamp like this appears its value is entirely in the eye of the beholder. Doubtless, it would have a lot going for it. That the head is Hitler's is enough to generate worldwide interest. The more 'beholders' who want it, and there would be many, the more the stamp will be worth. Only by exposing the stamp to the marketplace can one begin to ascertain a price.

"When your father first came to see me I was getting ready to leave for a few days' vacation. But the thought of such a unique stamp existing—an error like he described—was too exciting. So I delayed my departure, scanned this sketch into my computer and placed it along with a message onto my Internet website. Then I sent an e-mail with the same information and illustration to my entire customer and vendor file, alerting them to the possibility of the find. The next morning, I left for Key West. When I got back yesterday, I found a number of responses—some from other dealers, some from collectors and a few from auction houses. None of them had ever heard of an invert of that issue nor did anyone have any price estimate for the stamp. However, they were all excited by the stamp's existence and wanted to examine it, believe me."

"So you've no idea of what it could be worth?" Jake said, slightly disappointed.

"Can't even begin to guess how much it might eventually bring. It could be worth hundreds, thousands, tens of thousands or possibly even hundreds of thousands of dollars. There's no real way of telling without actually offering it into the marketplace. Collectors are strange people. If they want something and have the money, well . . ." Kunze's voice trailed off. "Let's just say the demand for Third Reich collectibles is quite strong, both here and abroad. And an invert surfacing—especially this one—would be huge news in the stamp world."

Jake tried to absorb what the dealer was telling him. That a sliver of paper might be worth a small fortune was not nearly as farfetched as the notion that his father might have owned it.

"This is all academic," Jake finally said. "I'm afraid. I know nothing about any stamp my father may or may not have told you about. Believe me, I wish I did."

Kunze lowered his head in a gesture of defeat. He struggled off the barstool, folded the sheet of paper he had shown Jake and handed it over.

"Please, keep the drawing. I've more copies. I'm sorry to have intruded at such a difficult time for you. Please accept my deepest condolences. If by any chance you ever locate the stamp, by all means call me. I'd be interested in either buying it from you or, as an alternative, helping you to sell it for the best possible price."

Jake also stood. "Thank you, Mr. Kunze. I enjoyed meeting you. Unfortunately it looks as though you've come out here on a wild goose chase."

"Not to worry. This is my business and sometimes the most interesting part—at least the most *fun* part—is the hunt. I hope you'll take me at my word and contact me if you ever find the stamp."

"Absolutely."

Kunze took a short step away, then turned back toward Jake.

"You might want to keep in mind that even if you find the stamp, without expert advice, there's a good chance you won't realize its full value. Stamp collectors, like stock market investors, always try their best to buy low and sell high. So, if you do find the stamp and want to sell it, be very careful. The buyers will try to take advantage of you. You have my card."

Jake watched as the big man lumbered toward the

lobby. Kunze had laid a bombshell in his lap. Was it possible, Jake mused, that his father did own such a stamp, and if so, where could it be?

An epiphany shot through him like an electrical charge.

His first instinct had been right. Whoever broke into the apartment *was* looking for something.

And now Jake knew what it was.

They were looking for the Hitler error.

CHAPTER 12

"JEEZUS, JAKE . . . WHAT WAS THAT GUY'S STORY?"

Toby tossed the question over her shoulder as she brushed past Jake on her way to deliver drinks to a couple seated at a corner table. By the time she was back, two new arrivals filled the stools on either side of Jake. Answering her questions would have to wait.

Jake sipped his drink, toying with an idea. If whoever trashed Moe's apartment was looking for the stamp, then he had more questions for the stamp dealer.

The housephone was at the end of the bar, far enough away to give Jake a bit of privacy. One of the numbers on Kunze's business card was for his mobile and Jake dialed it. The fat man answered on the second ring.

"Mr. Kunze, Jake Green here. Sorry to bother you but after you left something occurred to me. Are you aware of the circumstances surrounding my father's death?"

"The people with the truck—the ones moving the furniture from your father's apartment simply said he had passed away. I just assumed . . . his heart . . . age . . . you know?"

"My father did have a heart attack. But it was brought on while his apartment was being ransacked. His place was pulled apart. Swastikas sprayed all over the walls."

"My God! Are you saying he was murdered?"

"Not in the usual sense of the word. The police think he died of natural causes while the apartment was being vandalized."

"And you don't?"

"No. Not vandalized. I think that whoever did it was searching for something specific, because nothing—at least nothing as far as I can tell—was stolen. But every inch of the place, and I mean all of it, was ripped apart."

Jake could hear an acceleration of Kunze's breathing.

"After our conversation, it occurred to me that there might be a connection between the German stamp and the vandalism."

"That's terrible, Mr. Green. Goodness . . . I . . . I'd no idea. Terrible, *terrible* . . . I can't imagine . . . I certainly hope it was nothing caused by me. I mean, the stamp may be valuable but to do that, to cause a death, it's hard to believe."

"You said you were on vacation. When did you get back?"

"Yesterday. About noon," Kunze replied then paused. "Wait! You don't think . . . ? I was in Key West . . . at the Wyndham Casa Marina. I swear . . . you can check with them . . . I don't know what to say to you."

"I wasn't trying to imply anything. Thanks. Listen, I'll be in touch if I learn something." Jake hung up and dialed the hotel operator.

"This is Mr. Green. Could you please look up the num-

ber for The Wyndham Casa Marina in Key West and con-
nect me. Charge it to my room."

    Trust . . . but verify.

CHAPTER 13

UNLESS THERE WAS ANOTHER OBESE GUY WITH A RED PONYTAIL running around Key West, Jake's call to the hotel confirmed Kunze's story.

The astonishing encounter with the stamp dealer had been totally unexpected. Jake needed time to figure out what it meant, try to digest it.

For the rest of the evening he nursed a drink and played out the conversation with Kunze in his head.

Toby's voice dragged Jake from his thoughts. Glancing around, he realized the small bar had emptied.

"So what was the fat guy's story?" Toby asked. It was the first time she'd spoken to him since his call to Key West.

"Still trying to get my head around it. But it was pretty damned strange."

Toby did not hide her curiosity. "I love strange. If you're free to talk about it, tell me everything, right from when he sat down."

Jake told Toby Kunze's story. She listened intently, elbows on the bar, chin resting on her closed fists.

"Of course Kunze isn't certain there's really such a stamp," Jake concluded. "He never actually saw it. But if there is, and it really has Hitler's head upside down, it could be worth a hell of a lot."

Toby's expression turned serious. "Do you suppose he thinks you have the stamp?"

"I don't see why he would."

"He'd have reasons. First of all, you're the son. You cleared out the apartment. Lots of reasons."

Jake didn't respond. Toby was right.

"Do you?" She asked.

"Do I what?"

"Have it? The stamp?"

"Of course not. I went through my dad's stuff pretty thoroughly."

"But at the time you weren't looking for anything specific, right?"

"Certainly not an old German postage stamp," Jake said.

"Any chance he had it? You'd know better than anyone."

Jake took a deep breath. "If you'd asked me that question before I met Kunze I'd have said, no way. But now? Damned if I know. I'm sure my father didn't tell me everything that went on in his life, any more than I told him everything that went on in mine."

"What about a safe deposit box?"

"I'm going to check at the bank tomorrow. But I had his Power of Attorney and got copies of his monthly statements. I never saw any charge for a deposit box.

"Which leaves the question, where's the stamp?"

"The more I think about it, the more I have to believe that whoever trashed the apartment was looking for something, and . . ."

". . . and," Toby said, finishing the thought, "since nothing else was missing, the stamp is the only something that makes sense."

"Right."

She stepped back to the small alcove at the end of the bar, filled two mugs with coffee, and returned. Her face was slightly flushed and her eyes were shining; clearly, she was enjoying the challenge of solving this puzzle.

"You know," she said, "if you're right, the swastikas and spray painting were probably nothing more than a diversion."

Jake smiled. The same thought had crossed his mind.

"Don't laugh at me. I'm serious."

"I'm not laughing at you. I was just amused at how alike our minds work because I was thinking the same thing."

For a moment they were silent. Finally, Toby said, almost to herself, "You have to wonder how he ever came across a stamp like that? And where?"

"Who knows? Hell, he could have won it from one of his pool-playing buddies. Or picked it up off the street."

"If he did have the stamp and those bastards found it, I imagine that's the end of the story," Toby said, sounding slightly disappointed.

"Unless . . ."

"Unless what?" Toby replied.

"Unless . . . they didn't find it."

CHAPTER 14

TOBY CLOSED OUT THE CASH REGISTER AND SHUT OFF THE SOUND system.

"You must be tired," she said.

"After all that coffee?"

"I should have made decaf."

"No, really, it's fine. Besides, sleeping's the last thing I want to do. We could both use some fresh air. How about we go somewhere and talk until I get sleepy?"

Toby glanced at her watch. "It could be dawn by then," she said, smiling.

"Is that so bad?" he asked. "Have you seen the dockside area?"

"Nope."

"It's very romantic."

"Oh, really?"

"In a travel brochure sort of way. Bobbing boats, water lapping on fiberglass hulls, the occasional cigar smoker."

"Sounds perfect." Toby pulled a bottle of Champagne from the bar's cooler and slipped it into her canvas bag, along with two fluted glasses.

*   *   *

A series of low, mushroom-shaped lights threw a pool of pale yellow along the length of the hotel's dock. Other than their footsteps, the only sound was the slow creak and grind of boats straining against their moorings.

Jake and Toby settled on a bench facing the water. He opened the wine and filled both flutes. They leaned back, enjoying the warm breeze.

Toby closed her eyes. Her head rested on the back of the bench; her legs pointed straight out toward the water. "You're right, this is heavenly. Just as advertised."

Jake studied the woman relaxing next to him. Familiar, yet practically a stranger. He'd known her . . . how long? Hours, at most? But he was drawn to her. To the decency and compassion she'd shown him. *Dammit,* he thought, *it wasn't supposed to happen this way.* God knows he'd gone through the dating Kabuki with more women than he cared to remember. He was well acquainted with the usual drill. He'd tell his story. She'd tell hers. The thrust, the parry. He never could decide who was auditioning whom. And the results, at least to date? A blur of forgettable one night stands. Several a bit longer. One or two even bordering on meaningful. But none close to what he was looking for, if he even knew any more what that was. In any case, all the machinations and effort hadn't worked.

This encounter with Toby had broken the pattern. There was nothing measured about his feelings toward her. No parry, no thrust. Just a strong and uncomplicated gut reaction. An adolescent level urge to make love to her, to be close to her, touch her, smell her, kiss her.

"You know," Toby said, tearing Jake from his fantasy. "If they did find the stamp in the apartment, you can forget about ever getting it back."

"Right, and someday I'll probably hear that the damned thing brought in a small fortune at auction, and have a nervous breakdown."

"That'd be enough to wreck your day." She turned toward him, her face within touching distance. "Are you going to tell the police?"

"About what?"

"Kunze. His connection to your dad and his showing up here tonight."

"Would you?" Jake asked, trying to imagine how Detective Stein might react to the information.

Toby turned the question over. "No . . . I don't think so. You said Kunze was hot to buy the stamp or at least help sell it. So why try and get it from your father by force?"

"That's how I see it, too. Kunze couldn't have had anything to do with what happened to my father. He posted the information about the stamp on his website. I know he was in Key West when the break-in took place. He tracked me down hoping I had the stamp. Any connection between him, the break-in, my father's death and the German stamp is purely circumstantial. So, I don't think telling the police about Kunze will do anyone a damn bit of good. Certainly not Kunze."

Toby hesitated. "But what if . . ."

"If what?"

"What if he's lying? What if the part of Kunze's story about your father not having the stamp with him when he came to the store is just that, a story? What if Kunze did get it? What if the posting on the website and the e-mail to his customers and even his coming out here to talk with you is just so much smoke?"

"To what purpose?"

"For one thing, it would be a nifty piece of misdirection. Like when a magician gets his audience to look one way while he's doing something sneaky, like pulling an elephant, or something, out of a hat. Think about it. By posting the stamp on his website and going to the trouble of tracking you down, he directs suspicion away from any involvement he might have in trashing the apartment and your father's death."

"But Kunze was out of town when Moe was killed."

Toby paused, turning over what Jake said. "Okay, try this. Your father walks in with the stamp. Kunze takes one look and immediately recognizes the stamp's value. He convinces your dad to leave it with him so he can get an accurate appraisal. He figures it's worth what? Fifty, maybe a hundred thousand? So he hires someone to kill your father and rip his place apart, make it look like vandalism."

The alarming image played like a film flickering across Jake's imagination. He could picture the stranger ringing Moe's doorbell. Old people are always a little lonely so a friendly smile and almost any story could have gotten someone into the apartment. And then his father, sitting, watching, horrified, as his home and his life are ripped to shreds.

Jake forced the images from his mind. "My father had a heart attack," he said, defensively. "He wasn't touched. It was only considered murder because he died while the robbery was going on."

"Okay, so Kunze got lucky! The guy he hired didn't have to do the nasty part. Nature took care of it."

Jake took several deep, calming breaths, then put his arm across Toby's shoulder. "I don't buy it. But I do admit, you have one hell of a devious mind."

She flushed. "I read a lot of detective novels."

"Clearly," Jake poured more Champaign. They sat in comfortable silence for several minutes.

"So," Toby finally said. "Let's change the subject."

"Okay. To what?"

"Well, for starters, I don't know anything about you."

"You know how I broke my nose."

"I mean important stuff. Like, what do you do? You said you went to Yale."

"Architect."

"Really? A regular Howard Roark?"

Jake couldn't hide his surprise. "You've read *The Fountainhead?*"

"Sure. Ayn Rand. Bartenders read more than the *Old Mr. Boston Bar Guide.*"

"Sorry. I didn't mean it to come out that way. The book changed my life. It's what got me pumped-up about architecture. In high school—senior year—I was an avid reader. I 'rescued' a stack of novels I found sitting on a curb. One was *The Fountainhead.* I read the whole thing over a weekend. It blew me away. Howard Roark became my hero."

"You were hooked."

"Hooked and reeled in."

"Then what?"

"Then I discovered Michelangelo."

"His architecture?"

"And, his broken nose."

Toby laughed.

"No, really. I came across the picture of a bronze bust of Michelangelo and there it was—his nose, flattened out just like mine. That clinched it for me. It was love at first sight."

"This is a joke, right?"

"Absolute truth. I researched it. Happened when he was an art student in Florence. Lorenzo Medici became his patron and protector. Another student named Torrigiani got into an argument with Mike and broke his nose. Medici was more than pissed and poor Torrigiani had to escape to England to stay out of prison."

Toby made a sceptical face.

"I was convinced that my schnozzle was the present-day incarnation of Michelangelo's nose," Jake paused a beat. "Hell, I was only a kid."

"I don't believe a word of it," Toby laughed, "but go on."

"Got my degree from Yale just in time to be drafted."

"Vietnam?"

"Yeah."

"Combat?"

Combat. Oh, yes, I was in combat. And, if by chance, a day goes by without the memories, the nightmares will remind me.

"For almost a year. But I got out in one piece. I worked for Skidmore, Owens & Merrill for a few years, then started my own company."

"Married?"

"Was. My wife died a long time ago. Cancer. My daughter, Adrian, was seven. She's grown and lives in London now. An artist." Jake took his daughter's picture from his wallet.

Toby peered at the photo. "I saw the large version of this at the apartment. I figured it might have been your wife. She's lovely. Who takes care of your company while you're down here?"

"I sold the company to my partner a few years ago."

"Oh? But you're too young to be retired."

"I think of it as being recommitted. I do some teaching, but mainly I can be picky about the kind of architecture I practice."

"Like what?"

"Well, for the past year I've been working on a project for the Government to develop inexpensive portable shelters that can be airlifted and dropped into disaster sites. Like after a tornado or an earthquake."

"I'm impressed."

"What about you? Somehow, I don't believe bartending's your lifelong ambition."

"No way. But it gives me some breathing room. I've had

a rough year or two and needed something brainless to do while I sorted out some stuff. I worked my way through college tending bar and remember enough about mixology to earn a living. But, you're right, it's not a permanent thing."

"Wait. Go back some. Where are you from?"

Toby put her hands on either side of Jake's face. "It's 3 A.M.," she said wearily. "I'm beat. Been on my feet for ten hours. You can understand. What I'd like now is a hot shower and a night's sleep."

"Yes, of course. When I get going, it's hard to stop. You must be exhausted." Jake felt confused. Was he prying? Had he misinterpreted? Was her need to leave really about being tired? "Come on, I'll walk you to your car."

She reached in her bag then scribbled on a piece of paper. "Here's my cell number. Call me tomorrow. Okay?" She covered his hand with hers and reached out with her lips toward him. It was neither a platonic nor an erotic kiss. Something in between. "You're a good man, Jake. I'm glad we met. Happy I was able to be with you, especially at a time like this."

Her lips were alluring in the moonlight.

"Me, too," he said, surprised by the level of passion her kiss had aroused.

"If you like, I'd really enjoy seeing you again. Maybe in New York. What do you think?"

"I'd like that a lot."

"Let's talk soon and see what we can arrange." Breaking the intimacy, she leaned away. "And, by the way, you don't look anything like Brando. I mean, have you seen him lately?"

"He's dead."

"I rest my case," Toby laughed.

CHAPTER 15

JAKE MADE TWO STOPS ON HIS WAY TO THE AIRPORT. The first, to purchase a piece of luggage into which he packed the personal effects salvaged from his father's apartment. With a bit of pushing and shoving, the new bag was able to accommodate the container with Moe's ashes, as well.

With the bag stowed in the trunk of his car, Jake drove to his father's bank. It was a small branch office sitting at the end of an undistinguished strip mall.

Apparently Moe had been much liked by the manager, who expressed sadness at the old man's passing. In this part of Florida, with its large population of retired seniors, death had become as indigenous as palm trees and air-conditioning.

"Your dad was a wonderful man. We'll miss him—and especially the treats," the manager said.

"Treats?"

"Sure. He'd bring them every time he came. He knew who liked Gummy Bears and who preferred red licorice whips. Bless his heart he had us trained to salivate every time he walked in the door."

"I never knew he did that. Thanks for telling me," Jake said. "Do you happen to know if he had a safe deposit box in addition to the checking account?"

The manager pursed her lips. "No, I don't believe so."

"Would you check? It's important."

The young woman walked to a nearby desk and pecked at a few computer keys. "Nope, he never had a box. At least not with our bank."

"At any branch?"

"At any branch."

*   *   *

Back at the car, Jake realized he'd parked almost directly in front of Carl Kunze's store.

It seemed silly to be so close and not stop in. A small sign hanging in the window of the front door indicated the proprietor was out and would return at 2:30 P.M. Jake knocked anyway. No response.

Maybe it was just as well. After all, Jake didn't have anything of importance to say to the man.

And he had a plane to catch.

CHAPTER 16

JAKE WAS HAPPY TO BE HOME.

He walked from room to room. The air was still and cool. Everything was as he'd left it. It felt as though he'd been gone for a long time. Had it only been a few days? He shuffled through the waiting stack of mail and checked his phone messages. Several were from Helen Faye, her concern growing with each recording. He responded to her apartment number knowing she would be at the office or doing rounds at the hospital, assuring her he was fine, without adding any details of his father's death. Citing work, travel and anything else he could think of, he added an awkward explanation of why he'd not be available to see her for a while. He needed to explore the possibilities with Toby. Without any distractions.

While a pot of coffee was brewing he unpacked his bags and showered. The urn containing his father's ashes went onto the coffee table in the living room. Moe's personal effects were spread out in neat piles on the large drafting table that dominated Jake's den.

Now, he sat sipping coffee, and contemplating the odd assortment of things he'd taken from the Florida apartment.

He wondered if he was looking at a roadmap that could lead him somewhere, or simply staring at a pile of life's sentimental leftovers?

Could he possibly make any sense out of the senseless?

Did my father really have the stamp? If so, how did he get it? Was it taken from his apartment? Did I unwittingly toss it out, along with the rest of the stuff I threw away? Or, is it somewhere on the table in front of me, hidden among his effects?

All difficult questions, but Jake tried to apply the kind of logic he used as an architect. A wall had to be built in a certain place because that's where pipes and wires needed to be buried. Logical. The quotidian use of a room dictated where the doors would be positioned, light switches placed. Logical. The best height for kitchen counters related to the size of the cook. A zoning law forced a decision about a building's height and footprint. All logical.

It was logical to believe his father had the stamp. To think otherwise would be to assume the old man had been around the bend, that the stamp was nothing more than a dementia-induced fantasy. Not logical.

Jake knew how much Moe hated not being financially successful. The older he got, the more obsessed he became with having something, anything of value, to pass on to Jake or Adrian.

But what if it turned out that Moe did have *something*? The German stamp. Regardless of where or how he got it, he must have wondered what it might be worth. Why not go to the stamp store near his bank to find out?

The choice of Kunze? Probably serendipitous.

After visiting the dealer, Moe's apartment was ransacked and vandalized. Moe had a massive heart attack and died.

Whoever trashed the apartment was looking for something—the "something" had to be the stamp. It was the only logical conclusion.

But could a sixty-year-old fragment of paper motivate someone like Carl Kunze—a simple shopkeeper in South Florida—to invade a man's home? To steal a postage stamp?

Not logical. If Kunze wanted the stamp so badly he could have bought it or negotiated to buy it. At very least, help broker the sale. Any of those choices would have netted him a tidy profit.

What about Toby's theory? Was it possible that Moe gave the stamp to Kunze, who then hired someone to kill the old man? Was he cold blooded enough to do that, then drive down to Key West and relax in the sun while Moe was being murdered?

Would he risk doing that for the stamp—even before he knew the value of the invert as a collectable?

Was Kunze devious enough to fabricate an elaborate alibi by posting the find on the Internet and then seeking out Jake at his hotel?

Illogical.

On the other hand, if Jake was right and Kunze didn't have anything to do with the ransacking, who trashed Moe's apartment? And how did they—whoever they were—know that Moe Green had the stamp in the first place, let alone how to find him?

And why Moe? If Carl Kunze posted the news on his website and e-mailed his customer file, wouldn't the reasonable assumption be that it was *Kunze* who had the stamp? And wouldn't it have made more sense for Kunze's store and Kunze's home to be searched?

As far as Jake knew, there were only two people who

could have told anyone that his father had the stamp. Moe himself or Carl Kunze, and now it was too late to ask Moe anything.

The last thought gave Jake an idea and he dug Kunze's business card from his wallet. He went to his desk, booted his computer, logged onto the Internet and punched in the dealer's website address. Maybe there was something on the site that could shed some light, provide some answers.

Kunze's website opened. Jake stared at it in horror.

CHAPTER 17

IN THE MIDDLE OF THE SCREEN WAS A BOXED NOTICE:

!!ATTENTION ERROR COLLECTORS!!

Representing my client, Mr. Morris Green of Boca Raton, Florida, I am seeking information pertaining to a possible find—a Third Reich circa 1943 invert (see sketch below) commemorating Fuhrer's 54th birthday, features inverted profile of Adolf Hitler in center circle over legend: DEUTSCHES REICH, with vertical Torchier to left and vertical sword on right. Red color, 12.38 RM postage. E-mail responses to this address only, please.

The posting amounted to his father's death notice.

Jake recalled Kunze mentioning that he'd e-mailed his entire customer file, informing them of the possible find. God knows how many collectors had received the information. And on the Internet, word could spread exponentially.

Jake was now certain how someone, somewhere in the world had learned of the stamp and came looking for it. What he didn't know was why.

Regardless of the answer, Moe Green was dead.

The questions were all too obvious—and the answers, all too ominous.

Did the people who killed his father get the stamp, or was the stamp among his possessions, now spread across Jake's drafting table? He had looked through the files and photos several times and found nothing. He would have to do so again.

But what if the stamp wasn't in the apartment when the intruders came? Would they continue their search?

Of course they would.

And Jake had to be the obvious next target.

He jumped at the sudden, shrill sound of the telephone. "Hello?"

"Hi, it's Toby. Did I catch you at a bad time?"

"No. I was just going through my dad's things again. The phone startled me. I'm glad you called," Jake said, wishing she was there so he could show how truly delighted he was "I was beginning to think I made you up. You okay?"

"Great. I slept eleven hours!"

"I really appreciate your hanging out with me last night. After my week from hell, it was a blessing not to be alone."

"My pleasure. If you're still game, I'd love to pick up where we left off . . . hopefully sooner than later."

Jake's fist made a pumping movement. "Tell you what, how about an all-expense paid trip to New York? This weekend works for me."

"Oh, God, I'd love to, but I've got to give the hotel enough notice to get a replacement. Let me talk to my boss and get back to you with a firm date, okay?"

"Perfect."

"Did you get to the bank?"

"Yeah, but no deposit box. I told you I didn't think he had one."

"Listen, my dear, I almost forgot. Two guys came in a little while ago asking after you."

Jake froze, inhaling sharply. "Really?"

"Said they met you at the bar a few months back; that you were interested in going deep-sea fishing with them?"

"Deep-sea fishing? Hell, I get seasick on a water bed."

"It sounded suspicious."

"What did they want to know?"

"When you were here last. Did I know where you went when you checked out. That sort of stuff. I didn't tell them anything. Just thought you should know."

"Jesus! Do you think they were police? Was one of them a detective named Stein?"

"Dunno. Never showed me a badge or any ID."

"What did they look like?"

"Not your white bread ordinary. One guy was tall, over six feet, with bushy hair and a big moustache. The other was short, skinny with one of those road-kill hairpieces. Kind of comical. Mutt and Jeff."

"Americans?"

"Only the tall guy said anything. Foreign. European. Could have been German, but his English was good."

"They give you business cards or phone numbers?"

"Nope. They had a drink, asked their questions and left."

Jake didn't try to cover his concern. "I'd like to know what that's all about,"

"I probably shouldn't have said anything. I don't want to worry you."

Jake didn't respond.

"Another subject. Find anything new in your dad's stuff?"

"Nothing so far. But now I know how they found out he had the stamp and where to find him."

"How's that?"

"Kunze's website. It's all there. Kunze had it laid out like a Yellow Brick Road, for God's sake—clear as could be. Anyone looking at it learned that dad had the stamp and that he lived in Boca. A call to the information operator, and they had his address. It was just sitting there, his fucking obituary."

"Did it actually say that your father had the stamp in his possession?"

"Not in so many words. But it would stand to reason."

"Then couldn't someone assume that Kunze had it?"

Jake thought about Toby's point then dismissed it. "I don't think so. Dad had only just met Kunze. The dealer was practically a stranger. I doubt he would have just handed the stamp over to him."

"You know that, but no one else knew that."

"Even so, I think the odds are pretty good in favor of someone with such a unique stamp, keeping it close. Real close . . . where he could see it and touch it."

Silence on the line, then finally Toby responded, "I guess that blows my theory about Kunze having the stamp. So, what are you going to do next?"

"I wish I knew. I'm convinced Kunze didn't have any devious motives when he posted the message. It was stupid, but innocent. I'd guess he was just covering his ass—making sure he had something 'official' that would link him to the stamp and my father in case dad ever sold it to anyone Kunze had previously contacted. Proof that Kunze was owed a commission."

"That sounds right. Listen, I hate to rush but the hotel

doesn't like me making personal calls at the bar. You have my cell number, so it's best if you always call me on that."

"No problem."

"I miss you. And I think your nose is very sexy. Let me figure out when I can get to New York, okay? And one more thing."

"Shoot."

"I wouldn't worry about those two guys. A year's worth of martinis says they weren't stamp collectors."

"Thanks, Toby. You're a sweetheart. Take care."

Jake hung up, his emotions tugged in two directions: fantasy and fear.

First, there was Toby. Her call made him realize how anxious he was to see her again.

Then there were the two men. Regardless of Toby's reassurance, the possibility that they might be coming after him was terrifying. Not because he had the stamp, but because he didn't.

*   *   *

Jake returned to the computer screen. Kunze's website stared back.

Toby's call told Jake something he would have preferred not to hear. If the two men were the ones who searched his father's apartment, then their visit to the Monkey Bar made it clear that they hadn't found what they were looking for.

Were the sins of his father being visited upon him?

Fuck, no! His father was a sweet old guy whose only so-called sin had been an attempt to give something of value to his son. And look where it got him!

Jake was suddenly gripped by raw fear on a level he hadn't felt since Vietnam. A feeling of consuming terror that came from being totally without control over a situation. Nothing more than an object to be pushed forward or aside, stepped on or eliminated. All at someone else's will.

He went to the kitchen and poured two inches of bourbon; then, using the building's intercom, rang the doorman.

"Walter? It's Jake Green. If anyone you don't *personally* recognize comes in asking for me—tell them I'm out of town. Even if it's someone you do know, ring me first, before you let *anybody* up. Understood? Good, thanks. And pass that on to whoever comes on duty to relieve you."

Jake checked the front door to make sure the deadbolt was set, used the rest of the Bourbon to swallow two sleeping pills, took a hot shower and went to bed.

CHAPTER 18

RINGING DRAGGED JAKE SLOWLY OUT OF HIS SLEEP.

He groped toward the phone, knocking the offending instrument to the floor, finally managing to get the receiver to his ear.

"Daddy? It's me. Are you okay? What's the matter?"

"—Adrian? *Christ!* Is anything wrong?"

"No, nothing. I didn't mean to scare you. I thought you'd be up by now."

"I took a sleeping pill."

"Oh, God, I'm sorry."

Jake squinted at the illuminated numbers on the bedside clock. It was almost 9 A.M. "What's up?"

"I recalled something very important. Poppy told me you're supposed to call his lawyer."

"What are you talking about?"

"Remember when I was in Florida visiting Poppy last year? Well, he gave me his lawyer's name and number. A man named Alan Carson. I was to remind you to call him if anything happened to him."

"Happened?"

"You know—like if he *died*. Anyway, I just came across his name and number, and it all came back to me."

Jake jotted down the details. He asked if everything else was okay, made sure she didn't need money, said good-bye and headed for the bathroom.

He stood for a long time under the spray of the shower, his head slowly clearing.

Even though Moe had no doubt mentioned him, Jake had forgotten about the lawyer, just as his father knew he might. So Moe stored the information with Adrian as a kind of Palm Pilot to back-up Jake's memory.

Could Carson have the stamp? Was it going to be that simple?

Jake's hopes soured.

CHAPTER 19

AMERICA'S NEW NATIONAL PASTIME MUST BE PHONE TAG, JAKE thought as he tried reaching his father's lawyer again, getting nothing for his effort beyond a repeat of the recorded message saying that Alan Carson was out of town.

Just as he hung up, the phone rang in his hand.

"Jake? It's Arthur Scanlon. God, it's been a long time."

Scanlon was a former client. Jake hadn't heard from the man since Jake's firm converted waterfront warehouse space into corporate offices for Blarco Industries, one of Scanlon's many holdings. For the year or so while the work was being completed, the two men had fallen into the habit of having dinner a few times each month, along with their respective dates. Once the job was over, their social get-togethers stopped as well.

Jake was pleased to hear from Scanlon again; he had

enjoyed the younger man's company and his first instinct was to assume the unexpected call came in reference to an architectural problem, and he wondered if Scanlon was aware that he'd sold the firm. Although to an aggressive businessman like Scanlon, a small impediment like that would make little difference.

"It certainly has been," Jake said. "Almost four years. How you doing?"

"Hanging in. How is your daughter? You're not a grandfather yet, are you?"

"Nope. She's in London, painting."

"Not a bad life. Don't you wish you had a rich daddy?"

"You have more experience at that than I do."

Arthur Scanlon laughed heartily at Jake's barbed response. "I was down at Blarco the other day, you remember the job?"

"Vividly. Please, don't tell me they want their money back?"

"Not a chance. They're doing fine, happy as pigs in shit with the space you designed."

"So what can I do for you, Arthur? You know I sold the company."

"Yeah, I heard. Actually, I want to discuss something that falls into the Small World category. Really prefer to do it in person. Could lunch tomorrow work for you?"

"Why don't you tell me what it's all about first?" Jake said, slightly annoyed by Scanlon's peremptory tone.

"I want to talk face-to-face. Come on, where's your sense of adventure? What do you say?"

Jake recalled Arthur's bulldozer ability to obtrude, and diplomatically surrendered. "Okay. Where and what time?"

"In front of the Metropolitan Museum at one."

"I'll be there."

Like his father, Jake was a packrat but in his case his papers were all organized and cross-indexed. He kept his old business files in the small owner's locker in the basement and he decided to refresh his memory about Scanlon and his company before they met for lunch.

Jake had kept a detailed dossier on every client. His partner, and now current owner of the architectural firm, jokingly called Jake's thick folders, Eighty-Fours . . . as in *1984, Big Brother Is Watching You.*

The more I know about a client, the better I can predict what designs he will or won't buy, Jake would say.

It took him less than a minute to locate the Eighty-Four he wanted. Back in the apartment he leafed through the clippings, reprints and notes in Scanlon's file.

Arthur was the son of S.J. Scanlon, the late co-owner of Crane Industries. He attended The Fieldston School in New York City, prepped at Choate. Got his B.S. from Columbia; took a year at The London School of Economics, then went to Wall Street, trading commodities for Merrill Lynch. Clippings pictured him with a series of attractive women, smiling out from yellowing society pages. Named as one of a dozen "Most Eligible Bachelors" by *New York Magazine,* he'd somehow eluded capture.

Jake picked up the lengthy obituary that appeared in *The New York Times* announcing the death of S.J. Scanlon, Arthur's very rich father. It was interesting reading, although the business world, he knew, was rife with information that contradicted the essential elements.

According to the *Times,* Solomon Jerzy Skanlowski was a Holocaust survivor. When the death camps were liberated he had found his way to Paris and made his first fortune in oil. The reasons behind his rise from a Displaced Person to a mega-millionaire were mysterious and suspicious. Numerous rumors hinted of possible business ties with ex-Nazis; more than likely true, since Europe's reconstruction was a commercial cesspool, deep enough to accommodate businessmen of varying stripes.

By the time Solomon Jerzy Skanlowski met Barbara Murray, the American woman he would marry, he'd already become S.J. Scanlon. He'd also acquired a French partner, Phillipe Scoville, and together they began buying under-funded, potentially profitable companies, which they organized under a conglomerate umbrella they named Crane Industries.

Barbara Murray was the only child of an overpowering, wealthy, close-knit New England family. The idea of the couple living abroad was out of the question.

S.J. and his partner solved the problem by cutting the growing company in half, each part to be run separately by one of the partners with the proceeds combined and shared equally. S.J. would, of course, be in charge of the American portion.

Two years after Arthur was born, his mother and both her parents died when the plane Brice Murray was piloting crashed on its way to Palm Springs.

The Murrays' formidable estate would have gone to their only child but since Barbara also died in the crash, the fortune went to her husband, S.J. Scanlon. At the time, several short-lived tabloid stories hinted at a possible connection between the crash and Crane Industries' need for a fresh infusion of capital.

Growing up, Arthur had little contact with his father and was mostly raised by nannies. Occasionally there were visits from S.J. but as Arthur grew they went from infrequent to rare. In later years the relationship, according to insiders, turned hostile.

Jake pulled out a clip from a *Fortune Magazine* article, which ran shortly after S.J.'s death. A paragraph was highlighted with yellow marker:

"It was a bright spring day. Arthur Scanlon, seated with a client at New York's 21 Club, was enjoying a rare lunch away from the confines of his trading desk. At precisely that same moment his father, S.J. Scanlon, lay dying in the conference room of his company's Paris office. During dessert, unbeknownst to the younger Scanlon, he inherited

half of Crane Industries Worldwide. When asked to com-
ment, Scanlon would only say, 'All things considered, it sur-
prised the hell out of me.' "

Even with S.J. Scanlon dead, Crane remained a closely
held corporation, the ownership shared equally. Only now,
it was divided between Arthur Scanlon and his newly acquired partner in Europe, Phillipe Scoville.

Jake closed the file, wondering what the lunch was
about. He felt certain that Scanlon wanted something. People like Arthur Scanlon always did.

CHAPTER 20

AT HALF-PAST NOON JAKE STROLLED INTO CENTRAL PARK AND HEADED north toward the Metropolitan Museum of Art.

The broad steps leading up to the museum's entrance were draped with the usual lunchtime crowd. He picked out a spot, sat, and tried to relax.

A silver BMW sedan broke out of the traffic and came to rest at the curb in front of the museum. Even before the passenger got out, Jake knew Scanlon had arrived.

If one were asked to relate Scanlon to an animal, it would be a whippet. His skin was taught, pale, and hugged his body without, it seemed, an ounce of fat. His brown hair, gray at the temples, was fashionably short, his alert eyes a vivid blue. He was impeccably dressed—black silk turtleneck, lightweight gray slacks, black loafers, and a silk and linen tweed sports jacket.

Jake stood. Scanlon waved and charged up the museum steps. "Ah, Jake. God damn, you look good!"

"I hate good," Jake said, smiling. "The three ages of man are childhood, middle age and, you look good." The men shook hands. "You haven't gained an ounce. I hate you for that," Jake, added.

"Part of my inheritance. Dad left me a shit load of money, but Mom left me an industrial strength metabolism."

"Speaking of that, where are we eating?" Jake asked.

"One of my favorite lunch spots." Scanlon guided Jake toward one of the vendor's carts positioned at the base of the steps. "The only important question is, how do you like your hot dogs? I always get mustard and kraut on mine, okay with you?"

They ate sitting on the museum steps. "What's the mysterious thing you want to discuss?" Jake asked.

"First off, my condolences. I was sorry to hear the news about your father."

Jake froze, his mouth full. Scanlon's words carried the threat of an unopened switchblade. No obituary had appeared in any of the New York papers.

"How on earth did you . . . ?"

"That's the small world part. Carl Kunze told me."

The switchblade opened. This was crazy. A coincidence was one thing but Arthur Scanlon connected with Carl Kunze?

"You know Kunze?" Jake asked, trying hard to mask his amazement.

"Sure. Carl and I go way back. One of my passions is stamp collecting."

"I didn't know that."

"I've been doing business with Kunze for years."

Jake's mind raced. He felt it best to let Scanlon lead the discussion.

"Kunze called to tell me about the Hitler error," Arthur continued.

Jake kept his voice in neutral. "I see."

"Do you realize how seldom a stamp like that presents itself? It's damned exciting. To be perfectly candid, I'm interested in it. Very interested."

"Kunze must have told you I don't have the stamp," Jake said. "In fact, I'm not even sure there is a stamp. Kunze said he never saw it, and I sure as hell haven't."

"Let me tell you a secret. The bulk of my collection is purchased from dealers and at auctions, probably always will be, but sometimes I only get a *whiff* of something wonderful, little more than a vague rumor, and I go after it. Some dealer hears that the brother-in-law of so-and-so says that a stamp was found in the back of a picture frame owned by an old maiden aunt, etcetera, and etcetera."

"Serendipity."

"Exactly."

"Like my father walking into Kunze's store?"

"Sometimes that's the way it happens," Scanlon shrugged. "The hunt is the exciting part. Seriously, I usually get what I go after."

Jake was trying to decide just how far to trust Arthur Scanlon. Under all the suave bonhomie and sophistication was the tough gristle of a pragmatic businessman. As long as Scanlon knew there was a stamp and he decided he wanted it, Jake was certain he would steamroller over him to get it.

"This time I'm afraid you've hit a dead end. I wouldn't have the slightest notion where to begin looking. But if it ever turns up, I'll let you know. Beyond that, there isn't much more I can tell you."

Jake watched Scanlon's face harden with resolve, his knotted jaw muscles working. It was clear that he wasn't accustomed to giving up easily.

"Hear me out," Scanlon said. "When someone gets to a

high enough level of collecting—not just stamps, any-thing—what you find is a small, tight world controlled and held together by the common need for information. What might be coming up for sale? Who wants to buy what? Who's peddling fakes? Which way are prices moving? All kinds of information. Christ! If collectors were dealing in publicly held equities instead of the things we collect, we'd all be be-hind bars for insider trading. I've got some connections. I'd like to tap into them and maybe find out if there really is a stamp like your father claimed to have, and if luck is on our side, I may be able to . . . locate it. Let me help. You've got nothing to lose."

Jake wasn't so sure he had nothing to lose. He thought of his father's ransacked apartment. Scanlon's call and this meeting were too coincidental. Scanlon certainly sounded sincere and friendly enough, but on the other hand . . .

On the other hand, what?

Was he being paranoid?

Jake thought back to Toby's phone call and the men in Florida who had questioned her.

Damn right! I've every reason to be paranoid.

Trust Arthur Scanlon? Jake could certainly use all the help he could get. Why *wouldn't* Scanlon know Kunze? He was a stamp collector. Kunze was a stamp dealer. Fuck it!

Dammit, I'll give it a shot.

"Okay," Jake said without much enthusiasm. "If you can find out about the stamp, be my guest. I sure as hell don't know how to go about it."

"Great!" Scanlon clapped Jake on the back, a business-man's deal sealer. "Start by telling me about what hap-pened down in Florida."

Jake, still wary, felt no need to give the man all the de-tails.

"Exactly what did Kunze tell you?"

"Just that your dad came to his store, told him about

the stamp and a few days later had a heart attack and died."

"That's about it. There isn't a lot I can add. After dad died, Kunze tracked me down at my hotel and told me about the stamp. I've gone through my father's things. No stamp."

Jake said nothing about the ransacking and his suspicion that a connection might exist between it, the stamp and the death of his father.

Scanlon sat silently for a minute or two. It gave Jake a chance to finally ask a question.

"I'm puzzled. Kunze told me about an American invert. The Jenny something or other. He said it had been sold at auction for more than $100,000."

"To be precise, it was $192,500. I'm sure that someday, when it comes up for sale again, it will top a quarter million."

"That's hard to believe."

"Well, *believe* it! You can get a better idea of how valuable inverts are when you understand that the same stamp—minted the conventional way—sells for a few hundred bucks."

Jake paused. "If such a stamp were stolen the owner would report it and that would make it almost impossible to put up for sale, right?"

"Correct. At least not a sale through any public channels."

"But even if some nut stole the stamp simply to put it into an album to enjoy privately—would that be something worth killing someone for?"

"Not by any sane person," Scanlon said, then looked hard at Jake. "Are you saying you think your father was killed for the stamp?"

Jake felt a flurry of panic. "No. Not at all," he lied. "Just thinking out loud."

CHAPTER 21

ALAN CARSON RETURNED AT LAST.

The lawyer's small suite was in Midtown, Manhattan, on the second floor of a post-war building on Madison Avenue. Carson himself was a short, slightly built gentleman in his late seventies, as impeccably dressed as a Brooks Brothers mannequin, suddenly come to life.

"Ah, Mr. Green," the lawyer said when Jake came into his office. "Please forgive me. My secretary is out. I should have been in the reception area to greet you, but frankly, I forgot you were coming. It seems I misplace my memory each day, right along with my car keys. Lucky my door was open, eh?"

Jake smiled. "Lucky I barged in."

"Please say you'll join me for coffee. A friend down the hall brews a mean bean and, against my dear wife's wishes, I usually treat myself to a cup or two in the morning."

"Sure. With a touch of milk, please."

Carson pulled two large mugs from a desk drawer and left.

Jake had time to look around.

This isn't an office, he quickly concluded, *it's a tackle shop*!

Fish were mounted on every wall. Not huge game fish, like marlin or sailfish or barracuda, but small fish secured to wooden plaques, each with a brass plate, identifying the catch.

Jake examined them. Small mouth, large mouth and stripped bass, redfish, bonefish, trout and tarpon. Each specimen was frozen in a lifelike pose, hooked for eternity in a futile fight for its life.

A tall, glass-fronted oak cabinet held vertical racks of fly rods, at least a dozen. A row of gleaming reels rested on a deep horizontal shelf. Framed pictures of Carson captured him at various stages in his life, most showing the lawyer hip deep in water or on a variety of boats, fly rod whipping out or pulling in a catch.

Carson's desk had been transformed into a workbench for tying flies. There was a vise clamped on one end, a half-finished fly in its grip. Hovering over the vise—the size of a small pizza—was a combination lamp and magnifying glass.

"I see you've been examining my toys," Carson exclaimed, as he reentered.

"It's overpowering. Where do you practice? Or is the law just a front for your fishing activities?"

Carson grinned. "Yes, it has sort of taken over, hasn't it?" He handed Jake one of the coffee mugs, sat behind his desk, and motioned for Jake to pull up a chair, facing him.

"Really sorry I wasn't available when your father passed on. Truth is, I'm almost fully retired, and only handle work for a few old friends and, of course, one or two remaining clients like your dad. Most of the time I'm here I tie flies."

"Sounds like a good life."

"In fact my wife and I are off next week to Cozumel. The bone fishing on the north end of the island at Rio de Plata is some of the best in the world. Do you fly fish by any chance, Mister Green?"

"No, I'm afraid my only involvement with fish is as an end user." *Enough small talk,* he thought. "I'm curious as to why my father needed a lawyer in New York and not in Florida?"

Carson leaned back and pressed his palms together. "People do strange things when it comes to preparing for the end of their lives. Maybe he simply felt better knowing the paper work was in the hands of a lawyer who lived near his son. Your father's instructions were clear. When he passed, you were to contact me. If you didn't, I was to contact you, although I was always a bit vague on how I would know when he passed. Luckily you called."

"Luck is the right word. It was years ago when my father told me about you and his instruction had disappeared into my mental ozone. If my daughter hadn't reminded me, that would have been the end of it."

"Anyway, Mr. Green, you're here. So let's get started."

Jake inched his chair closer to the lawyer's desk and took a sip of the coffee. It was, as promised, very good.

Carson pulled a thin file from a drawer. "I had Mrs. Feder, my secretary gather everything we had on your father. He and I only spoke, face-to-face, once. Summer of 1982. He was in New York to visit—with you, I imagine. A friend of mine living in Florida gave him my name. I was able to handle most of the necessary work in that single meeting. You can see by the small size of the file that what I did required very little paper work. His will was straightforward. You were to inherit everything and unless his fortunes had changed dramatically after I saw him, I assume there isn't a great deal of value involved." Carson riffled through the thin file. "We spoke by phone several times about some small details and after that, we used the mail to send papers back and forth for notarized signatures. There was a Living Will and the General Durable Power of Attorney—you were sent copies of both at the time they were drawn up."

"Yes, I've those in my files. As for the will, I've some idea of what's in it, although I never actually had a copy."

"Go through it by all means but I think you'll find it's about as close to being an 'off the shelf' document as one finds." Carson pushed the document an inch toward Jake, then took a swallow of coffee. "Let me ask you a few questions about other issues that could affect your inheritance."

Jake couldn't help laughing. "My inheritance? I've already cleaned out Dad's apartment and taken the few things I wanted to keep. The only value is purely sentimental."

"How about insurance policies, investments, safe deposit boxes, checking and savings accounts, real estate; that sort of thing?"

"No safe deposit box—I checked with his bank. No insurance. No investments or real estate, no saving account. I believe there may be a small Social Security Death Benefit coming. If I'm lucky, that, combined with what's left in his checking account, may cover his unpaid bills and possibly part of the cremation expenses. Mr. Carson, my father had very little. I was his only means of support; me plus his monthly Social Security check."

The lawyer pushed a single sheet of paper across the desk. "In my secretary's absence I wrote out this inventory. You'll see it lists each of the specific documents I executed for your father. Look it over and make sure it's in order. Then, if you'll just initial next to each of the items, I think we can wrap this up."

Jake felt as though a weight had descended on his body. He read the pathetically short list several times, hoping it would change; like a man looking for lost keys again and again in the same pocket. His expectation of finding the stamp had grown ever since Adrian called with Carson's name. The lawyer may not have been his last hope for finding the stamp but he was Jake's best hope.

Jake scribbled his initials next to each item: his father's Last Will, the Living Will, and the Power of Attorney—and handed it back toward Carson.

"I appreciate all you've done, Mr. Carson," he said, rising. "I hope you catch lots of fish in Mexico."

"Thank you. Again, my condolences on your loss."

Jake left.

He was halfway down the hall when Carson ran up to him carrying a large manila envelope. "Forgive me. My memory, you know. There is something else. This envelope arrived here right after I left for Canada."

"An envelope?" Jake was instantly alert.

"Yes. From your father."

Maybe it's here after all!

"Mrs. Feder put it in my drawer rather than in your father's file. I forgot it was in there and she wasn't here today to remind me. It's addressed to me but to your attention. Your father phoned the office the day after it arrived, just to make sure it got here."

Jake took the envelope. "Did he say what might be inside?"

"No. You see, I didn't speak with him and, as you can see, it's still sealed. It's intended for you . . . and, well, that's all I know about it."

"What if I'd . . . been . . . ?"

"Dead?"

Jake nodded.

"Unless you'd made other arrangements, it would have gone to your daughter. Apparently, your father told Mrs. Feder that if both you and your daughter were deceased the contents of the envelope, and anything of material value, should be given to the Holocaust museum at Yad Vashem in Jerusalem."

"Yad Vashem?" If Jake had found it hard to believe his father had a valuable stamp, he was stunned to think that Moe, a man not particularly involved with things Jewish, would have any interest in willing something to the Israeli Holocaust Museum.

"Like I said, I hardly knew your father. When I heard about Yad Vashem I just assumed he was religious. By the way, you might as well take along your father's file, as well. The papers are better off with you than buried in some warehouse where no one will ever see them again."

Jake thanked Carson and proceeded down the hallway toward the elevators, trying to contain his excitement. He looked at the postmark on the envelope. His father had mailed it the day after his meeting with Carl Kunze!

That would have been after Kunze made it clear that the invert could be worth money. Possibly, a lot of money.

So when Moe mailed the envelope, he knew he might have something of value.

But why would he mail it to Carson? Maybe he wanted to be certain that the stamp was indeed valuable before saying anything, Jake reasoned. And he might not have wanted to keep it in the apartment. What if he were to die?

So Moe decided to mail it to his lawyer; even followed up with a phone call to make sure it arrived.

The stamp must be in here, Jake thought.

Better not open the envelope until I get home.

Jake hit the down button and waited for the elevator, clutching the envelope tightly under his arm. If he had the stamp he had to accept the possibility that whoever wanted it could easily have followed him. And if they did, they might even be waiting in the lobby, watching the elevators. His heart was pounding again.

The elevator arrived; its ornate doors slid open. Jake hesitated, suddenly bothered by the thought of two men asking Toby questions; he stepped back. The doors slid closed.

He scanned the hallway and spotted the fire exit. Without hesitating, he walked to the exit door, hoping the stairwell would lead out of the building onto the sidewalk, bypassing the lobby.

Jake opened the door. No handle on the inside, which meant once the door closed he wouldn't be able to get back in.

He took a deep breath and entered the dimly lit stairwell.

CHAPTER 22

JAKE CONTEMPLATED THE DOOR AT THE BOTTOM
OF THE STAIRWELL.

If lucky, he'd find a sidewalk on the far side. He pushed
down on the horizontal bar mechanism and slowly pushed
it open.

"Dammit!!" He was in the lobby next to a news stand
and there was no going back. He emerged, moving as close
as possible to a large rack displaying newspapers and magazines, trying to keep his body shielded behind it while he
examined the lobby—looking for what, he wasn't sure. Two
guys from Florida that he'd never seen before? Across from
him was a reception desk, a uniformed guard seated behind
it and, behind him, a large, wall-mounted glass-encased directory listing all the building's tenants and their various
floor locations.

People were streaming in and out through the two

large sets of revolving doors situated to his left, leading onto Madison Avenue. To Jake's right, people flowed into and out from the bank of elevators.

Jake felt foolish, peeking out from behind the magazine rack, and he moved quickly toward the revolving doors then stopped, suddenly.

Standing among a cluster of nicotine-challenged, mostly female, smokers were two men.

One, tall with a moustache, the other, short and skinny, possibly sporting a bad hairpiece, although from where Jake stood it was hard to tell.

Was it possible they could be the two who questioned Toby? Why take the chance?

Jake swallowed back a wave of nausea; sweat broke out and rolled down the small of his back. The only safe assumption was that they were, which meant he'd be wise to get out without being seen.

He removed his blazer and slung it over his shoulder, hoping they wouldn't be looking for someone in shirtsleeves. Then he crossed the lobby and approached the security guard.

"Is there another way out of the lobby besides that one?" Jake asked, indicating the revolving doors.

The guard pointed to a steel door, on the far side of the elevator bank.

"Thanks." Jake started toward the door.

A large hand clamped firmly onto Jake's arm. "Only for emergencies. You crack that sucker without me pressing this here button, it sounds the alarm."

Jake only hesitated for a minute then dug a $10 bill out of his pocket. "Look, I got a problem. I was seeing my lawyer about a divorce and my wife followed me. She's outside. You know how it is. I don't want her to see me. What do you say?"

The guard gave a furtive look to his right and left,

snatched the $10 and pressed a meaty finger onto the red button that shut off the alarm.

"There you go, man. Knock yourself out."

Jake emerged onto the glare of a pedestrian-choked street, his pulse racing, clutching the envelope. There were no cabs; he headed on foot toward Central Park.

The park's roadways were closed to automobile traffic, clearing the way for joggers, strollers, groups of cyclists, and horse-drawn buggies carrying tourists or lovers, at a leisurely pace.

Jake paused every few minutes to look around—but did not spot the men. His pulse came under control, and his pace slowed.

As he considered the situation at the lawyer's office, Jake realized he'd been in minimal danger. Dead, he'd be of no value to anyone. A dead Jake Green meant no stamp, and no hope of anyone ever getting it.

Was he being followed? And why? To see if he might visit a stamp dealer? Or go to a bank and retrieve the stamp from a safe deposit box? Or, if he already had it, put it into a bank box?

He had no answers.

If the two men were following, he wanted a better look at them, so when he left the park he settled onto a bench, in the shadow of a large elm tree, and waited. He sat for almost ten minutes but they never appeared.

At last convinced they were not going to show up, or, were entirely the product of his imagination, Jake went to his apartment.

It was time to open the package.

CHAPTER 23

JAKE NEVER SUSPECTED HE WAS BEING FOLLOWED TO ALAN Carson's office. In fact, three people had been in pursuit, the whole time.

Two of them, the men Jake had seen, stopped short of the revolving doors, watched him enter the building, then waited outside. The third, a woman, more experienced at the game, had followed Jake into the elevator.

Jake had examined her reflection in the mirror of the elevator's interior wall until it stopped on the second floor and he exited. Attractive, he noted.

The woman went to the third floor, then returned to the lobby.

She checked the building directory. The second floor only had three tenants: an advertising agency, a commercial casting company, and the office of Alan Carson, Attorney at Law. She guessed that Jake was on his way to see the lawyer but it really didn't matter since her primary concern was not *who* he was seeing but rather, how he would get out of the building.

She learned of the emergency exit and positioned herself outside on the street. Not, however, in front of the building where the two men stood amidst a knot of smokers, but on the corner where she had a perfect view, of both the front entrance and the exit on the side street, as well.

The woman only had to wait thirty minutes before Jake came through the emergency door. She watched as he briefly looked for a cab.

After a few minutes he began walking. She followed.

CHAPTER 24

AN HOUR AFTER JAKE LEFT THE LAWYER'S OFFICE, ALAN CARSON WAS packing his briefcase preparing to leave for the day, when heard the outer door to his suite open.

He walked into the reception area. "Can I help you?"

"I'd appreciate that. Could you tell me if Mr. Green is still here?"

"No, no . . . he left quite some time ago."

"That's too bad. If you could spare a minute, it would be most helpful. I'm a close friend of his and need a little information. Please, it could be very important."

The request seemed harmless enough. "I've got to be at Grand Central in forty-five minutes."

"This will only take a minute."

"Okay, but just a minute. I don't want to miss that train." He motioned to his office. "Come in."

The lawyer was far enough away not to hear the new-comer lock the door to the outer hallway.

Then Joshua turned and followed Alan Carson into his office.

CHAPTER 25

JAKE USED THE METAL URN HOLDING HIS
FATHER'S ASHES TO PROP UP the large envelope. Then
he sat on the couch staring at it.

He was afraid to open the damned thing. Afraid that
stamp wouldn't be there and just as afraid that it would.

He got up, walked to the kitchen, warmed a bagel, and
took it into his den. The light on his answering machine was
blinking and he pressed the retrieval button.

*"Hi, daddy, it's me. Did you get hold of the lawyer? Call
me when you get a chance. I'm so excited—I actually sold a
painting—for real money—well, almost real money . . . actually 100 pounds sterling! Ha. Ha."*

A short beep, then a second message: A recorded plea to
vote for a certain councilwoman.

Another beep.

"This is Toby. Please call as soon as you can. I'll be

working until one. You have my cell number. It's really important."

Toby! He'd almost forgotten her. He dialed. "Toby here." Jake could hear customers in the background. It was 5:30 P.M. Happy Hour.

"Hey, kiddo. How are you?"

"I'm up to my neck in thirsty customers right now—and besides, too many big ears around. My break's coming up in ten minutes. Are you home?"

"Yes."

"Good. I'll call you back in ten."

Waiting for Toby's call was a good excuse to postpone opening the envelope.

The phone rang. "It's me," Toby said.

"You sound stressed. Is anything wrong?"

"Carl Kunze is dead!"

The words slapped Jake like a physical blow. He sucked air until he thought his lungs would burst.

"Murdered. It's all over the God-damned news. I called when I heard but you weren't home."

Questions flooded his mind. "*Christ!* When? What happened? Do they know who did it?" Jake stood up, then sat again.

"He was found in his store early this morning—tied-up, gagged and shot once in the back of the head. The news reported he'd been dead for some time and apparently roughed up pretty bad—probably to get him to open the safe. Police say it was clearly a robbery. Cash from the register gone and the safe was open and empty. Who knows? Maybe there's no connection to anything. But the timing sure seems suspicious. Poor bastard."

The dealer's murder had blindsided him. How could his death not be connected to the stamp?

"Jeezus! My father and now Kunze."

"What if they suspect *you* have the stamp . . . ?"

"I think they already do. The two guys you told me about, from the bar. I think I may have seen them."

Toby gasped. "Where? When?"

"Today. When I went to see my father's lawyer."

"What happened?"

"Nothing. I came down to the lobby and saw two guys standing outside who looked like the ones you described. Not sure, but no way I was going to take any chances. I snuck out through the emergency exit."

"You've got to call the police. Tell them what happened. Ask for protection."

"I thought about that but I can't even prove there's a stamp. Why would the police believe two people would be killed for it? They'll think I'm some nut case."

Toby was silent.

"Maybe it's best if you don't call me here," Jake said.

"Really?" Toby sounded hurt.

"For all I know, my phone's tapped. It's best if I call you. I'll use a pay phone or my cell phone. Okay?"

Toby agreed. "But what about New York?"

Jake hesitated.

"Come on, Jake. You shouldn't be alone."

"It could be dangerous. Why would you want to put yourself in that position?"

Toby didn't hesitate. "Who's going to mix your drinks, big shot?"

She was wonderful. "If you put it that way . . ."

"Call me often," Toby said. "Twice a day. Okay?"

CHAPTER 26

KUNZE WAS MURDERED AFTER MEETING MOE GREEN.

Moe Green died after meeting Carl Kunze.

If the killings were linked—as they certainly were—the next dot to be connected was clearly marked: Jake Green.

Christ! It's only a stamp.

None of it made sense. Hell, if he had the damned thing he'd gladly give it to him . . . or her . . . or them.

Jake grabbed a letter opener, sliced along the top edge of the envelope, and began to empty its contents.

He pulled out a slim book, about 1/4-inch thick and the size of a comic book, turning it in his hands. It was a beginner's album for collecting U.S. postage stamps.

A short note from Moe greeted him on the first page.

Dear Jake. You might want to start collecting again. As

*a kid you always enjoyed filling your album. Remember?
Love, Dad.*

He riffled the pages and saw lots of illustrations. The
idea was to collect real stamps that matched the pictures,
then mount them in the correct spaces in the book.

He found nothing in the book.

It's got to be in here!

He went through it again, more slowly, this time rub-
bing his fingers across each illustration, as if he could will
the German stamp to appear.

It wasn't there. Jake tossed the album onto the coffee
table.

He went back to the envelope.

Still a chance to find it.

Jake pushed aside several slightly faded black and
white photographs, and pulled out a quarter-inch thick
stack of white bond paper, held together by a black
spring-binder clip. As he did, a flutter of tiny translucent
slivers fell from the pages, sparkling like mica.

Hinges! Stamp hinges. Delicate gummed glassine slivers that collectors use to mount their stamps into albums.

Jake counted nine of them, which he tucked into the
centerfold of the empty album.

Confused, he sat looking at the contents of the envelope—his legacy, his inheritance. What was he to make of
it? Why had his father mailed them to him? What was he
trying to tell him?

Jake picked up the clipped sheaf of paper.

If this document didn't tell him the whereabouts of the
stamp, chances were, he would never find it.

He ran his hand over the cover page where his father
had written Jake's name, touching what his father had
touched.

He turned over the top page.

A letter. His father had written him a letter!

A smile began to bend up the corners of his mouth.

He riffled through all the pages and when he had seen each one, front and back, he began to laugh.

CHAPTER 27

THE LETTER CONSISTED OF PAGE AFTER PAGE OF
. . . NUMBERS.

Thousands of numbers, each clearly written in Moe's tiny, meticulous hand, filling each sheet, on both sides, to the bottom of the last page.

Just numbers. Not a single word. Their code!

He immediately recognized his father's familiar salutation: *4-5-1-18-19-15-14: Dear son.*

Tears of laughter ran down his cheeks, pulling sobs from someplace deeper than he had ever known and, covering his face with both hands, he shook with sadness.

Leave it to my old man to go out with a stunt like this.

He cleared space on his desk, adjusted the reading light and went to work.

It was a long letter.

CHAPTER 28

DEAR SON,

I'm writing in our code simply because it makes me feel good—closer to you, and at this point in my life it also helps me to pass the time—sort of like building a boat in a bottle but more personal. Besides, it may give you a twinge of nostalgia when you decode it. (And keep us involved with each other a little bit longer.)

I can't tell you how long I've been thinking about writing this. As the years went by I kept notes to myself—recollections as they came to me—names, dates and events. So I wouldn't forget. It became a hobby. Some of the time it was painful. There was so much to remember and not all of the memories were good. Keeping notes took the place of having to talk about my years in the Army—the most painful and glorious period of my life.

It's time for me to put it all together.

This is a tough letter to write for many reasons—there's a little matter of my being dead when you read it.

And maybe it's just as well since while I was alive, I never had the stomach to discuss with you or your mother events that took place in my life—during the war—the horrible things I saw and some of the things I did. She went to her grave not knowing. Probably best.

I hope you will understand my desire to keep quiet about it . . . and will not judge me too harshly.

As you know, I was in the Army. You didn't came along until I was back in civilian life. During basic training, all of us were given aptitude tests to see what jobs we'd get. It was typical Army BS—real stupid since regardless of the results they just sent us wherever they needed bodies—mostly into the infantry and overseas.

There were exceptions. My test scores were high and when they discovered I spoke a little German (it was actually more Yiddish) I ended up with an assignment at a top-secret language school in California. Not even mom knew what kind of school I was going to. And when that was finished I was put onto a troop ship to Europe where I was attached to a special Intelligence unit as a translator.

My job was to interrogate Nazi prisoners, so our group of interpreters followed the Army as it advanced through Italy, on its way to Germany.

Along with the combat troops, we just moved from place to place—wherever they needed translators.

In the winter of 1944, as the war was starting to wind down, the Allied Armies were pushing into the Third Reich, down from the north and up from the south, out of Italy.

The Russians, who were moving into Poland, had liberated the Majdanek Concentration Camp in July. That's when the rumors people had heard about Nazi atrocities were backed up with the facts. By early 1945 all the Allied Armies were liberating concentration camps as fast as the troops could get to them.

It was in April of 1945 when I personally witnessed the results of Hitler's final solution.

I know you had a hellish experience in Vietnam, but Jake, the first camp I went into was something I could only pray I would someday forget. (Of course, I never could.) We found the camp by accident.

I was heading up a group of a dozen or so translators. At the time, we were attached to a tank unit from Patton's 3rd Army. We'd camped for the night in a field at the edge of a thick forest. In the morning the wind shifted and a terrible stench filled the air. About a mile farther on, we discovered a camp—Salzwedel, one of several satellite camps attached to the larger Neuengamme concentration camp. You've seen pictures of what went on in those camps so I won't try to describe it for you—besides, I haven't the vocabulary. The Salzwedel labor camp was populated mainly by women whose job it was to make landmines for the German Army. The women were barely alive and those who had died (along with those still alive but too weak to move) had been thrown into lime pits, layer upon layer, to decompose.

Let's just say that whatever you think a place like that was like—whatever your mind could possibly imagine—it was a hundred-times worse. The smell! It was something that has haunted me ever since.

After Salzwedel my unit started splitting up. As we reached each new camp, one of our group would drop off to work with the Army interviewers while the rest of us would drive to the next camp and so on.

We drove south from Salzwedel in a convoy of Jeeps and dropped off translators at the various camps that had just been liberated. Since I was the ranking non-com of the group, I would be the last one assigned.

We arrived at Dora-Mittelbau right behind the liberators who had come in the previous day. I dropped off a few of our guys then drove about 8 or 10 kilometers south to Buchenwald.

The original plan was for me to help out a few days at Buchenwald before moving on to the Ohrdruf-Nord and Flossenbuerg camps and, finally, to Dachau.

But the plans were changed.

CHAPTER 29
(Germany. 1945)

AT 0300, A BORED CORPORAL WITH BAD BREATH ROUSED Moe Green from a deep sleep by poking him in the eyes with the beam of his flashlight.

He shoved an onionskin copy of a fresh set of orders under Green's nose. They instructed him to report to the US Army base Commander at the *Ohrdruf-Nord* concentration camp by 0800 that same morning.

That gave Moe five hours to make the journey, more than enough time to travel the 25 kilometers separating *Buchenwald* from *Ohrdruf-Nord,* as long as no bridges were bombed out or roads blocked.

Moe dressed, stuffed his possessions into a duffle bag, and made his way to the mess tent where he filled his canteen with a mixture of boiled field coffee and the remains of a bottle of filched Cognac and gulped down a plate of powdered eggs.

Then, he jumped into a Jeep, driven by an obviously weary GI, and they headed for *Ohrdruf-Nord.*

Moe knew from experience that this last minute command performance most likely meant VIPs were dropping in and required the Army's translating skills. Recently, the VIP junkets had grown more numerous as more Congressmen tried to grab a few photo opportunities now that they knew the bullets had stopped. Mostly, they were a pain in the ass.

Ohrdruf-Nord was a satellite of the huge *Buchenwald* concentration camp complex. Its prisoners had been literally worked to death, digging vast underground caverns that housed Nazi armament and rocket factories. But the camp had been abandoned ahead of the advancing US Army. Panicked, the Germans had fled north taking with them all the prisoners who could still walk, limp, or hobble. Those who couldn't were either shot or simply left to die.

*   *   *

At 0700, with a whole hour to spare, Sergeant Moe Green's Jeep stopped at the front gate of *Ohrdruf-Nord,* and after showing his orders and identification to the guards, he and his driver were waved into the camp.

Little had been permitted to change since the camp was liberated eight days earlier. This was, after all, a crime scene. Hundreds of bodies had been left exactly as they were found; the stink of decomposing flesh was pervasive.

A handful of survivors—the few *lucky* enough to have the strength to stand—shuffled about the compound or stood, clinging for support to the wire fencing, traumatized.

Moe reported to the American Commanding officer. His assignment was to translate for the visiting Generals, Patton and Eisenhower.

Halfway through the tour, General Patton, who'd led

the American Third Army in the bloody Battle of the Bulge, dashed behind a barracks to throw up.

Eisenhower, deeply shaken, insisted that all military and civilian personnel in the surrounding vicinity be forced to visit the camp, to see the horror, first hand.

That same afternoon, the mayor of nearby Ohrdruf and his wife were brought to the camp so they might witness what the Nazis had left on their town's doorstep. They arrived thinking they were there for an official audience with the two famous Generals.

The mayor, his wife and other local dignitaries approached the officers. Moe was prepared to translate. Then Patton and Eisenhower turned their backs and walked off, refusing to even acknowledge the civilians' presence.

Moe mumbled, "I don't think they like you," to the German couple, then trotted to catch up with his charges.

Months later, over beers with a Stars And Stripes reporter, Moe was told that the mayor of Ohrdruf and his wife had killed themselves.

The next morning the American major in charge of the camp ordered Moe to take one of the liberated prisoners with him to Dachau, for special debriefing.

The prisoner was a woman.

CHAPTER 30

(New York. The present)

MOE'S LETTER WAS REVEALING A FATHER JAKE
NEVER KNEW. A STRANGER.

He wished that his father had somehow found the
nerve, or the need, or the desire to talk about these things
while he was still alive.

One of the photographs showed his father—decades
younger at the time the picture was taken than Jake was
now. Moe stood, uniform pants tucked into the tops of his
muddy boots, a faded field jacket buttoned up to his chin
and cinched at the waist by a wide webbed belt from which
hung a canteen and a holstered .45 Caliber Colt sidearm.
His steel helmet was tilted at a slight angle, chin strap
hanging down. Jake had a similar picture of himself taken
in Vietnam.

The big difference was that in Moe's picture, Eisenhower

and Patton flanked him. In the background, jutting into an edge of the photo, barely visible, a skeletal face was staring out from a small window. No one in the picture was smiling.

Moe's letter continued:

By the time we got to Dachau it was dark. I took the woman to the Adjutant's Office where she was checked in. My driver and I were billeted in one of the Army tents that had been put up near the outer perimeter gate. One of the soldiers told me there was food in the mess tent but the awful smell—the same as the smell at Ohrdruf-Nord—was so intense there was no way I could possibly stomach a meal. Another translator who'd arrived a few days before was kind enough to share his bottle of Cognac. I drank hoping to blot out the stench long enough to fall asleep.

My first morning I was assigned to work with a young major, a Judge Advocate named McCord who was interviewing those survivors physically and mentally strong enough to go through the process. The major and I conducted the interviews in what had formerly been the living room of the camp commandant's personal quarters. A WAC stenographer captured the interviews for posterity. McCord was gentle and considerate with every person he interviewed. We were all three often in tears.

Sometime after noon on the third day the young woman I'd driven from Ohrdruf-Nord was escorted into the room by a nurse and helped into a chair.

She was pitifully thin but not as emaciated as the majority of the survivors.

Her name was Zofia Plassenburg.

Zofia had only been at Dachau for a short time. She was suffering from malnutrition but her green eyes were alert in their dark, sunken sockets.

Helped along by the major's questions, which I translated, she unfolded her story, which I repeated in English, as best I could.

CHAPTER 31

US Army Survivors' Debriefing, Dachau, CASE FILE #D365, Female, PLASSENBURG, ZOFIA. (Grunberger) AGE, 28, BORN: MUNICH, GERMANY, 1917. Present: USA Maj. McCORD, John, 334870; USA Staff Sgt, Green, Morris, 356123; USA Cpl. Noonan, Mary, w78934WAC.
Session #1, 11/April/1945, 0900/1000.

Q. Good morning. My name is John McCord. Sergeant Green will be your translator. Corporal Noonan will take notes. For the record, would you please state your name.

A. Zofia Plassenburg.

Q. We would like to ask you some questions. You don't have to answer if you choose not to but it would be most helpful.

A. They ask me questions at other camp.

Q. Yes, we know. Captain Meder, whom you met at Ohrdruf-Nord, gave us your background information. We're interested in the war years in Berlin. You are one of the few Jews who actually remained in the city throughout the war. Not shipped to the camps, that is.

A. Yes.

Q. How long was your imprisonment at Ohrdruf-Nord?

A. Not long. Two months maybe.

Q. And before that?

A. In Berlin.

Q. Your husband was killed?

A. The air raid. Our apartment building was destroyed by the Allies. He was inside. So was Nazi officer he working for, *Obersturmbannfuhrer* Josef Hauptmann.

Q. Josef Hauptmann? We'll get back to him. In Berlin, how did you avoid being captured . . . were you in hiding?

A. There was no need to hide. I had papers. My husband made them for me.

Q. To pass as a non-Jew?

A. As long as he was alive, yes.

Q. I'm sorry, I don't understand. Could you explain?

A. My husband, Mendel Plassenburg is—was, maybe best engraver in Germany. Before I meet him, when he was just 17, the Postal Section of the Civil Service brings him to Berlin to engrave stamps and currency. We married in 1936.

Q. I imagine it was very difficult living in Berlin in those years—being Jewish. With the rise of Hitler.

A. The Nazis needed Mendel's engraving skills. They willing to postpone hatred. So they leave us alone.

Q. And that bothered you?

A. Yes.

Q. You felt guilty?

A. Yes.

Q. And your husband? Did he feel the same way?

A. Mendel was artist. Politics were beyond him. With his tools he was fine. He worried only for me.

Q. What about the "Nuremberg Laws"? Didn't they prohibit Jews to work in public service?

A. I told you, the Nazis needed him. They only reduced his salary. And, like all Jews, we had to have our papers stamped with the red J. That's when he made me forged documents.

Q. To pass?

A. Yes. Then Mendel's job changed. He was moved to a different section. A building on *Friedrichstrasse*. To something called Operation Bernhard, run by Nazi named Bernhard Kruger.

Q. As an engraver?

A. Yes. Can we stop now please. I am very tired.

Q. Of course. But just one more question. What did he engrave for Operation Bernhard?

A. Plates. For printing money.

Q. Reichmarks?

A. No. American Dollars and British Pounds.

CHAPTER 32

(Germany. 1945)

**US Army Survivors' Debriefing, Dachau, CASE FILE #D365, Female, PLASSENBURG, ZOFIA. (Grunberger) AGE, 28, BORN: MUNICH, GERMANY, 1917. Present: USA Maj. McCORD, John, 334870; USA Staff Sgt, Green, Morris, 356123; USA Cpl. Noonan, Mary, w78934WAC.
Session #2, 12/April/1945, 1400/1500.**

Q. Good afternoon, Mrs. Plassenburg. Did you get some rest?

A. Yes, thank you.

Q. Fine. Yesterday you were telling us about Operation Bernhard. You say its purpose was to counterfeit American Dollars and British Pounds. Do you know why?

A. Mendel said to, I don't know word . . . yes, thank you, Sergeant Green . . . to *disrupt* the economy of Allies.

Q. So you lived a relatively normal life?

A. For a while. But the bombing was getting very bad. This Kruger person was afraid. So he move the counterfeiting to *Sachsenhousen* Concentration Camp.

Q. Located where?

A. Thirty or thirty-five kilometers north from Berlin. Mendel, of course, was taken there. I was permitted to stay in our apartment. Like I say, they needed him. Two years I don't see my husband. It was very difficult.

Q. And he was forging the money?

A. That's what I believed. But when Mendel came back I found that at *Sachsenhousen* his work had been changed. They stop with money and are counterfeiting documents. Passports, identity papers, drivers' licenses. It was early part of 1945. Kruger was making everything that high ranking SS officers need to escape from Allied Armies.

Q. Why would they let your husband come back to Berlin?

A. A general named Von Erbin arranged for Mendel to work in Berlin for several weeks. To forge some papers for him and for two other officers.

Q. Do you know who the others were?

A. No. Mendel did letters and identity papers. The names and signatures on letters and papers were filled in . . . forged by someone else. So he would not know.

Q. And then?

A. He was taken back to *Sachsenhousen*.

Q. And you were left to survive on your own?

A. Survive? Yes, barely. No one questioned me too close since everybody knows all Jews are gone, so they think I was not a Jew. Besides, at that time no one cared. Everyone just trying to stay living. There was no work. My only work was with underground.

Q. The resistance?

A. Yes. I knew it was only a matter of time before the Nazis had all the forged papers they needed. Then they would

kill Mendel. His only hope was for war to end quickly
and maybe he would be spared in confusion of Nazi defeat. All I could do to help was work with resistance.

Q. Can you tell us about that?

A. In the spring of 1943 my cousin asked for my help starting a Berlin cell for The White Rose.

Q. We've heard about that. It originated in Munich, didn't
it?

A. Yes. By students who hated Nazis. Three who started
organization were captured by Gestapo and executed by
guillotine. When they die, the group was flooded with
new recruits.

Q. Zofia, I'd like to save details of the White Rose and the
resistance for another session. I'm interested in Mendel. What happened to him? You said he was sent back
to *Sachsenhousen.* You also told us he was killed in your
apartment building when it was bombed. Which means
he returned to Berlin again. Is that correct?

A. Yes. Not long after doing work for Von Erbin, Mendel
was released once again by another officer, one who
worked for Von Erbin, *Obersturmbannfuhrer* Josef
Hauptmann. The man who died with my husband.

Q. Your husband, he had been released to forge more papers?

A. No. Not to forge papers.

Q. To do what?

A. To engrave a stamp.

CHAPTER 33
(Germany. 1945)

**US Army Survivors' Debriefing, Dachau, CASE FILE #D365, Female, PLASSENBURG, ZOFIA. (Grunberger) AGE, 28, BORN: MUNICH, GERMANY, 1917. Present: USA Maj. McCORD, John, 334870; USA Staff Sgt, Green, Morris, 356123; USA Cpl. Noonan, Mary, w78934WAC.
Session #3, 14/April/1945, 1000/1200.**

Q. Zofia, we'd like to start this morning discussing your husband's work with the German officer you mentioned before, Josef Hauptmann . . . and the stamp.
A. Not too much to tell. This Hauptmann would come on his motorcycle to get Mendel and take him to building on *Friedrichstrasse* to work. He would bring Mendel home at night. Sometimes they work there through the

139

night and Mendel would be brought home to sleep during day.

Q. Do you know anything about the stamp he was engraving? What it was for? Why he was making it for this Hauptmann person?

A. No. I asked Mendel and he said I was better off not knowing. He was afraid that if he did, Hauptmann would kill us both when he finished. Hauptmann was a ferocious man. You could see in his eyes that he was killer.

Q. And they were both killed?

A. Yes. The night he died, Hauptmann had come to pick Mendel up. It was bitter cold. I am making tea when a bomb hits the building next to ours. The entire back of the structure fell away. In light from the flames I can see all the rooms, with the people dead inside. One man was still in his bath. He is dead. The water was boiling. It was total confusion on the street. The fire trucks came. They tried to put out the flames but it was no use. The water was turning to ice wherever it fell. Finally, the whole building collapsed. The windows in my apartment had blown out and I was wrapped in a blanket trying to stay warm. I went back to making tea. That's when I smelled the gas. I didn't know where it was coming from. I thought maybe a broken line. From the building that had just fallen down. The fumes were getting heavy. I know I can not stay, whether building survives or not. I filled a suitcase, dressed in many clothes and left a note for Mendel on the kitchen table. I also took proof print, which he brought home, of stamp he's engraving. I knew he would want it safe.

Q. Where did you go?

A. The resistance. The Headquarters was always moving. We could not stay in one place more than week or two. We'd find safe houses, attics, or basements. Wherever we could set up printing press and be safe. At that time we were using bombed out basement of the *Ka De Wa*.

Q. I'm sorry, I'm not familiar with that.

A. It is what everyone used to call the *Kaufhaus Des Westens* department store. It took up a whole square block but had been bombed bad. Nothing left above ground but rubble. There was a small, well hidden entrance to the basement. Even if you knew exactly where to look, it was still hard to find trap door. Inside was a big space full of broken beams, piles of brick, stone and glass. Hundreds of naked, flesh colored mannequins were scattered all over—some half buried—in dark it was very scary. We had some mattresses. I tried to sleep but the noise from the hand cranked printing press kept me awake. Just before dawn I left to go back to apartment. To see if it had survived and try to find Mendel. The gas filled the building like giant brick balloon. When it exploded, not a single piece was left larger than a bread loaf. I found one of my neighbors, Frau Becker. She was dazed, in shock, out of her mind . . . maybe all those things. She kept saying she was dead and told me I was also dead. She was no help. I made my way where building's front entrance would have been. I began to look through the debris. Then I saw piece of green metal sticking out. I tried to clear more space away from the metal. My hands were bleeding by the time I uncovered Hauptmann's motorcycle. If Hauptmann's machine was outside when the building blew up then he and Mendel were inside, both dead. I felt very guilty that I had not stayed and waited for Mendel. But truthfully, I felt just as guilty that it didn't have impact on me it should. Maybe I had presumed him dead so many times and mourned him so many times, that when he died, it was no longer shock, you know? Is that possible? Anyway, I went back to the basement and thought about what I would do next. I went through my things, counted what little money I had and decided to try and get to Munich where some of my family might still be alive. The stamp print was all I had left to remember Mendel. I placed it between two small pieces of paper, rolled like a cigarette, and slid it inside empty brass cartridge shell. I plugged opening with some candle wax. That is when the Germans broke in. They came with automatic rifles and Doberman dogs. I hid the cartridge in my underclothes just before they arrest me.

CHAPTER 34

JAKE HAD TO STOP. HE WENT TO THE KITCHEN, WASHED HIS FACE, POURED A DRINK AND RETURNED TO the living room. He took a swallow and settled back to continue reading his father's letter.

I became fascinated by this German woman. Each day she gained more strength and, to me, became more beautiful.

Translating requires concentration and so I was intently focused on her throughout the sessions, to the exclusion of anything else.

None of the sessions was very long because after an hour or so, Zofia was too exhausted to continue. Her story unfolded in small installments over many days.

From the end of the very first interview, I fell into a routine of escorting Zofia to wherever she needed to go—back to her barracks, to the infirmary or the mess tent. Sometimes we would just go walking. The gates were open and the sur-

rounding countryside was beautiful. Zofia couldn't walk too far without stopping and if it wasn't too cold we would find a sunny spot, sit on a blanket, smoke my American cigarettes, and talk.

We were falling in love.

When the major's official questioning of Zofia was over, I continued to see her every day. God, she was strong! The women I had known before her seemed childish, by comparison. Yes, even your mother, although she had many qualities Zofia didn't. Maybe it was Zofia's experience living through the war, or the camp, her husband's death. . . . I don't know. What I do know is that my feelings for her were deeper than anything I had ever felt.

My ongoing work with the major wasn't too demanding—no more than four or five hours a day. So Zofia and I spent a lot of time together. She told me about growing up, her family and her friends. I told her about my life in America.

I don't know if you can understand what I am going to say, Jake. But my feelings for Zofia had nothing to do with my feelings for your mother. It was like I was in one of those parallel universes they talk about in science fiction. I had never been unfaithful to your mother—before or since. I can only characterize it as a kind of madness. Zofia and I were surrounded by things that humans should never have to see or experience. And so we were not so much drawn to each other, as pushed toward each other by the circumstances—the war, the concentration camps and the carnage. In that kind of hell, love—no matter how wrong it may be in normal circumstances—is, by any comparison, beautiful.

Zofia's recovery after the camp's liberation progressed quickly. When a small group of civilians representing a Zionist rescue organization arrived at Dachau, recruiting survivors to settle in Palestine, Zofia was a prime prospect. She was intelligent, had lost all of her close family and had no desire to return to Berlin. Her decision to join seemed like the most natural thing in the world.

The night before she was to leave, I borrowed Major

McCord's Jeep and drove with her to the town of Schwabhausen where there was a small inn, a place where some of the translators went to get a "home cooked" meal and a bottle of wine.

The ride was festive, if that word can be used. It was the first time Zofia had been away from the camps since the Nazis arrested her. After dinner Zofia and I went to our room. Spending the night together seemed natural and comfortable.

Zofia made it clear she had no intention of interfering with my marriage—but had she made even the slightest effort to ask me to stay with her, I believe I would have.

Forgive me, but in that place, at that moment in my life, I was close to throwing everything away just to be with her. At the time, I truly wanted or needed to be safe, inside a little bubble—just me with Zofia. You were in Vietnam so it's possible you can understand what I mean.

In the morning we headed back to Dachau. The sky was dark; it was cold.

By the time we drove through the gates there was a layer of fresh snow across the camp, a bright, clean veneer that, for the moment, masked the horrors.

Zofia went to her barracks and got her few possessions; most of what she had she wore on her back.

A half-dozen recruits were in the process of boarding the truck to begin the long journey to Palestine.

Some were already on board, others stood speaking with friends—hugging and crying. Most were wrapped in Army blankets; but here and there, some still wore parts of their prison garments.

Zofia and I hung back, wanting to wait for the very last minute.

I gave one of my dog tags to Zofia. She clutched it tightly, the knuckles of her hand turning white.

She was wearing a field jacket I had gotten for her. Out of one of the pockets she pulled a brass cartridge and gave it to me. She said it was all she had. It was something her hus-

band had made and she wanted me to have it. I thanked her and slipped it into my pocket.

Finally, everyone but Zofia was on the truck. One of the leaders shouted for her to get aboard. She obeyed and he pulled her up into the canvas-covered truck bed.

I stood by the tailgate, feeling inexplicable sadness and babbling some nonsense about letter writing and seeing her again. I knew how excited Zofia was to be getting out of Dachau. I mean, who the hell would not be thrilled?

Imagine, Jake, she had lost everything; her husband, her family, her country and now she faced an unknown future, in a strange land, with a strange language, and for what? The opportunity to start a new life, that's what.

I actually envied her. I wanted to go to that empty land and help fill it with life.

But I didn't. And, truthfully, I've regretted it to some degree ever since.

I watched the truck until all that was left were the black tire tracks in the pristine snow.

We both knew we would never see each other again.

Later, in my tent, I shook the paper out of the cartridge she'd given me and found a German stamp. She had told me about her husband, a master engraver, and the kind of work he did. The stamp was more than just something he had made when he worked for the government. It was his art, and therefore it was part of him. It must have meant a lot to her. I placed it between clean pieces of paper and put it in with the rest of my gear.

I've kept the stamp all these years. Without it, the whole experience—the camps, Zofia, our time together—would all begin to fade along with my memory. But, occasionally, when I take the stamp out and look at it, I'm reassured that all those things really did happen. The stamp is physical proof that it wasn't just my imagination. The older I get the more I need that reassurance.

I'm not sure if the stamp is worth anything—although I intend to contact someone to try and find out.

So, who knows, if I'm lucky, maybe I can leave you some-

thing of value after all. If nothing else, the stamp was of value to me. If, in fact, it proves to be worthless, which will probably be the case, please keep it anyway, for in many ways it is as much me as my ashes.

Meanwhile, my son, remember, I love you dearly. You are, and always have been, the light of my life. God bless you.

Love,

Dad

PS: I'm sending this to Alan Carson for two reasons: First, I don't want you to read it until I'm gone. And second, in case the stamp is worthless, which it probably is, I won't have to suffer the embarrassment of telling you in person. As soon as I find out if the stamp has any value I'll let him know. Either way, you'll find out when I'm gone and maybe have some fun figuring out where it is.

Jake held his father's letter, his mind trying to absorb the story.

My father confesses he was in love with a woman who was not my mother. How am I supposed to feel?

He picked up the second photograph from the envelope. It showed Moe standing next to a woman. She was taller than he by several inches and wore an oversized Army field jacket. Her hair was cropped close to her head, or, more than likely, beginning to grow back from being shaved. The picture had caught them both in mid-laugh. Jake wondered what had amused them so. On the reverse of the picture was written, *"Z and Me. 1945."*

Jake understood there were instances when married people were unfaithful. He believed it was possible to love more than one person at the same time.

So it wasn't anger he felt toward his father, but rather, *sadness.*

Sadness that Moe had lost a woman he'd loved so deeply. Sadness that he felt he had to bottle up his story all those years. Sadness that his father needed to die before he could reveal these things to his son.

Am I being unfaithful to the memory of my mother? he wondered. *They're both dead, so does it really matter?*

*   *   *

Most importantly! There is a stamp.

According to Moe's letter it should have been in the envelope he sent to Carson. *But I've not been able to find it.*

Jake still had no idea where it might be.

It was clear now that the value of the stamp went far beyond a mere collectable.

They've killed two people and I'm next in line because they think I have it.

Jake sat motionless while the living room grew dark.

CHAPTER 35

JAKE OWNED A PISTOL, A WALTHER-PPK, EXACTLY LIKE THE ONE HE'D won from a French Army officer in a poker game in Saigon.

A month after the game, Jake was leading a patrol when it was ambushed by a half-dozen Viet Cong. Fighting was up close and fierce. Jake's rifle jammed. It was the pistol that saved his life.

A week later he was taken prisoner by the VC and held in a jungle camp for almost a week before he could escape. When he came back to the States he sought out several gun dealers and finally found a PPK to match the one he'd had in Vietnam.

He kept it in a bank's safe deposit box near Grand Central Station. It was the closest bank to his former business and when he sold out to his partner, he didn't bother to change to a different branch. Three or four times a year he'd fetch the gun, travel to Brooklyn and spend a few hours shooting at The Bay Ridge Rod & Gun Club, a private indoor pistol range. Afterwards he'd strip and clean the piece, assemble it and deliver it back to the bank.

Jake knew damned well that his little ritual helped exorcise his demons, pushed away the terrifying memories of combat that visited him in the night. A safe way to scare himself silly. The hair of the dog.

Just standing at the firing line, staring at the menacing silhouette of a crouching adversary, was all it took to bring back the fears.

But the reassuring feel of the PPK, the kick of its recoil and the smell of burnt gunpowder, would lessen his panic. At least until the next nightmare.

Now, Jake figured, was a good time to bring the gun home.

*   *   *

It was early morning when he left his apartment on West 67th Street. A woman was standing on the far sidewalk, reading a newspaper. Something about her looked vaguely familiar. Possibly a neighbor.

New Yorkers are walkers in the same way as Angelinos are drivers. A woman, just standing, was a paper-thin reason enough to give Jake an uneasy feeling—a sense that something was ever so slightly askew. Like a picture frame not quite straight.

What was the old joke? Just because you're paranoid doesn't mean people aren't out to get you.

What if I walked over to her and said, Listen, I don't have the fucking stamp. Shoot me if you want but it won't change anything.

Jake shook off the thought, tucked his own paper under his arm, and walked west toward the subway entrance on Broadway. The woman stayed put.

He walked at a steady pace, trying not to look back, working hard to convince himself that the whole notion of being followed was stupid.

Finally, when he couldn't take it for another minute, he glanced back. She was gone.

Ten minutes later he was standing on the subway platform waiting for the train when he spotted the woman again, maybe fifty-feet down the platform.

You're going to drive yourself crazy.

Moments later he boarded a train and lost sight of her. At Times Square Station, he was swept along by the flow of people as they hustled toward the Shuttle—a train that made the short run back-and-forth between Times Square and Grand Central Station.

Common sense told him that even if he did see her again, it didn't mean she was following him. She could just as easily lay claim to the one being followed. Every day thousands of people traveled the Broadway Subway line to Times Square and shuttled across to Grand Central. She and Jake were just two of many.

On the other hand, there were the two men he saw outside Carson's office building.

Much more clever to use a woman to follow him.

He boarded the Shuttle.

As the doors were starting to close, instinct told him to step back onto the platform. The train pulled out. People in the car looked out at Jake like he was just another New York nut case. He felt foolish.

He turned slowly to his right as if the moving train was twisting him around. And then he saw her, thirty yards away, alone on the empty platform.

They watched each other for a full half-minute before he started walking toward her. Her eyes locked onto Jake's as he narrowed the distance, but she never moved.

It was the woman from outside his building. And as he

got closer he realized it was the same woman he'd admired in the elevator when he visited Alan Carson.

She was almost as tall as Jake, and younger, he guessed, by maybe ten years. Athletic body. Dark hair worn very short and shot with steaks of gray, olive skin, large, wide-set green eyes, high cheekbones. As he approached, she ran her hand back through her hair, and smiled, pleasantly.

Jake started speaking when he was ten steps away and continued until he was close enough to catch the smell of her perfume.

"Excuse me, this may sound crazy but are you *following* me?"

Her smile broadened. "Yes, as a matter of fact, Mr. Green, I am."

Jake felt the blood draining from his face. He was being ambushed again only this time he didn't have a pistol.

"How do you know my name? Do I know you?"

"No, no, we've never met."

The woman's tone was friendly. From her accent it was clear she wasn't American. But he couldn't place it.

"However," she went on, "I know quite a lot about you."

"Really?"

"Yes, really. But I suggest we not talk here, if you don't mind." Her eyes examined the crowd drifting onto the platform to catch the next shuttle. "Unless you have some pressing business, why don't we go somewhere a bit more private? There is a great deal to discuss. I know a place where we can talk."

Jake didn't know whether to stay or run. "Okay, so you know a place. And what? I'm supposed to trot along after you just for the hell of it? I don't know you and if you wanted to talk privately you could have just said hello outside my apartment. We could have saved the subway fare."

"I wasn't trying to hide. I just had to make sure no one was following you . . . or me, for that matter," she said.

"What makes you think anyone was following me? And why would anyone be following you?"

The woman glanced around to examine anyone within hearing distance. "Because, Mr. Green, I can shed some light on what happened to your father."

Jake felt his stomach flip and put his hand gently on the woman's arm. "Fine. Let's go. But I prefer to pick the place."

CHAPTER 36

FIFTEEN MINUTES LATER THEY WERE FACING
EACH OTHER IN A DIM corner of the Algonquin Hotel's
Blue bar.

Neither had spoken during the short walk from the
subway station. Now, with hot coffee next to them, Jake
was ready for some explanations. "Okay. Who are you?
What do you know about my father? Why are you following
me, and what is this all about?"

The woman made adjustments to her coffee with cream
and sugar, a convenient bit of business that afforded a
chance to organize her thoughts, he guessed. It also gave
Jake time to examine the woman; a time lag he sensed
might have been planned.

She was wearing a knitted jacket in muted earth tones
over a cream-colored silk blouse and a short charcoal
leather skirt. Her legs were long, shapely and bare, ending

in fashionable yet sturdy brown suede pumps. No make-up that he could detect. Tasteful understated earrings and a Cartier Tank Watch, her only jewelry. A strong jaw tapered toward her chin, which bore an inch-long, comma-shaped scar at its tip.

The effect was pugilistic. Considering his own boxer's nose, he figured they'd make a hell of a couple.

She reached into her handbag, which lay at her feet, her open jacket revealing the swell of her breasts against silk. She pulled out a small notebook, her smile telling him she'd seen where his gaze had fallen. He blushed.

"To begin with, my name is Davida Snyder."

"Go on."

She riffled a few pages of the notebook. "Your name is Jake Green. You're forty-nine years old. Your wife died of cancer fifteen years ago and you have a grown daughter living in London. You earned your Architectural Degree from Yale, graduated with honors and served as an infantry officer in Viet Nam. You were a POW for a blessedly short time—one week, I believe, before you escaped. You worked for the architectural firm of Owens, Skidmore and Merrill for five years. Soon after your wife died, you started your own company but sold out your interest to your partner, Kate Scotto, and left the practice a few years ago. You currently have a small design project for the government. You love opera, you travel often, most recently to London to visit your daughter, Adrian; you have no immediate romantic attachments. There's more but I think you get my point."

Jake had no idea what the point was. "All true. So what?"

She retrieved her purse, removed a thin, black leather case, one-handed it open and held it out to Jake.

The card tucked behind the window showed the woman's unsmiling picture. Her hair was longer but without doubt it was Davida Snyder.

An agent of Mossad.

Mossad! Jake was incredulous. Totally off balance. What could Israeli Intelligence have to do with him? He took a deep breath, decided to play along, let the woman lead.

"Am I supposed to believe this is for real?" He handed the ID back to Davida. "I'd like a bit more proof than something anyone with a decent computer could pump out in about ten minutes."

She handed over her cell phone. "Tell you what, call the Israeli Embassy and tell them you must get in touch with me. That it's an emergency. Within five minutes they will call me here. Go ahead, Jake. Try it. We won't talk until they call."

"Wait! Don't tell me. You just *happen* to have the number speed dialed into your phone."

"As a matter of fact I do but I doubt you trust me enough to use it. Nope. After all, what if I had an accomplice pretending to be the embassy you're reaching? It's better if you call information and get the number yourself."

Jake felt foolish but not so foolish as to give this woman a free pass.

Less than three minutes after he spoke to the Embassy, Davida's cell phone rang. She answered it, then handed the phone to Jake.

His eyes fixed on the woman as he listened to the operator's voice give the message that he'd called. Any question of Davida Snyder's authenticity was resolved. But the real question still burned: What did she want with him? What did she know about his father's death?

"Okay, I believe you. I'm ready to listen."

"I do work for Mossad but not as a spy. I'm with one of their divisions. The *Golem*.

"*Golem?*"

"Yes. Maybe you remember the word from Hebrew school."

"A *Golem* was a mythical character. Like a monster."

"Close enough. A *Golem* was a sort of Frankenstein monster, fashioned from dirt and clay, who had the power to protect its creator. The story goes that a plague was ravishing the population of Prague. The king blamed it on the Jews, and, the people, with the king's blessing, retaliated by persecuting them."

"Blame the Jews. How novel."

Davida sighed. "An unfortunately familiar theme, isn't it? Anyway, there were two rabbis who consulted the sacred books of the *Kabala* to find the recipe for making a *Golem*. Then they went to the Moldavka River, gathered up clay and whipped one up."

"And the Jews of Prague were saved."

"That's the story."

"So you're its modern day version."

"In a manner of speaking."

"What does your *Golem* do exactly?"

"We hunt down Nazi war criminals."

Jake flashed Davida a look of respect. He knew about people whose names had become synonymous with hunting Nazis; people like Simon Wiesenthal. But Wiesenthal was an old man and from what he'd read, claimed there were no more Nazis to find.

This woman is a hunter. A young and very attractive hunter.

"I don't imagine too many of the Nazi war criminals are still alive?"

"Enough to keep us busy."

"Then what's your role in *Golem?* I'm having trouble picturing you wrestling Herr whatever-his-name-is, to the ground."

"Not a woman's job? I'm surprised. I didn't peg you for a sexist. My official title is Director of Field Research. I have talented people working for me who do all the boring stuff, like combing through old documents, studying microfilm, starring at computers screens. Once they pick up the scent of one of the hundreds of Nazis who are still hiding out, I get to do the fieldwork."

"Fieldwork is a euphemism for what, exactly?"

"I take their information and try to zero in on the target."

"And when you do?"

"Other people, the ones with the guns, take over."

"Fascinating. You said you knew something about my father."

Davida took a sip of coffee. "Does the name *Zofia Plassenburg* mean anything to you?"

CHAPTER 37

"YOU'RE SPILLING," DAVIDA SAID.

Nonplussed, Jake dabbed at the stain on his trouser leg.

Davida took the coffee cup from Jake's hand. "Here, take my napkin. I assume from your response that the name's familiar?"

Jake nodded.

"Can you tell me how you first heard of Zofia Plassenburg?"

Jake wondered how much to tell this woman, then decided there was no way of knowing. Play it by ear, he thought, and see where it leads. "I didn't hear her name. I saw it last night."

"You *saw* it?" Davida leaned toward Jake, obviously excited. "Where?"

"A letter. My father had written me a letter."

"An old letter? I know your father was killed, last month. I'm very sorry."

"How did you know?"

"I'll get to that. Tell me about the letter. Have you had it a long time?"

Jake hesitated, then decided it made no difference. "My father sent it to his lawyer. I got it from him yesterday. It described his experiences in the war."

"And that's when he mentioned Zofia?"

"Yes. He was in the army, a translator. He met her in the concentration camp, at Dachau when she was being debriefed. Apparently, he spent a good deal of time with her . . . they became . . . good friends," Jake felt himself flush.

"Did your father mention what happened to Zofia after Dachau?"

"Just that she left the camp with a Zionist rescue group headed for Palestine."

"And?"

"And nothing. That was it. She got onto a truck and left the camp. He didn't say anything more about her. I've no reason to believe he ever saw her again."

"There was no way he could have known," Davida whispered to herself.

She might as well have been shouting. "No way he could have known what?" Jake asked.

Davida leaned close. "When Zofia left Dachau she was *pregnant*. It was a small miracle, given what must have been her physical condition."

"And why should that be of interest to me?" Jake demanded, already knowing the answer.

"She was pregnant with your father's child."

Jake repeated Davida's words, *"My father's child,"* as if they'd been said in a strange tongue he'd never heard spoken before.

She's telling the truth. I just don't want to hear it.

Jake's initial shock gave way to a realization.

"That means I have, a . . . ?"

"Yes, Jake. Her name was Sarah. She was killed. In Israel, in the 1967 war. Sarah was in the Army. She was barely twenty-years old when she died."

Jake sank back in the upholstery of the wing chair, his mind a kaleidoscope of thoughts. He'd always harbored a fantasy: to have a brother or sister. It made no difference which. To find out that he'd had an older sibling, and now she was gone, was bitter sweet. Sarah, he calculated, would be 56. The realization of what he'd lost, saddened him.

"Do you have a picture of her?"

"Not with me. I'll get one for you. But tell me more about your father's letter."

"Not much to tell. I went to see my father's lawyer, Alan Carson, a man I'd never met before. He had a package that my father had mailed to him. It was to be given to me when he died. It contained a letter from my dad, written in code."

Davida's expression asked the question.

Jake chuckled to cover his momentary embarrassment. "We had this little, dumb code . . . when I was a kid. It was sort of silly. Anyway I decoded the letter and read it." *Just last night.*

"Can you tell me what he said?"

"Mostly stuff about the war. What he did. Like I told you, he was an Army translator working at the liberated concentration camps. He described the relationship he'd had with the Plassenburg woman."

Davida said nothing. Jake was forced to fill the void. "That happened almost sixty years ago. And here I am, less than twenty-four hours after reading about her, and you miraculously show up, follow me, evoke her name, and tell me that I once had a half sister. This whole situation is a bit fantastic, wouldn't you agree?"

Davida ran her hand through her hair. For a fleeting second her expression reminded Jake of Adrian who, years ago, wanted to try the high board at a pool, sure she wanted to jump but at the same time petrified to leap into the unknown.

Davida jumped. "I don't blame you for being confused. A lot of things are happening. You'd have no way of knowing. It's a complicated situation that involves your father, Zofia and Mendel Plassenburg, and some high-ranking Nazi officers. Most of the players are dead now. Zofia and her husband, your father, and at least one of the Nazis."

"My father's letter mentioned some German officers. They were using Zofia's husband, something about engravings."

"I'd like to see that letter as soon as possible. There were three officers involved. One was killed in a Berlin air raid in 1945. The other two fled Germany after the war with new identities. We're hoping they're both alive. But we're certain at least one of them still is."

Jake understood the individual words Davida was saying, it was their juxtaposition to one another that was causing his heart to pound.

My father and Nazi officers do not compute.

"What connection could my father have with German officers? Mendel Plassenburg? The *Golem?* You mentioned that you started your fieldwork after having some idea of where a criminal might be found, so where's the criminal?"

"What I said was, as soon as my people picked up the slightest scent of a war criminal, I was called in to begin the fieldwork."

"So in this case, what was the scent they picked up?"

Davida paused. "A fortune in stolen diamonds."

CHAPTER 38

"DIAMONDS?"

Jake inhaled until his lungs wouldn't hold any more, then slowly let the air out, a conscious attempt to remain calm. "Go on," he managed to say, finding it hard to keep his voice steady.

"Diamonds that were 'appropriated' from hundreds of thousands of Jews before they were murdered in Nazi death camps. Understand, Jake, I'm talking about a fortune."

Jake ran his hand over his face, trying to clear his head. *Am I dreaming?* he thought. "Like how much of a fortune?"

"In today's dollars, at least a half-billion. It could easily be twice that much. It would depend on the quality of the individual stones."

Maybe it was the human instinct to avoid danger—fight or flight—but whatever it was, Jake stood up

163

and walked slowly to the large lobby window that looked out on West 44th Street. He rested his forehead on the cold glass.

What am I getting sucked into?

A bike messenger zipped past his field of vision in a blur of Spandex. A woman in a lipstick red coat paused, hunched forward, hands cupped, lighted a cigarette and walked on. A couple out of earshot on the other side of the street pantomimed an argument. After a moment of fragmented thoughts— a disjointed montage—Jake returned and sat silent, looking at Davida.

"It's a lot of money," he said.

"You can see how it could motivate certain people to do just about anything."

"Sure. But I'm still not clear about what it has to do with tracking Nazi war criminals."

"The three Nazi officers who stole the diamonds left them behind, hidden somewhere in Germany. We've no idea where. One of the men, and possibly two, are still alive and are now after those diamonds."

"You mean to say, they don't know where they are?"

"No. Like us, they haven't any idea where they're hidden."

"And my father got involved in this, how?"

"You said there were lots of coincidences and you were right. Your father meeting Zofia was, of course, a coincidence triggered by the war. But what insured his involvement was the stamp she gave him."

"You know about the stamp?" Jake said, no longer capable of hiding his astonishment, as if watching a master magician pulling silk scarves out of thin air.

"Yes. I know about the stamp. That's what this is about. The *Golem's* not after diamonds. We're hunting the Nazis. When the stamp surfaced, it pulled them out of hiding. They need to get their hands on the stamp because it's their only link to the diamonds."

"And my father's stamp is your connection to them." Jake lowered his forehead into his hand, chuckling.

"Is something I said funny?"

"No. Sad. But in a funny way. My father, bless his soul . . . all his life, all he ever wanted was to have something of value to leave to me. Money, real estate, it made no difference . . . and here he was, walking around for sixty years with a half-billion dollars in his wallet."

Davida nodded at the irony. "You can be thankful he waited for sixty years to see what it was worth. The minute he brought the stamp into Carl Kunze's shop he triggered something that ended in his death. If he hadn't done it, he'd still be alive and you and I wouldn't be here."

"You know that Kunze was murdered?"

"Yes."

"Why doesn't that surprise me?"

"This is what we do, Jake. We're very good at it."

Jake leaned forward, elbows on his knees, his thinking growing clearer. "After my father was killed, I went to Florida to clean out his things. Kunze tracked me down at my hotel and told me about the stamp. From then on, I suspected there was a connection with the stamp and dad's death. Then when Kunze was murdered, I was positive."

"You're right about the connection. And that's why I'm here. And, believe me, this part is no coincidence."

"Okay. You're throwing a lot of stuff at me at once. I get that it's complicated and dangerous. Tell me precisely what that means.

"Do you trust me?"

Jake considered the question. "Let me put it this way, I *believe* you. Trust takes time."

"Fair enough. I understand the difference. But time's something we don't have much of at the moment. This may have to serve as a small step start toward trusting." She reached in her bag and handed Jake a thin piece of metal.

Even before he touched it, Jake knew what it was.

Then he held it in his clenched fist, trying to *feel* his father—a novice clairvoyant attempting, but failing, to channel his subject.

Jake reached inside his shirt and pulled out the chain around his neck. Attached to it was the gold plated twin of the dog tag Davida had just given him.

"Tell me everything that's going on," Jake said in a voice choked with wonder.

CHAPTER 39

"THERE CAN'T BE MUCH RELEVANT INFORMATION IN THE LETTER YOUR father sent," Davida said.

"What do you mean?"

"During the period your father was describing, neither he nor Zofia had any idea of the stamp's significance. But even so, you can understand how the events taking place now were being set into motion."

Jake nodded. "My father wrote that Zofia gave him the stamp just before she left for Palestine. According to his letter, he thought of it as simply a memento, about the only personal possession the poor woman had. And that's when he gave her the dog tag you showed me."

"Exactly. Her innocent act of giving him the stamp inadvertently started the clock ticking."

"Toward his death."

"Yes. Unfortunately. Toward his death."

Jake handed the dog tag back to Davida. When she took it her hand lingered in his and he covered it with his other hand.

"I have to know everything, Davida . . . all of it. I don't care how long it takes but I need the details. I can accept the fact that my father is dead. What I can't accept is not knowing why he had to die."

CHAPTER 40

DAVIDA BEGAN IN A LOW, EVEN VOICE.

"It was 1945. The *Haganah* was working overtime to populate Palestine by smuggling thousands of refugees coming out of the Nazi death camps."

"Illegal, right?" Jake said.

"Completely. The *Brichah*— its name comes from the word for escape in Hebrew—was the organization transporting survivors from the camps to various ports of embarkation in France and Italy.

"The truck carrying Zofia was the first out of Dachau. It headed south for the French port of Sete. It took weeks to get there. By the time they arrived she was in worse shape than when she said good-bye to your father. And, soon after that, she found she was pregnant."

"With my sister."

"Yes. It would have been suicidal for Zofia to sail in that

condition. It was far too dangerous and physically demanding a trip. She went to work with the local *Haganah* and kept at it, even after Sarah was born.

"Finally, in 1947, Zofia decided it was time to go to Palestine. By then it was only a matter of months before the United Nations would officially establish the State of Israel. She was determined that Sarah grow up in the new Jewish State, and not in France.

"The *Haganah* arranged for Zofia and Sarah to be smuggled into Palestine aboard a Cuban freighter. Zofia devoted the rest of her life to helping build the country. Twenty years later Sarah lost her life fighting for it."

"Can you tell me anything about the girl?" Jake said.

"Only second hand. It seems Sarah was an unusual child. Aggressive, headstrong, always in trouble. Heart-stopping beautiful but missing the intellect Zofia would have preferred. Zofia worried about her a lot. Sarah's death was tragic but not totally unexpected, given her destructive history."

Jake listened and tried to feel something toward this woman Davida was telling him about. A woman who shared his blood, genes, and father. It was no use. He felt nothing and was embarrassed by his ambivalence.

"And the diamonds?" Jake asked, anxious to move on. "How were they stolen? What happened to them? How did it all get back to my father?"

A low rumble of thunder rolled across the waist of Manhattan.

Fifteen seconds later, a far-off crackle of lightning.

The Blue Bar's interior darkened from the pending storm as the waiter arrived and poured fresh coffee.

Davida began her story.

CHAPTER 41

"UNDERSTAND THAT WHAT I'M GOING TO TELL YOU IS MOSTLY supposition," Davida said. "Put together with bits and pieces of general historical information and timelines; official Nazi records, extensive testimony from survivors like Zofia, and German police reports."

"All of which is how reliable?"

Davida rested her chin on her hand. "The scenario was constructed by Israeli Intelligence, so I'd have to say that directionally, it's damned reliable, maybe 90 percent. Is it exact in every detail? Probably not."

"But you know the diamonds were stolen, right?"

"Absolutely. And we know who stole them, how it was done and, most importantly, we know that the stamp is the key to finding the diamonds and the Nazis."

Jake leaned back, waiting for Davida to elaborate.

"I told you that three Nazi officers stole the diamonds. We know who they *were*."

Jake gave Davida a puzzled look. "When they escaped Germany their identities were changed. But back then they were Rutger Von Erbin, Axel Dengler, and Josef Hauptmann. Friends. More like brothers, who first met at one of the Fuehrer Colleges."

"The what?"

Davida shrugged. "Hitler had this notion that if his Third Reich was going to last for a thousand years he better damned well have a continuous pipeline of men sufficiently marinated in Nazi ideology to run it. So he had colleges created all over Germany—old castles converted into schools. They were collectively known as *Ordensburgen* and populated with the most promising specimens from the Hitler Youth movement. Von Erbin, Dengler, and Hauptmann first met at the *Ordensburg Vogelsang*. The school records show they were roommates for three years.

"We believe Von Erbin was the leader. We know from the school's transcripts that he showed great intellectual capacity, was athletic and politically astute. After graduating, he rose quickly in rank with a series of clever maneuvers, carefully cultivated friendships, and the meticulous avoidance of mistakes. By the time he escaped from Germany he had become General Von Erbin.

"Dengler was a bull of a man, a threatening physical presence, boring and plodding. A numbers guy. A pragmatist. He was routinely promoted based on his apparently encyclopedic knowledge and attention to details. In 1944 he was put in charge of all supplies for maintaining the day-to-day operations of the hundreds of Concentration Camps located on German soil. Everything from toilet paper to poison gas pellets."

"Just your basic, rabid Nazis."

Davida pressed her mouth into a thin line. "Not really. From what we can gather, despite the schooling, the three were apolitical, looking out more for number one than for the Reich."

"And Hauptmann? Where did he fit in?"

"Hauptmann was the only one who seemed to enjoy being a soldier."

"How so?"

"He became Waffen SS. They were all volunteers, you know. You had to love fighting to be part of that. But even so, he was apparently motivated by the action and not the politics. Seemed to thrive on danger. He probably would have been just as happy fighting for the Russians or even the Americans. Hauptmann was only loyal to himself and to his two close friends, Von Erbin and Dengler."

"And the diamonds?"

"We believe it was Dengler who first learned about them. As the number-one supply master, he was constantly traveling to the concentration camps. It's fair to say that's how he knew."

"Why were the diamonds there to begin with?"

"A by-product of Hitler's final solution. European Jews were in trouble from the beginning, when Hitler was little more than the leader of a street gang. Each day things got worse. Some families sensed the danger early on and were fortunate enough to get out. But most figured Hitler for just another tin-hat tyrant. A twentieth-century bully who, worse case scenario, might boot them out of the country someday. So they stayed. But just to be on the safe side, many of them methodically converted their assets."

"Into diamonds," Jake said.

"Yes. It made sense. A fortune in diamonds could be hidden in the hem of a dress or the lining of a shoe. And the Jews knew the diamond business. They controlled it. So the gems they acquired were the best money could buy." Davida saw the question on Jake's face. "You don't agree?"

"It's not that. But if they knew what was going to happen to them, and even planned for the worst, why did so few get out?"

Davida hesitated. It was a fair question. "I think that

the enormity of Hitler's ultimate plan was impossible for civilized minds to grasp. Genocide was simply *inconceivable.*"

"So they sat with their diamonds and waited?" Jake asked.

"Until it was too late. Eventually they were rounded up, taken to the camps and stripped of everything, including the diamonds. The gems remained at the camps, along with gold and silver. Bars, coins, dental work— gold fillings and gold teeth! And enough jewelry to fill more than one Tiffany store."

"Wasn't it heavily guarded?" Jake asked.

"According to testimony from survivors, everything was just lying around in storage sheds. At one camp the diamonds were kept in a shoe box. Can you imagine? A fortune in diamonds in a fucking shoe box!"

"So they stole the diamonds."

"In a manner of speaking. But not right away. Clearly, they wanted the gems."

"But?"

"Von Erbin needed a plan. He came up with one that was simple and audacious, but for it to work, he needed the means and the opportunity. Which meant direct access to the command levels of the Wehrmacht bureaucracy. At command level, just about anything was possible. Unfortunately, Rutger Von Erbin wasn't yet there."

"What was his rank?"

"*Obersturmbannfuhrer,* a colonel. For his plan to work, he needed more clout. He had to be a General Officer."

"I was in the military and I can tell you, becoming a General is no mean feat. You've got to be real good and damned lucky."

"In Von Erbin's case, it was better to be lucky than good," Davida went on, "His lucky day came when he was damned near blown up, along with Adolf Hitler."

CHAPTER 42

IN THE EMPTY APARTMENT JAKE'S RINGING PHONE SOUNDED PLAINTIVE and hollow.

The machine picked up.

I can't take your call right now. Leave a message.

Sam Stein waited for the tone.

"Mr. Green, this is Detective Stein calling from Boca. I gotta speak with you, soon as possible. There've been some developments relating to your father's death that we need to discuss, preferably in person. You have my card with the phone numbers, but just in case, I'll repeat them," Stein recited the numbers. "Please get back to me as soon as possible, Mr. Green. It's most important."

Then Jake's apartment fell silent once again.

CHAPTER 43

JAKE WATCHED A COUPLE ENTER THE HOTEL, LAUGHING AND SHAKING rain off their coats, then he leaned back in the wingback chair.

"Blown up with Hitler? You're kidding?"

"Absolute truth."

"I want to hear this but I need some food," Jake said.

"Thought you'd never bring it up. I'm famished."

"Okay we eat here?"

"Isn't it expensive?"

Jake smiled, working on a faint memory, dislodged by her comment. It had been a running gag between him and his late wife, Norma. Regardless of who suggested the eatery or where it was, the rejoinder would always be the same: *Isn't it expensive?*

"My treat. I wouldn't dream of asking the Mossad to pick up a check. I'll go see how soon we can get a table."

Jake talked to the host at the entrance to the dining room, returned and sat back down.

"We can get a table in about 30 minutes. So continue the story. Von Erbin is almost killed."

"Not long after Von Erbin learned about the diamonds from his friend Dengler, a war hero by the name of Claus Von Stauffenberg was assigned to Berlin in an important staff job."

"I read about him a long time ago. Von Stauffenberg was the one who tried to assassinate Hitler."

"Right. His was the eighteenth and final attempt. Von Erbin knew Von Stauffenberg and made it his business to rekindle a relationship with him in Berlin. It wasn't long before they were drinking buddies.

"Von Stauffenberg's job required him to attend briefings with Hitler, which typically took place in the Fuehrer's bunker at Wolf's Lair, 150 miles Southeast of Berlin.

"Early on the morning of July 20th, 1944, Von Stauffenberg and a co-conspirator, by the name of Lieutenant Von Haeften, flew from Berlin to Rastenberg Airfield then drove to Hitler's Wolf's Lair.

"It was a hot, muggy day. Hitler insisted the meeting be moved from his thick-walled concrete bunker, to an airy briefing hut known as the Tea House where all the windows were thrown open to catch the breeze.

"Only after he arrived and armed the bomb in his briefcase did Von Stauffenberg find out where the meeting was. For a moment he panicked. The explosion would be more effective in the sealed bunker than in a windowed room. But he was determined to go through with the assassination, regardless of where it took place.

"Von Stauffenberg placed his briefcase with the explosives next to the table leg closest to the Fuhrer. That's when he saw, to his surprise, that his friend, Rutger Von Erbin, was in the room, seated on the other side of the table.

"Von Stauffenberg tried as best he could to signal Von

Erbin to leave but his friend, not knowing of the assassination plans, misread Von Stauffenberg's signals and didn't budge. Von Stauffenberg activated the bomb, then excused himself.

"Von Stauffenberg and Von Haeften watched as the explosion blew the Tea House apart. Unfortunately, one of the officers present had inadvertently moved Von Stauffenberg's briefcase just far enough so that the full force of the blast was directed away from Hitler and he survived with only minor injuries.

"But Von Stauffenberg and Von Haeften thought Hitler had been killed and immediately flew back to Berlin.

"Later that day, they were arrested, along with many other conspirators, and executed by a firing squad."

"What about Von Erbin?" Jake asked.

"His entire left side had taken the force of the bomb blast, fracturing his arm, scorching his leg and partially burning one side of his face."

"Don't tell me," Jake said. "He was a hero."

"Exactly. Based on the simple calculus that anyone present at the explosion was automatically ruled out as a participant in the plot, Von Erbin was now considered by Hitler to be a trusted patriot and a month later Hitler shook his hand and promoted him to the rank of general."

"So now he had the motive and the means," Jake said.

"Yes," Davida said. "And his plan created the opportunity."

CHAPTER 44
(Germany. 1944)

THE PLAN WAS BLATANTLY SIMPLE.

First, Von Erbin arranged for both his friends, Axel Dengler and Josef Hauptmann, to be reassigned to his command. Dengler was stationed in Munich and Hauptmann, on the Russian front. Both men were more than eager to be reunited with their friend in Berlin.

Once together again, they examined every aspect of Von Erbin's plan. No matter how many times they reviewed it, attempting, *hoping* to find flaws, traps or inconsistencies, it held up.

Dengler and Von Erbin knew an SS Major, Bernhard Kruger, who was in charge of a counterfeiting operation printing bogus credentials for ODESSA, to be used by SS officers when the time came to escape from Germany. Von Erbin had once helped Kruger out of a bureaucratic jam and the Major owed the newly minted general a favor.

Kruger had a dozen talented engravers working under his command, which was now housed in Sachsenhausen. Von Erbin asked that the best engraver be assigned to his office for a short period of time. Kruger, assuming Von Erbin wanted papers forged for his own escape and anxious to pay back Von Erbin, was more than happy to oblige.

The designated engraver, a Jew named Mendel Plassenburg, did an excellent job. After two weeks, he not only completed all the needed "official" documents, but also created flawless passports and other papers that established new identities for the three officers.

Von Erbin, Dengler, and Hauptmann were delighted with the results and as a reward, allowed Plassenburg to spend a night with his wife, Zofia, in the tiny Berlin apartment. It was the first time Mendel had seen Zofia for almost two years. The next morning, the engraver was sent back to his job at Sachsenhausen in General Von Erbin's staff car.

Everything was now ready.

Germany was losing the war. Money was needed to continue the war effort. Hauptmann, carrying counterfeit documents "signed," thanks to Mendel Plassenburg, by Hermann Goering, would travel across Germany, stopping at pre-determined concentration camps and, using the forged documents, collect the diamonds stored there, ostensibly to be taken to Berlin to further finance the war.

Hermann Goering was chosen as the "author" of all the paperwork for several reasons. He had become a lubricious caricature—a bloated morphine addict, less accessible or stable than Hitler himself, and therefore doubly dangerous. He was known to commandeer just about anything that the Reich hadn't already been secured or stolen, and officers of all ranks, both SS and Wehrmacht, had learned that any attempt to stop him was met in the most violent way. Anything of value was prime for his personal acquisition.

An SS officer like Hauptmann, armed with proper offi-

cial papers signed by Goering, would command a high level
of fear, instant cooperation and very little suspicion.

Once the diamonds were in Hauptmann's possession,
his next job was to hide them. Where they would be hidden
was left up to him. The plan called for the location's coordinates to be incorporated into the engraving of a commonly
used postage stamp that Hauptmann would then carry
back to his partners, Von Erbin and Dengler. But there was
a chance that he might be killed before he could be reunited
with his partners.

The problem they faced was one of communications.
Hauptmann needed a way to get the information to Von
Erbin and Dengler as soon as possible. Most lines of communications in Germany were problematic at best. So the
plan called for using carrier pigeons, a successful method
for communicating, commonly employed by the Wehrmacht
as well as the Allied armies.

Two pigeons would be waiting for Hauptmann in
Berlin. As soon as he decided on the stamp to be used,
Hauptmann would send the information to Von Erbin and
Dengler with one of the pigeons.

The second bird was a backup.

If, for any reason, the pigeon failed to do its job and
Hauptmann were to be killed before getting back to his
partners with the information, the stamp itself was a final
fail-safe. Residing innocently in his billfold, it would at
least have some chance of being returned with his effects to
Von Erbin, his commanding officer and designated benefi-
ciary.

The selection of concentration camps Hauptmann
would visit was Dengler's responsibility. Thanks to his previous assignment as supply coordinator, he knew precisely
which ones had the gems.

Once Hauptmann left for the first camp, Von Erbin and
Dengler got to work. For one thing, the bogus Goering letter
carried by Hauptmann included a phone number, which the

recipient was required to use to verify the letter's authenticity. Dengler was responsible for receiving those calls via a special phone line wired into his quarters, manned by him and his secretary.

Meanwhile, Von Erbin was busy completing the arrangements needed for their eventual escape to France. A small farm on the outskirts of Berlin was an ideal "safe house." It was where the carrier pigeons had been raised and where, once released, they would return. Forged French passports, and other documents, proof of their new identities—civilian clothing, maps, and American dollars—would all be finalized, accumulated and stored.

The diamonds would remain untouched until after the war. And even then, it was impossible to know how soon they could be safely recovered. So Von Erbin worked his family connections to secure jobs in Paris, which would begin when the three friends arrived in France.

Von Erbin, Hauptmann, and Dengler celebrated the start of their scheme at a small basement restaurant frequented by the SS and Gestapo.

It was the last time the three friends would be together.

CHAPTER 45
(Germany. 1944)

LESS THAN A MONTH LATER HAUPTMANN'S PART OF THE PLAN WAS nearly complete.

He'd successfully collected the diamonds and hidden them. When he returned to Berlin he confirmed that Mendel Plassenburg was still alive and working at the *Sachsenhausen* camp. Hauptmann went to get him.

Plassenburg was a strange sight straddled on the back of the SS officer's motorcycle, an Army blanket wrapped around his prison clothing, arms encircling his benefactor's middle. He was so grateful for his sudden stroke of good fortune—the second in a handful of months—that he could hardly stop crying.

An icy snow had begun to fall. The flakes pelting Mendel's face obscured his vision and stung like bees; but to the engraver, they felt as gentle as a mother's kisses.

He vowed he would never go back to *Sachsenhausen.* Even though his job had spared him from the camp's full horrors, he knew he would rather die than return.

In Berlin, Mendel and Zofia Plassenburg were re-united. Hauptmann stood patiently in the doorway of their tiny apartment, smoking a cigarette until their initial excitement died down. He assured the couple that Mendel would be in Berlin for as long as it took to complete certain work, possibly a week, maybe longer; then he left the couple alone. After all, it had been some months since they'd last seen each other.

Hauptmann had no idea where Von Erbin or Dengler were; it would be too dangerous for them to have future contact in Berlin. He did, however, collect a package containing his French passport, a key and a straw *panier* containing two carrier pigeons that Von Erbin had left for him. Hauptmann didn't know where the pigeons were programmed to fly. It made no difference, of course, as long as they arrived safely.

Hauptmann returned to the Plassenburgs' apartment and took Mendel to the engraver's former place of employment—a building on *Friedrichstrasse.*

Sheets of corrugated metal covered the ground floor windows. The entrance door was still secured with a heavy, lock and chain Von Erbin had used after the Goering paperwork was completed. The windows on the higher floors were missing glass, smashed by the concussions from unrelenting Allied air raids; a tatterdemalion derelict with missing teeth.

The building's neo-classic façade had been stripped of its massive Eagle and Swastika relief; in the moonlight, the outline of its phantom image was faintly visible.

With the key left for him by Von Erbin, Hauptmann opened the lock, the men entered the deserted building, and started climbing.

The first three floors were divided into a maze of small

rooms, formerly offices for low-level bureaucrats. The fourth floor was a single cavernous open space, originally filled with printing equipment, including a dozen massive offset presses. Now all that remained was an ancient and heavy die-cutting machine and one small, sheet-fed press intended for printing test-runs of newly engraved plates.

The interior was freezing cold. A winter's accumulation of snow had found its way through the broken windows and collected against the inner walls or mixed with the odd bits of debris that remained from the former occupants. After a few minutes' rest, Mendel placed his box of supplies on the floor next to the printing press, then walked around the familiar machinery, touching it as one would a family pet.

In the months since printing the letters and documents for General Von Erbin, the press had been unused. Plassenburg cleaned and oiled it and the die-cut machine, until they were once again in decent running order.

Then he and Hauptmann sat smoking, while, for the first time, the soldier explained to the master engraver exactly what he wanted accomplished.

A postage stamp!

No problem, Plassenburg assured him. Ah, but the tricky part was incorporating numbers into portions of the engraving so that they would not be easily detected, should anyone ever choose to examine the stamp through a magnifying glass. *I can do it,* Plassenburg said.

Hauptmann showed Plassenburg half a dozen common German postage stamps, all currently in use.

Plassenburg examined the stamps through a loupe.

"I think this one, sir."

"Why?"

"You see, there's the torch and then the sword. I think I can carve the numbers around them in a way that would be almost impossible to pick out if one didn't know what they were looking for."

The postage stamp Plassenburg chose to counterfeit

was one of a 6-stamp commemorative set, featuring the head of Adolf Hitler.

It wasn't long before Mendel Plassenburg devised a clever design that twisted the numbers around the sword and the torch, flanking the Hitler head pictured on the center of the stamp. Hauptmann was delighted with Plassenburg's solution, and returned the weary engraver to his apartment and his wife.

Hauptmann then rode to the SS barracks at *Lichterfelde* where he was given billet in a small basement room.

Day after day Hauptmann and Plassenburg went back to the building to work. It was difficult for the frail engraver to keep from shivering in the cold and he had to stop every few minutes to chuff warm breath on his freezing fingers. His bird-like hands were unsteady, making the engraving work difficult. He sat hunched over, surrounded on all sides by darkness and shadow, the only illumination coming from his work lamp, which threw a bright, yellow beam onto the surface where he worked.

"Dammit, Plassenburg, how much longer?" Hauptmann spit the question out.

"Please, *Herr Obersturmbannfuhrer,* I work as quickly as I can. It is most delicate to prepare the plate for a good pressing of the proof."

The weary officer threw his arms up in frustration, pivoted on the worn heel of his boot and strode to a window. Berlin stretched out in the darkness before him, darker even than the midnight sky. Silhouettes of buildings—some whole, many others bombed into little more than empty, broken shells—etched a jagged outline against a broad horizon; glowing faintly with the red and orange of distant fires not yet extinguished.

Hauptmann removed a silver flask from a pouch on the leather belt that cinched his overcoat. He unscrewed the top, took a swallow and shivered, waiting for the Cognac to push some of the chill from his bones. He studied his reflection mirrored in the single pane of window glass that remained. For an alarming moment, his drawn face appeared to mimic the Death's Head emblem embroidered in heavy silver and black thread on his cap. Almost five years in this stinking war had sucked the flesh from his face and faith from his soul. He was only twenty-five years old but looked and felt as haggard as a man of fifty. Still, now was no time to lament. His ordeal was almost over.

Tomorrow was what he had to keep firmly planted in his mind.

Tomorrow was what all the planning was for.

Tomorrow was all that really counted.

"I think it is ready, *Herr Obersturmbannfuhrer* Hauptmann," Mendel Plassenburg said.

The officer moved quickly to the engraver's side and straddled the stool. A magnifying glass attached to the end of an articulated arm was positioned over the engraving; he removed his cap and pushed his face toward the glass. "Yes. Yes, yes. Excellent. You've done it perfectly—it is seamless! Mendel, you are truly an artist."

Outside a rising wail of sirens signaled the nightly air raid. Minutes later the dark sky was crisscrossed with moving shafts of light, probing for Allied bombers. Batteries of anti-aircraft guns could be heard in the distance throwing blankets of flak into the sky.

"*Herr Obersturmbannfuhrer* Hauptmann—*please* . . . there is a flack tower nearby with a shelter . . ." The engraver's voice tailed off.

"A flack tower? You're a fucking old woman, Plassenburg," Hauptmann said. "We haven't finished yet. There's a problem."

Plassenburg tensed. "A problem?"

"Yes. We need to be able to distinguish this version of our stamp from the others. I don't like having to use a magnifying glass to know I have the right stamp."

Plassenburg breathed with relief. "It's interesting that you mention that," the engraver said, his fear now replaced by surprising enthusiasm. "I tested something. As you see, I've constructed the engraving in two pieces."

Hauptmann said nothing.

"This little piece is the engraved head of the Fuhrer, the surrounding portion is a separate plate."

"Why?"

"If I made an error, you see. I would not have to do all of it over."

"So what is your point?"

"Like I said, the head is a separate plate so when I rotate it, like this—upside down . . ." his voice trailed off, the explanation speaking for itself.

Hauptmann stood, hand on chin, considering the engraver's idea.

"There have been such errors before," Plassenburg continued. "Printed by accident. The stamp would stand out without the need for a glass . . . it can't be missed. A collector's item."

The officer thought for a moment then patted the engraver on the back. "Brilliant, Herr Plassenburg. Absolutely brilliant! That's exactly how we'll do it."

The building began to shake. Bombs were erupting across the city. Fires ripped the darkness, marching in long lines like exploding strings of giant firecrackers.

The engraver was on the edge of panic but knew any plea to seek shelter would be futile. So he prepared the machinery with a dexterity born from years of experience and the will to live. An hour later he had a satisfactory print of the engraving.

Hauptmann examined Mendel Plassenburg's work under the powerful glass. Flawless. The numbers had been ingeniously integrated into the engraving and were clear, but only if one knew where to look.

When the print dried, he wrapped the single sheet of

paper in several layers of clean tissue, added cardboard stiffeners, wound it with oilcloth, and slid the small packet into an envelope, which he secured with tape. Then, he slid the envelope inside his tunic, next to his skin.

"Destroy the plate," the officer said. "Use the acid."

Within minutes the two parts of the plate were no more than an unidentifiable lump of melted metal on the sheet of glass.

The officer switched off the desk lamp. Only one detail remained.

"Mendel. A while ago . . . what was it you said? That you had . . . *tested something* . . . that solved the problem of identifying our stamp?"

The engraver's survival instincts had been honed from years of captivity so his expression never changed, but he felt as though blood was draining from his body.

"You printed another copy didn't you?" the officer asked, his voice low, almost conversational.

"No . . . please . . . I . . ."

"Just tell me where it is and we can both get on with our lives," the officer whispered. "There can only be one copy. The one I have here."

"Please . . . *Heir Obersturmbannfuhrer* Hauptmann, I did make one copy. Last night when you went out for food but it was only to check the accuracy of my engraving and experiment with the inversion. I took it home to study it. I was going to burn it tonight, when I returned to the apartment. I just wanted to be certain the work was right for you, that it was perfect. I meant nothing more. I'll go with you now. You'll see. My Zofia will tell you that I was going to burn it . . . I swear."

"Where in the apartment is it?"

"In my desk. In the top center drawer of my desk."

"And where are the other prints you made?"

"I . . . made . . . no other prints, *Herr*

Obersturmbannfuhrer. Just the one in my apartment for the test . . . I swear on my wife's eyes."

In one swift motion of his right hand the Luger came out of Hauptmann's holster and into the engraver's mouth. His left arm circled the small man's shoulder, holding him tight toward the revolver. "You will tell me—where are the other prints? I'll count to three, Plassenburg, and if you don't tell me where they are I'll kill you."

The engraver was paralyzed.

"One."

Plassenburg moaned.

"Two."

The engraver wet his pants.

"Three." The officer waited a moment, and then withdrew the barrel of his pistol from the engraver's mouth. "I believe you," he said.

He unscrewed his flask and handed it to Plassenburg who eagerly sucked at the liquid, feeling the snake of heat move to his empty stomach.

Plassenburg did not notice the Luger pointed at his lowered head. When he did look up, his eyes asked why, even as half his brain and the back of his head splattered across the printing press.

CHAPTER 46

HAUPTMANN HOLSTERED HIS LUGER. HE WROTE A SHORT MESSAGE ON A slip of paper, removed one of the pigeons from the carrier, the one he called *Bormann,* placed the paper into a tiny capsule attached to the bird's leg, and set the bird aloft from one of the shattered windows.

He'd made the decision to split the information, using both pigeons, rather than one. The message was therefore shorter than called for in the plan. It only described the stamp: *"12.38 RM red one of six Hitler head Deutsches Reich. Identify by inverted head."*

Once Hauptmann destroyed the second copy of the stamp, he would be the only one who knew where the diamonds were hidden. He considered how easy it would be to never send the second message, to disappear, to forget Von Erbin and Dengler and keep the diamonds for himself. How many other men in his position could turn their backs on that kind of temptation and remain as loyal to their friends? A small number, of that he was certain. But he was one of them.

Hauptmann wrote a second message consisting of the coordinates needed to find the diamonds.

He released the bird; the one named, *Rommel,* through the same window, and watched it thrash into the night sky, following *Bormann.*

Hauptmann exited, replacing the chain and lock on the front door, increasing the probability that Plassenburg's body would not be discovered for a long time. The officer's motorcycle was where he'd left it and he kicked it to life.

From a block away Hauptmann could see a cluster of fire trucks around Plassenburg's house. A fire would be just fine, he thought. As long as the second print was destroyed it made no difference how. As he got closer, however, he realized the engraver's residence was still standing; it was the building next to Plassenburg's that was burning. In a few more minutes he would get the second print from the engraver's desk drawer, destroy it and be off. Several days of hard travel still lay ahead of him. Maybe he could rest for a few hours in the engraver's apartment. Plassenburg's wife might be persuaded to provide a few hours of companionship. Hauptmann hadn't been with a woman in almost a year; he decided he might as well enjoy her before he killed her.

He leaned his motorcycle against the brick wall outside the entrance of Plassenburg's building. There were no lights because of the blackout, but he knew the apartment was on the third floor.

He held the end of his scarf to his nose and mouth to protect against the ash and smoke from the fire next door and trudged up the three flights of stairs, then stood for a moment in the hallway outside the apartment. He smelled gas.

Gas!

Something primal in him sensed what would come—as birds intuit an immanent earthquake and fly from a tree just before the first shock-waves hit. Moments before the explosion ripped upward from the bowels of the building, he swiveled and lunged back toward the stairs.

Obersturmbannfuhrer Josef Hauptmann died an instant before pain could register.

A half-hour earlier, not far from where Hauptmann died, a gray and white pigeon, thrown from the sky by an exploding bomb, fell into the burning remains of yet another building. The bird twitched for a few moments before being eaten by the flames.

It was the second pigeon Hauptmann had launched—the pigeon carrying the latitude and longitude co-ordinates in a little capsule on its leg.

The pigeon called *Rommel*.

CHAPTER 47
(New York. The present)

IT TOOK A MOMENT FOR JAKE TO REALIZE DAVIDA WAS NO LONGER talking.

It's late, he thought, looking around. A rain-soaked but boisterous pre-theater crowd had invaded the Algonquin's lobby bar and the noise level was high.

"You realize I've got a million questions but I can hardly hear myself think." Jake checked his watch. "Our table should be ready."

They were quickly seated in a quiet corner of the dining room, each ordered a vodka martini, green salad and a steak and sat in silence until the drinks were placed in front of them.

"I'm stunned," Jake said, raising his glass. "Here's to the most amazing story I've ever heard. I still can't imagine how you pieced it together?"

"I can't take much credit. This story goes back long before I was involved with Mossad or *Golem*. The process we use to track down criminals like Von Erbin and Dengler actually began in 1942. When your father helped debrief Zofia, the information was not wasted, it was used to feed that process."

Imagine, my old man, helping out Mossad. "It would have made him proud to know that what he did was important. It's a damned shame he never could bring himself to talk about it while he was alive. I think we would've both benefited."

Davida nodded. "Zofia's knowledge was of great interest to Israeli Intelligence. Of interest to American Intelligence, as well. Invaluable stuff."

"But she never told Mossad about giving the stamp to my father?"

"Think about it. At the time the stamp was a meaningless detail. She had no idea of its significance."

"I guess."

"She was able to confirm the plot to counterfeit British Pounds, to say nothing of their document forging operation that allowed hundreds, possibly thousands, of high-ranking Nazis to slip into hiding. As you can imagine, Mossad was particularly interested in that."

Jake and Davida paused while the waiter served their food. For the next few minutes they ate in silence.

"This is nice, Jake," Davida said, sipping her drink. "I'm starting to feel relaxed."

"I wish I could say the same. All this is coming at me pretty fast."

"There was no slow way to tell you."

"How long have you been on this case?"

"Me personally? Not that long.

"But your focus is now specifically on Von Erbin and Dengler?"

"Until we learned that the stamp had surfaced, they

were just two more names on a long list. But when the stamp popped up, I was put on it full time."

A new thought struck him. "Was Zofia involved with the search for Von Erbin and Dengler?"

"No. Her contribution was information. She was able to report, for example, that the third Nazi, Hauptmann, had been killed in the explosion that destroyed her building and killed her husband."

"But if you knew that both Mendel and Hauptmann were blown up at the apartment, why did you think there was still a stamp floating around? She obviously didn't tell anyone in Israel who she gave the stamp to. If she had, you could have gotten it a long time ago by contacting my father."

"That's true. The pieces of the story didn't all come together until some time after Zofia died. Mossad uncovered the police report of Mendel Plassenburg's death. The report claimed he had escaped from *Sachenhousen,* was tracked down by the Gestapo in Berlin, and killed."

"And that tied back to Hauptmann?"

"It took some digging. Mossad knew from Zofia's reports that Mendel was doing work for Hauptmann in the building where his body was found. They discounted the Gestapo story and, instead, theorized that Hauptmann murdered the engraver after his work was completed."

"How can you be so sure that Hauptmann was really killed in the explosion. What if he just buried his motorcycle there and took off. After all, he was the only one who knew where the diamonds were hidden."

"That was exactly the same question Von Erbin and Dengler were asking. It had to be verified beyond any doubt. And it was. The police eventually found Hauptmann's body. What was left of it. Its prints matched those in his SS file. The dental records matched, as well.

"The investigation was carried out on the orders of a

certain General officer. It doesn't take much imagination to guess the officer's identity."

"Von Erbin?"

"None other. Mossad became convinced that Hauptmann killed Mendel, then drove his motorcycle to the Plassenburg apartment."

"If Mossad knew that Hauptmann had been killed when he came back to get the second copy of the stamp, couldn't they have located my father in America and gotten the original stamp back from him? It wasn't as if he was in hiding. Hell, it took them seventeen years to find Eichmann. They could have found Moe in about seventeen minutes. He was in the phone book, for crying out loud."

"Absolutely. Just one little problem. Mossad didn't know what Hauptmann's reason was for going back to the apartment. The connection, between the stamp and the diamonds hadn't yet been made."

"Then why did Mossad think Hauptmann would go back to the apartment after killing Mendel?"

Davida made a small shrug. "Lust."

Jake remembered Zofia's picture. "I see."

Davida ran her hand through her hair, a familiar gesture. "Zofia was forthcoming about all of Mendel's projects. She had even mentioned the stamp's inverted image of Hitler and the fact that she had given it away. But we simply had no idea that a secret was engraved on the stamp . . . nor did she."

"And she never mentioned my father's name?"

"No. Don't forget, Jake . . . this was a long time ago. A different morality. Your father was a married man with a family. She was simply honoring his anonymity."

How different things might have been had Zofia not been so honorable.

"So she was protecting him?"

"Something like that. In retrospect, Zofia told us everything except the one thing we needed to know—the name of the man she'd given the stamp to, the father of her child."

"But you had my father's dog tag," Jake said.

"Yes. But it meant nothing at the time. When Zofia died back in 1980, her effects filled a large storage room. Mossad simply dismissed it as just another memento in a room brimming with more important stuff."

"I'm still having trouble figuring out how you made the connection to my father."

Davida considered Jake's question while she sliced off a piece of steak and popped it into her mouth. Jake watched her chew and waited for her to answer.

"The posting Kunze made on his website was the key," Davida began. "When our research people saw it, they were shocked. That's when I was put on the case full time. As part of my prep work, I had all of Zofia's things pulled out of storage and combed through it. But unlike Mossad back in the '80s, I now had the name of the person who owned the stamp. So, when I came across your father's dog tag, the connection fell into place."

Clear, simple words that explained and made sense. But what Jake was feeling in his heart was maddeningly capricious. His father and a camp survivor had stood, shivering in the snow, and traded a sliver of metal and a scrap of paper. Their action lit a fuse that burned for half a century. When it finally blew, his father and a stamp dealer were dead.

"How did you decide that the stamp was the key to finding diamonds? Or, that they were hidden in a lake outside of Potsdam?"

"We sort of backed into the scenario. When Kunze's website described a German stamp from the Third Reich it alerted Mossad's researchers. They fed the information into our computers and out popped references to Zofia and Mendel Plassenburg and the stamp. What they found made a connection between a German stamp that was engraved and a German stamp that was for sale—possibly one and the same stamp—and the two were separated by sixty years! The question was, *Why?*"

Jake thought about it, absently sipping his drink.

"As it turned out, it was all there in the computer. For years we'd known that diamonds were 'taken' from a number of concentration camps. We discovered from Wehrmacht records that Hauptmann had visited a few dozen camps and, with authorization papers signed by Hermann Goering, had 'appropriated' the diamonds, ostensibly to be used for the war effort. We believe Hauptmann hid them in one of the lakes near Potsdam."

"Come on," Jake said, each word wrapped in skepticism. "Why not a cave near Munich? Or down a well outside of Dresden?"

"Three soldiers were traveling with Hauptmann. Some children found their bodies in a lake near Potsdam. Ballistics confirmed they were shot with bullets fired from the same type of gun that killed Mendel. A Luger."

"Hell, every German officer carried a Luger. How do you even know the soldiers were traveling with Hauptmann?"

Davida's eyes flashed. She seemed to be relishing his interrogation. "The corpses were secured with wire into vehicles checked out from the SS motor pool in Berlin by Axel Dengler, obviously for Hauptmann's use. An unopened bag of cement was found in the boot of one of the cars. One of the vehicles was an amphibian, a *Schwimmwagen.* We think Hauptmann took the diamonds to the deep part of one of the Potsdam lakes and sank them. Then Hauptmann shot the three soldiers and sank them along with the vehicles. Hauptmann had a motorcycle in Berlin; we assume he carried it with him and used it to go back to Berlin. And, once back in Berlin, we know from Zofia's account that he got Plassenburg out of *Sachsenhausen* for a second time and had him engrave a counterfeit version of the postage stamp.

We're pretty sure that the key to finding the diamonds is revealed somehow on the stamp and that their location is
likely in some body of water in the Potsdam vicinity."

"Why not dredge?"

"There are hundreds of lakes, rivers, and canals in that
part of Germany. Dredging would be an impossible task.
Unless we can narrow down the location, we'll never be able
to find the diamonds."

"Did you at least check the lake where the dead soldiers
were found—wouldn't that have made some sense?" Jake
said.

"Of course. We had divers in there for two weeks. Nothing."

"So there's no chance of finding the diamonds, right?"

"Not unless we can locate the stamp."

CHAPTER 48

JAKE WAS SILENT, OBLIVIOUS TO THE CONFUSION OF RESTAURANT noises surrounding him; the clink of dinnerware, conversational chatter, and bursts of laughter.

Suddenly he saw what Davida was driving at. The real reason for her needing to find the stamp.

"The stamp's not what you're after, is it?"

She shrugged, her eyes never left his. "It's the magnet. Von Erbin and Dengler are the metal shavings. I've no doubt that the attraction will be strong enough to pull them out of hiding."

"If that happens, what will you do with them?"

What would be done with them? Davida's answer came from her body language. Her back went rigid, her jaw set and her eyes narrowed. *Whatever's necessary.*

Jake heard the answer as clearly as if she'd shouted. And for the first time since they met, Jake understood what drove Davida's passion for justice . . . or maybe, revenge. He'd felt it himself in Vietnam. He was feeling it now. It was a bond between them.

"What can I do? I need to be involved." Jake said, and found he was touching her hand.

"Nothing." She didn't pull away.

"Nothing?"

"You're already involved. Whoever is looking for the stamp will eventually find you."

"Is that supposed to be comforting?"

"I don't believe you're in real danger as long as you don't actually know where the stamp is."

Jake felt his insides shudder and it took effort not to raise his voice. After all, this wasn't her fault. "What about Kunze? He didn't know where the stamp was, and they still killed him."

"But you're the end of the line for them. Kunze was only one stop along the way. You're their only hope of ever finding the stamp. The last person they can afford . . . to kill . . . right now."

It was the "right now" part that was terrifying.

CHAPTER 49

IT WAS LATE BY THE TIME JAKE PUT DAVIDA INTO A CAB OUTSIDE THE Algonquin.

He was mentally exhausted but excited and intrigued by Davida's story and walked back to his apartment slowly, needing time, space and air to try and digest what he'd heard.

Wait and they will find you, she'd said. Hell, I'm about as difficult to find as a goat spiked out as bait for a hungry lion.

To make things more complicated, Jake found himself thinking about Davida. Not about their discussion, but about her. The cool professional, the complicated person.

He had just spent almost ten hours, sitting within inches of the woman, listening to her talk, yet she was so heavily fortified she revealed next to nothing.

He learned much about her world, but nothing about her life.

There had to be more to her than tracking old Nazi war criminals.

He wondered if, in her zeal, he was an expendable member of her hunting party? And, incongruously, if she was married?

It was almost ten P.M. when he arrived at his apartment house. Walter, the doorman was there before Jake could fish out his key. "A lady, Mr. Jake, she's waiting for you."

He entered the lobby. "I don't believe it!"

Sitting on a bench, feet resting on her wheeled duffle bag, was Toby Benjamin.

"I should have called. It was sort of last minute." Toby got to her feet and hugged him, her body pressed against his.

Jake's mind was spinning, struggling for traction. Of all the things to happen now!

He held her away from him, hands on her shoulders, and looked her up and down. "Let me guess: you ran away from home?"

"Actually, it was more like running to, rather than from. Your buddy Harry came back to work. They didn't need me behind the bar any more. I figured, why hang around?"

"Well, remind me to thank Harry," Jake said, picking up Toby's duffle and following her into the elevator.

They rode in silence, Toby snuggling against Jake's arm. He smiled at her. "I'm really glad to see you," Jake said, determined to dismiss Davida from his thoughts.

"I may never go back." Toby laughed. "No, I'm not planning on moving in. Just for tonight, then I'll find a more permanent place to park."

Toby stood in the middle of Jake's living room, taking it all in. "What a wonderful place! I love it. The art's fantastic."

"It's mostly WPA stuff . . . from the Depression."

"Sure. Works Projects Administration. Franklin D. Roosevelt. The New Deal. John Reed."

"You know the period?" Jake said, surprised.

"A little."

"Once you get settled I'll give you the complete tour. Meanwhile, what can I get you? A drink?"

"Yes. But first, a hot shower."

"No problem, and, seriously, you're welcome to stay—certainly until you find your own place or until we drive each other crazy."

"Thanks." Toby bussed his cheek. Her lips felt soft and cool. He pulled her closer and kissed her.

"I'm happy you're here," Jake said. The passionate response he'd felt for her in Florida came back quickly. Like riding a bike. "If I seemed detached, it's just that you surprised me. Now, as for the hot shower and cold drink—I've a good supply of both those liquids. But you must also be starved!"

Toby checked her watch. "It's late. Haven't you already eaten?"

"Dinner meeting," Jake lied. "But I'll get something for you. How does Chinese sound?"

"Love it."

While Toby showered, Jake ordered the food then checked his answering machine.

A message from Sam Stein! What could he need to discuss with me, Jake wondered? Kunze's murder? Possible. But Stein didn't know he and Kunze were connected. The subject of the stamp was never part of discussions with the Florida detective. It couldn't be that important. He'd call him in the morning.

*   *   *

They lay in Jake's large bed, beneath a soft duvet.

Toby rested on her side, propped on an elbow facing

Jake. Her hair was still damp, combed back. The front of her robe was loose, partially exposing an exquisite breast. "I missed you," she said, touching his face.

"I'd forgotten how beautiful you are," Jake whispered.

Toby shrugged out of her robe. Jake saw then touched a tiny red apple tattoo on her right hip.

"Ah, yes . . . my infamous tattoo. It's what happens when irresponsible youth mixes with the devil's brew."

Jake's body reacted mindlessly and then they were in each other's arms. Jake's passion was explosive. He made love without regard for his partner and that, in turn, seemed to excite Toby.

Later, he padded, naked, to the living room, poured Cognac, and brought it back to the bed. In the nearly dark room, they talked for an hour. Not once was there mention of the stamp or his father's death or Kunze's brutal murder.

CHAPTER 50

WHEN THE PHONE RANG IT WAS STILL DARK.

Jake woke with a start, grabbed the receiver. Toby didn't stir.

"Jake . . . just listen, don't say anything. Answer my questions with a yes or no. Understood?"

It took Jake a moment to clear his head, to realize it was Davida calling. "Yes."

"Are you alone?"

"Uh, No."

"Shit! Is the phone cordless?"

"No."

"Do you have a cell phone?"

"Yes."

"I'm going to give you a number and I want you to go someplace you can't be overheard. The bathroom, maybe. And call me back. Can you do that?"

"Yes."

"Now say something that will justifies making a cell call. Pretend there's a problem . . . maybe in London with your daughter . . . that sort of thing."

Jake's mind seemed mired. Finally, "Listen, darling, I know you're upset."

"Excellent. Now say you'll call me back in a minute or two."

"Yes. You're at your friend's flat? Okay, I'll call you back. Give me the number."

Jake took a pen from the night table and scribbled the number onto the palm of his hand.

Toby stirred. "What was that about?"

"Sorry, didn't mean to wake you. My daughter in London. Her boyfriend walked out. Now she may not be able to swing the money for her flat."

"You can call from here, Jake . . . it won't bother me."

"It's okay. I'll use the other room. Try to get back to sleep." Jake slipped into a robe. A minute later he was in the bathroom, sitting on the toilet seat.

Davida picked up a millisecond into the first ring.

"Jake?"

"Yes. What's going on?"

"Alan Carson was murdered."

Jake leaned forward as if he'd been punched in the stomach.

"Did you hear me?"

"Yes. My god! When?"

"A day or two ago. Tied up and shot. A twenty-two caliber to the back of his head. His body was just discovered."

"Just . . . like . . . Kunze."

"Yes."

"I was just with him the other day! That poor son of a bitch. I don't know what to say. I really don't. How did you find out?"

"The radio. You'd mentioned Carson yesterday. I went

over to his building. We work closely with the police, and my credentials got me up to his office. By then the body had been taken away."

A sliver of paper had become a serial killer.

"His death is terrible. But there's more."

Adrenalin flooded his body. "More?"

"There's a chance that you'll either be charged with Carson's murder or, at least, become the prime suspect."

"You can't be serious! Why?"

"I got a look at Carson's appointment book. According to his schedule, you were the last person to see him before he was killed."

True. It was his appointment. He'd been there.

"There was no phone number or address in the book," Davida went on. "Just the notation, 'J GRN.' There must be over a hundred Greens with first names beginning with J."

"That's the good news?"

"It'll take the police some time to check them out. But they'll get to you sooner or later. Evidently, no file with any J Green or J Greene was found."

"No. Carson gave me my father's file. He was closing his practice. He said he had no further need for it."

"That'll help. Unfortunately the guard in the lobby was able to give them a good description of you. That money you told me about—the cash you paid to the guard to leave the building through the emergency exit—well, it's going to look a little strange, don't you agree?" Jake could hear the concern in her voice.

"This is ridiculous," Jake mumbled, worry creeping up his spine. "Carson was my father's lawyer. I was there to finalize his affairs. The man was alive when I left him. Okay, so I left through the side door—what's the big deal?"

"It's suspicious that you went out that side exit. And paid ten bucks for the privilege."

Jake thought for a moment. "I'll tell them someone was

outside whom I didn't want to see. An old girlfriend. An irate husband."

"Don't be foolish. If you tell them there was a girlfriend they'll want to know her name. Where she lives. Eventually, you'll have to admit that you were trying to avoid two guys you thought were following you. And that will take them directly to Kunze and his death. And, Jake, trust me—this is not a patch of quicksand you want to jump into."

Jake's arms felt leaden and he rested them on his legs, his hands close to the tile floor. He fought back a wave of nausea. If this wasn't his familiar nightmare, it was damn close. No grenades this time, just a cell phone clutched in a clammy hand. But, nevertheless, he was about to be blown to bits.

Jake pressed the phone to his ear. "What possible motive could I have for killing Carson?" he said, feeling the full impact of his own vulnerability.

"Maybe you believed Carson was holding back on your inheritance. Anything's possible! We both know you had no reason to kill Carson, but on the other hand, you sure as hell don't have an alibi, either."

Jake remembered the message from Sam Stein. "The detective who was working on my father's case called."

"From Florida?"

"Yes. He wants to talk to me. Down there."

"He asked you to come to Florida?"

"His message said something had come up about the case."

Davida was silent. For a moment Jake thought the connection was broken. Finally, "Don't call him. There's nothing you can say that will keep him from being even more suspicious. Here's what you've got to do. Do you have a valid passport?"

Jake's anger flared. "What do you think I'm going to do, skip across the border?

"Do you have a passport?"

"Yes. But I'll be damned if I'm going to leave the country. I might just as well turn myself in."

"You'd be safer that way. I'm sure you'd eventually be cleared of any involvement but they'll press you hard because they've no one else to press. If Carson's killer was hired by Von Erbin and Dengler to track down the stamp, you can be sure he's a professional. And guys like that are almost impossible to catch. They cross borders as easily as you cross streets. The killer could be anywhere by now. So as far as the New York police are concerned, you're it."

"What's my alternative?" Jake said.

"Find the stamp! Because if we do, the killer won't be far away, and we can get you untangled from this mess."

"Untangled," Jake uttered in frustration. "What do you want me to do?"

"Pack. I've reserved a seat for you out of Newark on a Virgin flight to Heathrow. It leaves at 8:20 this morning. It's 4:30 now so if you move quickly, you can make it."

Jake contemplated the step Davida was asking him to take. What if Stein had found Kunze's killer? How would it look, his leaving the country? "You were that sure I would go?"

"I never thought you had a choice. Don't use a car service. Just grab a taxi. When you get to the airport, go to the Virgin desk and they'll issue your ticket. It's a round-trip with an open return. It's already paid for. Don't use credit cards. Does your building have a doorman?"

"Yes."

"Tell him you're going back to Florida to take care of your father's affairs. And, Jake, bring along everything of your father's that Carson gave you. I want to have it studied and analyzed."

"What do I do when I get to London?"

"Someone will meet you. When you come out of customs, they'll find you. Understand?"

"Yes. But, listen, Davida . . . I've got someone staying here at the apartment. I can't just leave her here."

A skipped beat. Then, "Course you can. Make up a story. She already thinks your daughter's having money problems. Stick with that. Tell her you're going to London. For god's sake don't bring her along." Davida's voice softened. "You can either leave her to go to London or leave her to go to jail . . . it's your call."

The connection broke. Jake sat holding the phone, terrified.

London. Would he be any safer there?

He had to figure out what he'd tell Toby.

CHAPTER 51

SHE WAS DIFFICULT TO MISS, THE ONLY WOMAN STANDING ALONGSIDE A slouch of limousine drivers, and the only person not holding a sign.

Jake broke into a broad smile.

"Welcome to Ol' Blighty," Davida said and encircled him with her arms. "After we spoke, I figured I'd best be here when you arrived. You sounded like you might appreciate a little support from someone with a familiar face."

Their bodies fit nicely and felt disarmingly comfortable. "True," Jake said, speaking into Davida's hair, slow to pull away. "Especially since this is my debut in fleeing my country of birth. How did you get here before me? Don't tell me you've got an Air Force at your disposal?"

"I got a hop on an Israeli Military Transport. Did you check any bags?"

"Nope. This is it." Jake indicated his garment carrier, handbag, and briefcase.

"Then let's get out of here." They walked toward the exit. "After I get you settled we'll do a few hours of homework. Serious homework. We've got lots to do and not much time."

A car and driver were waiting outside. Within forty-five minutes they pulled into the small crescent drive that fronted The Berkeley Hotel. A light rain that had begun soon after they left Heathrow was still falling.

"I've arranged a suite for you," Davida said. "My room's right across the hall. You're checked in already but they need to see your passport—front desk is up those steps. I'll round up some room service and meet you in the suite."

"Nothing heavy, please. A Scotch rocks. Make it double. And some eggs, toast and plenty of coffee."

"Won't it keep you awake?"

"The coffee and an earthquake, maybe."

*   *   *

The suite consisted of a bedroom and bath, a spacious sitting room and a small powder room. He had just finished unpacking when room service arrived.

Jake ate a piece of toast, took a swallow of his Scotch, then went to shave and shower. Thirty minutes later, he answered a knock on the door.

"You look better," Davida said, stroking his freshly shaved face as she passed into the room.

"Feel better."

"Where's the stuff from Carson?"

Jake handed Davida his briefcase. While she decanted its contents onto the coffee table, Jake phoned Adrian, got the machine and left a message telling her where he was. Then he downed what was left of his Scotch.

"Let's get to work," he said. "I've got my second wind but I don't think it'll last more than a few hours."

They sat, hip to hip on the sofa and began going through the materials.

She had laughed when Jake first told her of his father's coded letter. Now she read the decoded version intently.

"Nothing here explains what he did with the stamp," Davida said, putting the pages down.

Next, they studied the two photographs. "Good-looking guy, your dad. I'm trying to see the resemblance."

"Very funny. The letter came in this envelope," Jake said. "Also the stamp album and mounting hinges."

She spent several minutes examining the envelope, then retrieved hotel stationery and a pen from its leather folder. "Okay. Let's take a look at what we know and what we don't."

"Sounds reasonable."

"Let's start back when Zofia gave your father the stamp."

"And the dog tag."

"Right. Little gifts that neither one expected to see again. Obviously, he stashed the stamp and forgot about it."

"I don't think so," Jake said. "I'd bet that he never stopped thinking about it because he never stopped thinking about Zofia. He was coming to the end of his life so he wrote me the letter and tried to find out what the stamp was worth."

"But way before that," said Davida, "Hauptmann was blown up in Berlin. The other two most likely escaped from Germany. And then sixty years of silence."

An obvious question occurred to Jake. "How did Von Erbin and Dengler know when the stamp would come onto the market?

"Exactly the same way Mossad did. They became collectors."

"You're serious?"

"You'd be surprised how many Nazis we've found when they tried to sell a stolen painting or a piece of Nazi memorabilia. The market for everything from SS daggers to complete Wehrmacht uniforms is huge."

"I still don't understand why the stamp wasn't with the letter."

Davida got up and stretched. "The truth? I don't know why, either. It makes no sense. It should be."

"What if I threw the stamp out when I was clearing the apartment? It's possible, you know," Jake said, terrified at the thought. "I certainly wasn't looking for a stamp."

"Impossible."

"How can you be so sure?" Jake recalled the bags and bags of trash he'd tossed, without close examination.

"You couldn't have thrown it out because it wasn't there. Everything your father wrote indicates he sent the stamp with this letter to Alan Carson and planned on checking its dollar value later." She went back to the transcription. "It says right here, *I'm mailing this letter to Alan Carson and as soon as I find out if the stamp is worth anything I'll let him know.*' He didn't say, 'I'll find out what the stamp is worth and then send it to Carson.' He sent the stamp with the letter."

Frustration made Jake's head ache. "It wasn't in the package when I opened it and, as you can see, it's not here now."

"We need the stamp," Davida said with a mixture of finality and frustration.

Jake buried his face in his hands. "If I had the damned stamp, I'd give it to them."

"It wouldn't make a difference. Von Erbin and Dengler couldn't take a chance. Anyone who comes in contact with the stamp has to be killed."

The reality of what Davida said was too raw, too conclusive. "You're saying that regardless of what I do—find the stamp, don't find the stamp, give it to them . . . or not give it to them, they'll try to kill me?"

"Yes."

"So this business about being in London to untangle me is so much smoke."

Davida couldn't make eye contact. "I want to keep you alive and find Von Erbin and Dengler."

"But not necessarily in that order?"

"The only chance of getting what we want is if they do come after you."

"God dammit!" Jake exploded. "All this crap about being implicated in the Carson killing . . . it was all a bunch of bullshit to get me to London so you can use me someplace where Mossad can work a little more freely? You don't care about me. This is all about your sick, neurotic, obsession. You think you can become another Wiesenthal? Another great Nazi hunter? Looking for a Nobel Peace Prize? Fuck you!"

Davida didn't respond. Couldn't find the words to respond, he thought. In the silence Jake stood, walked to the window, then to the bathroom and washed his face. His hands were shaking. He went back to the sitting room, hoping Davida had left.

She hadn't. She was standing. She took his face in her hands. "Jake, please. Hear me out. I didn't get you into this. With me or without me, the die is . . . was cast, a long time ago. You may not want to hear it, may want to believe I'm using you, but the truth is, I'm your best hope. Please. Believe me we both want the same thing."

"Tell me . . . what *is it* we want? I'm so tired, I've lost track."

Jake was suddenly exhausted. The jet lag, the adrenaline provoking days—whatever it was, it had caught up with him.

"We want you alive. We want you cleared of any involvement in these terrible deaths. We want to find Von Erbin and Dengler and make them pay for their crimes. We just have to be patient. Wait for them to make a move."

Jake stood still for some time, thinking hard. "Maybe there's an alternative," he whispered.

"What's that?"

"What if we don't wait for them to come after me? What if *we* find them first?"

CHAPTER 52
(New York)

ARTHUR SCANLON WAS NORMALLY A CALM MAN BUT AFTER READING the FAX, he was apoplectic.

"I was expecting your call," Phillipe Scoville said. "I assume you had a chance to study the financials."

"*Study them!* Fucking right. You're in the middle of a god damned financial meltdown. What the hell happened since the last quarter?"

"The economy, Arthur. It's been very poor."

"The economy? Don't give me that shit."

He could hear his partner's breathing. "I can read a balance sheet," Arthur said, "and this one doesn't look good. My father trusted you and I've tried to show you the same trust. But someone's been playing with the numbers, and it ain't me."

"Are you implying I've done something illegal?"

"Illegal, immoral, dishonest, shady, underhanded, flimflam. Yes! This could sink Crane Industries. And you know damned well that even though we run our pieces of the company independently, we own Crane jointly. For accounting purposes there's no 'firewall.' If your end has the kind of liabilities this report indicates, it'll have to be covered by my half. And I'll be damned if I'll let this business go down as a direct result of your . . . I don't know what to call it . . . *surprising* losses?"

Philippe Scoville chose to say nothing. Scanlon was correct. The losses had been piling up for almost a year. There was no hiding them any longer. Not with the market what it was. Scoville reckoned Arthur would call for a board meeting. That was fine. He had enough board support to protect him for another few quarters. With any luck he could cover his losses by then.

Anything could happen in a few months.

Scanlon tried to keep his voice as even as possible. "I'm calling an emergency board meeting. I'll fly over to London tonight. Set it up for tomorrow afternoon. We've no time to waste. And Philippe—make sure someone from the auditing firm is there."

"Very well," Scoville said tightly. "I'll see you tomorrow."

He broke the connection but remained seated behind his desk for several minutes, staring into space. Then he called his lawyer.

"I want you to review the partnership agreement. Do it immediately. I'll have questions."

"No problem. Anything in particular you want me to check?"

"The original agreement divided ownership of Crane Industries equally between S.J. and me. It stipulated that when one of us died, his portion of the partnership would go directly to the other, unless the partner who died had a son.

When S.J. died, his share went to Arthur. Since I've no male heir, when I die, my half reverts to Arthur, as well."

"Correct. What is your question?"

"What happens if Arthur pre-deceases me? Does his half remain as part of his estate or does it revert to me?"

"I'll check it right away. But probably back to you."

"Make certain."

"Is Arthur ill?"

"It's a distinct possibility."

CHAPTER 53

SCANLON TOLD HIS SECRETARY TO MAKE THE ARRANGEMENTS for his flight to London on the company's jet. Then he left his office and walked the Midtown streets, trying to come up with a solution to the mess Scoville had handed him.

The exercise and fresh air helped him regain some composure, although he hadn't yet a clear idea of what he would say at the board meeting. He'd have plenty of time during the flight to work on it.

It was clear to Arthur that the board, sympathetic to Philippe's long and otherwise successful handling of the company, would recommend that Arthur cover the losses. And he would, he vowed, even though it would take every penny he had, plus everything he could borrow.

But only on the condition that Scoville agree to sell his half of the company to him. If Scoville refused, Arthur would sue. Ironic: Arthur was going to force his partner to accept money for what was now, thanks to his partner, a nearly bankrupt entity.

On 51st Street Arthur found himself in front of a small stamp and coin store. It reminded him of his promise to Jake Green.

Almost a week had passed since he and Jake lunched on the museum steps. Arthur felt guilty about not getting back to him.

At least he could apologize.

CHAPTER 54

TOBY BENJAMIN STEPPED OUT OF THE SHOWER AS THE PHONE RANG.

She jogged naked into the bedroom to answer, leaving a trail of wet footprints on the carpet.

"Green residence," Toby said.

"This is Arthur Scanlon. Is Jake there, please?"

Arthur Scanlon! Toby knew the name well. And what she knew could be summed up in one word: *Rich!*

"Sorry, he's not here. I'm Toby Benjamin . . . a friend he's letting camp out in his apartment for a few days while he's out of the country."

"Out of the country? I'm sorry I missed him."

"You were close. He left for London early this morning."

"Fortunate. I'm flying to London today. Do you happen to know where he's staying?"

"Matter of fact, he called a while ago. The Berkeley Hotel."

Hanging up, she tossed her nightgown into her suit-case.

She was already booked on a flight to London leaving in three hours.

Jake would be surprised.

CHAPTER 55

"LET'S SAY I FOUND THE STAMP."

It was the following morning and Jake and Davida were walking in Hyde Park.

Davida stopped short. "You *found* it?"

"No, but let's say I did. Just hypothetically . . . tell me what would we do . . . right now?"

"We'd want to make damn sure Von Erbin and Dengler found out about it."

"Right."

"I'm not sure I see where you're going with this," Davida said.

"Up until now they've had no choice but to work the leads as they developed. Once the stamp surfaced, they went after my father, then Kunze and then Carson, step by step, like following crumbs dropped in the forest. Right now they're facing a dilemma."

"Which is?"

"Me."

"You?"

"Yes. Because they can't be certain that I have it. And if I don't have it, they're finished."

Davida smiled in recognition. "No more crumbs to follow. So they're frozen, just waiting to see what you'll do. If you can lead them to the stamp."

"Like a deer in the headlights. But what if we eliminate the guesswork? Take away their uncertainty. Present them with the jackpot. Tell them where it is and how they can get it."

Davida stopped walking and turned toward Jake. "You're serious? Would you do that?"

"Why not?"

"Because it's dangerous."

"Like you said, one way or another, I'm their next target. We can wait for them, or we can take control. Make them play on our timetable and by our rules."

"Look, Jake . . . I do like what you're suggesting but, please, be clear, being in danger and going after danger are two different things."

Jake spotted a bench and led Davida to it. They sat. "When I was eight or nine, my pals and I would spend our summer vacation playing baseball. Endless pickup games on a lot that had never seen a blade of grass. Four or five guys on a side. We'd use baseballs that we'd have to tape every couple of days to keep them from falling apart. One day two older boys, big guys, maybe high school age, were watching us play. They called us over and one of them says, 'Any of you kids a Jew?' No one said anything. It was a Catholic neighborhood and I was the only Jew in our group. I just stood there, scared out of my mind. I finally mumbled that I was. One of them grabbed me and held me. The second older guy took a penknife and cut his initials in my arm, just deep enough to bleed. I never said a word. Didn't cry."

Davida grimaced at the picture Jake was painting.

"What's haunted me all these years—is that I didn't try to fight them."

"They were almost twice your age. What could you have done?"

"I could have gotten beat up!" Jake spit out the words. "Lost a fight. Something. But I just stood there and took it."

"And you see this as a similar situation?"

"For me it is. I don't have the stamp. But I can't just stand around waiting for them to come after me."

"To carve their initials in your arm?"

"Metaphorically? Yes."

Davida massaged her forehead as if trying to rub out a bad headache. Jake assumed she was going through the salient points of his idea, weighing the pros and cons. He was willing to put his ass on the line and wondered if, beyond catching Von Erbin and Dengler, she really gave a damn.

"I get your point," she said, finally. "So it will have to be a meeting that you . . . that *we* initiate and control."

"Exactly."

*   *   *

They wrestled with the question of how to set it up as they picked over lunch. Finally, Jake came up with the notion of an auction

"What makes you think they'd show up for something like that?" Davida asked.

"Greed."

"Greed's one thing. But in this case I believe survival would trump greed. Think how careful they've been to hide from the best intelligence organization in the world. Don't you think they might be a tad suspicious of an auction?"

"Here's how I see it," Jake said. "An old man in Florida contacts an obscure stamp dealer. Suddenly, after sixty years, Von Erbin and Dengler learn the stamp has surfaced and their diamonds are again more than an unattainable fantasy. What is there about those events that has the smell of a Mossad sting?"

"But what if they sent someone to bid for them?" Davida said.

"No!" Jake exclaimed. "Don't you see, that would be too dangerous. Think about it. Whoever they sent would have to know what to look for in order to make sure it was the right stamp. That person would then have the ability to go after the diamonds on his own. They can't chance that."

Davida gazed at Jake, not even trying to mask her admiration. "Damn! I think it can work. Absolutely!"

Jake hoped she was right, because he wasn't at all sure that it would.

CHAPTER 56

JOSHUA RETURNED THE GENERAL'S CALL.

"I'm getting impatient," he said.

"Everything's fine. You worry too much. I should have the stamp within the week."

The General's skepticism showed in his voice. "What did you learn from the old Jew's lawyer?"

"That he didn't have the stamp."

"Can you be sure?"

"Of course. I used chemicals."

"I've no intention of telling you how to do your job. But I can't help but worry."

"Don't. The police have no way of tracing the lawyer's death to me. If anything, they suspect the son."

"Just be careful. Green's the only one that can have the stamp. If the police take him in, we may never get it."

"By the time the police find him I'll have your stamp."

The General made no comment. "I have another job for you," he said. "Can you be in London tomorrow? I prefer not to discuss this any further on the phone."

"All right. How about lunch?"

CHAPTER 57

THE INTERCOM BUZZED. "SHIT!" ADRIAN GREEN SAID.

She hated being interrupted when she was painting.

Next to her front door was the keypad that connected to the building's entrance two flights below. "Yes?"

The small speaker crackled back. "Hi, I'm looking for Adrian Green?"

"She's not here. I'm the cat sitter."

"I'm a friend of Jake, her father. I'm passing through London on my way back to the States and wanted to take him up on his suggestion that I look her up. I have an art gallery in New York. In SoHo. If she was around I'd sure like to check out her work."

No words held more magic.

"Wait! Sorry. I'm Adrian Green. I was in the middle of working and didn't want to be disturbed. Let me buzz you in."

CHAPTER 58

JAKE RANG ADRIAN AGAIN BUT ONLY GOT HER ANSWERING MACHINE.

He'd call later. Right now he needed a nap.

The phone woke him. "Hello?"

"Jake? It's Arthur Scanlon."

"Arthur? Oh, *Arthur*. I was sleeping. Are you calling from the States?"

"No, in London. Flew in this morning."

"How did you know I was here?"

Scanlon explained he'd gotten the name of his hotel from Toby Benjamin.

"I must have called your apartment right after you spoke with her."

Jake's anger surged then passed. She'd have no reason not to tell Arthur where he was staying.

"How come you're in London?"

"Board meeting. Free for dinner tonight?"

Jake hadn't heard from Scanlon since their lunch in New York. He wanted to discuss it with Davida before making any commitments.

"I'm not sure I can make it. Give me your number and I'll get back to you."

*   *   *

Showered and dressed, Jake slipped a note under Davida's door telling her he'd gone to Adrian's flat, back before 6:00, and to meet in the lobby.

The taxi dropped him off in front of Adrian's building.

Jake pressed the button next to A. GREEN several times. Nothing. He buzzed PORTER.

"Yes, can I help you?" A metallic voice asked.

Jake introduced himself as Adrian Green's father. The porter buzzed him in.

No, the porter didn't know where Adrian was, adding she was a wonderful tenant and a pleasure to have in the building.

It didn't take much for Jake to persuade the man to let him into to his daughter's flat.

There was a note pinned on the front door.

IN AMSTERDAM FOR A FEW DAYS. BACK SOON.

At least he now knew where she was.

Using the Porter's key, Jake let himself in.

He had flown to London when Adrian first rented the flat. As an architect, he was used to seeing run-down places but this was one of the worst. Peeling wallpaper, floors encrusted with years of accumulated crud, a deplorable bathroom, a useless kitchen nook.

But Adrian had fallen in love with the space; it was large and, for most of the day, bright and sunny.

The difference, Jake now saw, was dramatic. The floors had been sanded down to the pale wood and the walls painted a bright white. Rolls of canvas and stretchers of various sizes were neatly stacked in a large, vertical bin. A half dozen paintings hung on the walls, others were stacked on the floor.

A stretched canvas, larger than any of the others, was propped against a wall, clearly a work in progress. He could tell it depicted Trafalgar Square, even though it was in Adrian's abstract style. The colors were bright, the oil paint applied thickly and aggressively with heavy brush strokes.

Jake studied the picture for some time. It was good, he thought, and felt a swell of pride.

A studio bed was in one corner, a TV on a stand pointed toward the bed. Books were stacked neatly in a large book- case. Art books were piled next to the bed, serving as a night table. An old-fashioned wind-up clock ticked loudly.

Nothing seemed out of order. Pleased and amazed to see hard evidence of how neat his adult daughter had be- come. Jake stopped at the Porter's flat on the way out to re- turn the key. He wrote down his hotel's phone number and asked the man to give it to Adrian when she came back, just in case she erased her message tape.

"I understand, sir. I'm a father myself," the porter said.

In the cab, Jake was struck by a fleeting thought.

Why would Adrian go to Amsterdam without cleaning her brushes?

CHAPTER 59

"DID YOU SEE ADRIAN?" DAVIDA ASKED. THEY WERE SITTING IN THE Berkeley Lounge.

"Nope. She went to Amsterdam for a few days."

Jake told Davida about Arthur Scanlon's phone call. "At one time Scanlon and I were, I guess you'd say, fairly close. Last week was the first I'd seen him in years. Turns out he's a stamp collector. Over the years he'd done some business with Kunze. When Kunze called to tell him about the German stamp, he recognized my father's name, made the connection, and called me."

"Can you trust him?"

Jake shrugged, clearly frustrated. "I'm not sure. I'm pretty certain that his only interest in the stamp is as a collector. Trustworthy or not, he could be helpful."

"How so?"

"Scanlon claims he knows everybody in the stamp

world. His own collection consists primarily of errors. A word from him to the right people—collectors and dealers—and the chances would be excellent that Von Erbin and Dengler would hear about the auction."

"But didn't you say Scanlon was interested in buying the stamp for himself?"

"That's what he said."

"Then why would he want to spread the word to a bunch of other collectors?"

"He knows I'll want to get the highest possible price. Selling it directly to him without opening it up to the broadest market would be idiotic. It's the last thing he'd expect—or even ask me to do."

"But, Jake, we don't have the stamp. Won't Scanlon want to examine it before he went further? Wouldn't anyone in their right mind want to study it before bidding on something so valuable?"

"Sure. But I think there may be a way around that problem."

Davida pulled a face.

"What if the bidding had to take place before seeing the stamp? Only the person with the highest bid would have access to it. If it doesn't meet their expectations, it costs them nothing and we allow the next highest bidder to see it."

Davida stared at him, clearly unconvinced. "Wouldn't that send a signal to Von Erbin and Dengler that there's something strange about the stamp that you don't want broadly exposed?"

"Maybe. But it'll also make it clear I haven't the slightest idea what its significance is."

Davida mulled over Jake's theory. "Possibly."

"No, not possibly, most probably. Because if I did know the stamp's real significance, I would . . ."

". . . go after the diamonds yourself," Davida said, finishing the thought. "And you think bidders will go along with that?"

"Only two people have to go along—Von Erbin and Dengler, and they don't have any alternative."

"I don't know."

"Give me an alternative."

She sighed. "Okay, Jake. Call Scanlon back and we'll meet him for dinner."

CHAPTER 60

THEY MET FOR DINNER AT MR. CHOW'S.

"You've found the stamp?" Scanlon cried.

"That's right. And I'll need you to help me sell it."

"Of course, whatever I can do," Arthur said, without hesitation. "I told you I'd be interested in buying it myself. When can I see it?"

"I know you're interested. I want to arrange an auction. A private auction. Of course, you're more than welcome to bid."

Scanlon shrugged. "I'll make you a generous offer. But I understand how an auction will get you the best price. It doesn't make me happy, but I understand."

Jake glanced Davida's way. Her face revealed nothing.

"An auction's not a problem," Scanlon said taking a sip of water. "If you're staying in London long enough, you could hold it at your hotel. I'd guess you'd have to give a few weeks' notice to potential buyers. The auction itself would-n't take more than a few hours. It's a simple affair. Prospects examine the stamp with high-powered loupes and decide if they want it, and what they're willing to pay."

Jake watched him closely. "Yes, that's the normal process. But I can't permit anyone to see the stamp until the bidding is over. And that's not negotiable."

Arthur's face twisted into disbelief. "Jake, that's crazy! No serious collector's going to buy a stamp without first examining it. I sure as hell wouldn't."

"Hear me out," Jake said calmly. "I didn't say it couldn't be examined before buying it. I only said it can't be examined before bidding on it. If the winning bidder doesn't like what he sees, he can withdraw the bid."

"*Christ.* Just for argument's sake, say that I'd agree. The question I'd ask . . . anyone would ask, is *why?* It sounds like a set-up for some sort of a scam."

"You may be right. It doesn't make much sense but it's the way it has to be."

Scanlon sipped his wine in resignation. "When and where is this crazy auction?" he finally asked.

"That depends. I've got everything I need except for one thing."

"An audience," Scanlon said, disgust clear in his voice. "The deep-pocket bidders."

"Right. And that's where I need your help."

"Great. You want me to bring in bidders to outbid me? Maybe you'd like me to be the auctioneer, too? Bring my own gavel? Hell, I'm going to the bathroom now. Not to pee. To throw up."

A step away from the table Scanlon looked back. "You realize that your dumb rule will discourage bidders. But, come to think of it, it gives me a better chance." Then he turned and walked away.

CHAPTER 61

"GO WITH ONE STRONG DEALER," SCANLON SAID,
RETURNING TO THE table, now resigned to accept Jake's
rules. "A fat commission's at stake so any dealer worth his
salt will deliver a small, discrete number of collectors
who've got the resources to make the highest bids. Atten-
dance is a matter of quality, not quantity."

"You mean give the dealer an exclusive listing; like in
real estate?"

"That's it exactly. The dealer is motivated because it's a
guaranteed commission."

Jake and Davida glanced at one another. The speed
with which the Nazis had learned about the stamp after
Kunze's Internet posting was proof that any legitimate
dealer could easily plug into the worldwide stamp market.
Scanlon had come up with a simple way to alert Von Erbin
and Dengler about the auction.

"Who do you have in mind?" Jake asked.

"Guy in Berlin. Wilhelm Kessler. He's probably the most influential stamp dealer in the world. Reputation's unmatched. Once he understands you're willing to give him an 'exclusive' on the Nazi invert, he'll jump at the chance to bring in a qualified buyer."

Jake looked at Davida. She nodded.

"Okay. We use Kessler."

Scanlon was right, Jake thought. The embargo on examining the stamp would scare off some collectors. But to Von Erbin and Dengler, it would seem little more than a speed bump on their rush toward the diamonds.

Once the Nazis heard about the auction, Jake couldn't imagine what, if anything, could possibly keep them away.

And that's what really mattered.

CHAPTER 62

ARTHUR SCANLON SAID GOODNIGHT, THEN SANK INTO THE BENTLEY'S back seat.

He was grateful for the hours of distraction their dinner offered, grateful for having a challenging problem to take his mind off his own potentially disastrous dilemma.

He'd met with his board of directors that afternoon, and expressed his outrage at the recent downturn in Crane Industry's fortunes. As a gesture to his and his late father's lifelong relationship with Philippe Scoville, he'd refrained from publicly blaming his partner. Nevertheless, he had recommended that the board approve the buyout of Philippe Scoville's portion of the partnership.

To Arthur's astonishment, Scoville did not object to the proposal.

Given the absence of such objection, the board agreed to the buyout and authorized the hiring of an outside auditing firm to compile a fair valuation for the company.

This meant Scanlon would need to raise cash, lots of it.

The sudden grim state of his firm's balance sheet wasn't going to help with the bankers, and he wasn't sure how he could raise the money, an impediment he chose not to share with his board of directors.

*   *   *

Arthur Scanlon wasn't the only one reluctant to share information with the board.

Philippe Scoville had some ideas of his own.

CHAPTER 63

TOBY?

Was it possible? She knew where he was staying but he never expected her to show up.

But it had to be Toby. The perfume. He smelled it as soon as he opened the door of his room. Of course! That's why the *Do Not Disturb* sign was hanging on the outside knob of his suite.

He walked quietly into the bedroom. She was asleep in the bed, her naked body outlined under the sheet; her auburn hair, a tangle of flame, across the white pillow.

Jake undressed in the bathroom and slipped into the bed next to her. She rolled toward him and they wordlessly embraced. Jake was startled at her level of passion. She grabbed at him, his hair, and his shoulders. Her arms circled behind him and her hands cupped the cheeks of his ass. And then she was below him, her mouth devouring him until he exploded with the intensity of the moment and of all the moments of the last hectic days. It was an ejaculation of tension and fear and frustration. It drained him to his center and when she finally rose up to hold him and caress him he began to weep.

An hour later they lay soaking in the deep tub. A pot of hot chocolate and two mugs from room service were within reach on a stool next to the tub.

"What I love about good hotels," Jake said, "is you can get whatever you want, whenever you want it."

"Yes, I got the call from room service yesterday and arranged to get here just as fast as Virgin Air could fly me."

"I'll send a letter of commendation to the management," Jake laughed. "I didn't see any of your stuff in the room. Aren't you planning on staying?"

"No, no, my darling. You need a rest, and besides, my old roommate, who's been living here for years, wants me to spend some time with her. You don't need me hanging around all the time. By the way, how did everything with Adrian turn out?"

Toby's question caught Jake off guard and for a moment he had no idea of what she was talking about. Then it came back to him—*Adrian's boyfriend walking out. Trouble trying to buy a flat.*

"Under control. You know . . . daddy comes to the rescue." Jake changed the subject. "How did you get into my room?"

"Picked the lock."

"Seriously."

"Just told them who I was."

"That was it? 'Hi, I'm Toby Benjamin' and, poof! You're in?"

"Hope you don't mind, I said I was Mrs. Green."

Mrs. Green. It sounded nice, Jake thought. Especially from the beautiful woman sharing his tub. It made him feel almost young enough to be her husband.

"*God*, no wonder I got such a lascivious look from the lady at the front desk. You've given my reputation a real shot in the arm."

She reached under the water for him. "Good. At your age you may need a booster," she whispered.

CHAPTER 64

"I DON'T KNOW WHAT YOU TWO DID LAST NIGHT BUT I HAD A brainstorm."

Jake and Davida had joined Arthur Scanlon for breakfast in the hotel's dining room.

"And that would be what?" Jake said, chewing a piece of toast.

"I think we should run this sale as a Dutch Auction."

Davida's expression telegraphed bewilderment. "What's a Dutch auction?"

"The opposite of a regular auction. Instead of the bids pushing the price *up* . . . a Dutch Auction pushes the price *down!*"

"The prices go down? I'm confused."

"Here's an example. Remember I told you about the Inverted Jenny?"

"Yup. Brought in almost $200,000."

"Personally, I believe the Nazi invert will bring a lot less. Maybe something in the $50,000 to $75,000 range."

"Arthur, get to the point."

"Sorry. The Jenny went up for sale at a regular, conventional auction. The bidding began low and rose as prospects increase their bids. Eventually, it sold to the highest bidder. Now let's say I'm selling the Jenny in a *Dutch* auction. I would set the asking price high at, say, $250,000. Anyone willing to pay that amount would take the stamp home. If no one bid at that price, the asking price would be lowered by set increments until it arrived at a price someone *was* willing to bid."

"What if more than one person bids the same amount?" Davida asked.

"Then the bidding would start moving up again until all but one of the bidders had dropped out." Scanlon folded his arms across his chest and sat back. "What do you think?"

"Christ, Arthur . . . you're missing the whole point. The auction isn't about how much we can get for the stamp," Jake said angrily. "It's about entrapping a couple of Nazi war . . . !" He stopped. "*Oh, shit!*"

Davida stared at him.

Jake lowered his head into his hand.

Scanlon leaned forward. "What the hell are you talking about?"

*　　*　　*

Having no choice, they withheld nothing.

They worked backwards, beginning with Moe Green's visit to Carl Kunze's shop, the vandalism and the old man's death. By the time Jake explained about Alan Carson, Scanlon could do little more than shake his head and stare at his breakfast companions in mouth-open shock.

Finally, he pulled himself together. "Just tell me what you want me to do," he said.

CHAPTER 65

"NOW CAN YOU SEE WHY THE DUTCH AUCTION IS A BAD IDEA," Davida said.

Scanlon shook his head, his expression pained. "No. Even with what you've told me, it's still a good idea. Let me see if I can explain it better. You assume the Germans must buy the stamp . . . correct?"

"That's correct." *Or steal it,* Jake thought.

"Okay. That means they'll have to make the highest bid."

"True. But what difference will a Dutch Auction make?"

"A lot," Scanlon said. "With this kind of auction, Kessler presents his prospects with an opening asking price high enough to knock out most, if not all, of the potential buyers. And what does that ridiculously high asking price guarantee?"

250

Jake realized the implication. "Of course! I see what you mean. Everyone will be eliminated!" Jake exclaimed. "With the exception of the only two guys who know the stamp is infinitely more valuable than the asking price, any asking price!"

"Whatever we ask will be little more than chump change, compared to the value of the diamonds. It's brilliant, Arthur!" Davida conceded, smiling.

Scanlon leaned back, having succeeded in making his point.

"I suggest you call Wilhelm Kessler and tell him there's to be a Dutch Auction."

"Agreed."

"How much do you think we should ask?"

"There's no reason to go below a quarter of a million. You want it high enough to scare off the deep-pocket collectors like me. And you know the Germans won't be scared off regardless of the price."

Jake and Davida agreed.

"One more thing," Davida added. "I think the auction should be held on my turf."

"Where?" Jake asked."

"Israel."

"*Israel?* You can honestly sit there and tell me you believe two Nazi war criminals would willingly go to Israel?"

"No, not willingly. But what if we could create a situation that demanded the auction be held there?"

"What situation?"

"Another bidder."

"But we don't have one."

"We'll invent one! And what if the new bidder's a rich American who intends to donate the stamp to the Holocaust Museum at Yad Vashem?"

Scanlon and Jake glanced at each other then at Davida.

"*Holy shit!*" Jake exclaimed. "That just might work."

"I love it," Scanlon added.

Jake leaned over, and kissed Davida on both cheeks. "You're brilliant! Another bidder adds the one necessary ingredient the auction was missing."

"Competition," Scanlon said.

"Right."

Davida looked at Jake and beamed. "And Israel becomes a credible location simply because it's such an *incred-ible* location. As far as Kessler's concerned, our rich guy insists we hold the auction at the stamp's intended new home at Yad Vashem."

"It works for me," Jake said. "Okay, here's what we'll do. Arthur, call Kessler and give him the ground rules. The asking price for the stamp will be a quarter million dollars."

"Who's going to be the mystery bidder?" Scanlon asked.

"Davida's rich American," Jake said. "As far as Kessler's concerned, you don't know much about the guy; you just know he's legitimate. Jake Green has asked you to help. He's an old acquaintance of yours, etcetera. That's all Kessler needs to know."

"What's the guy's name?"

Jake thought for a moment, and smiled. "Abrams. Reuben Abrams. He was my teacher in Hebrew-school. If he's still alive, he'd be over one hundred years old."

"Reuben Abrams it is."

Jake turned to Davida. "Can you make the arrangements for the two of us to get to Israel?"

"Hold on. I've got my plane here," Scanlon said. "That'll give us flexibility."

Jake caught the firm, negative shake of Davida's head. Clearly, she wasn't ready to trust Arthur. "You've been a great help. I don't want to drag you in to this any deeper," Jake said.

"Deeper? Bullshit! I'm up to my ass already. I know about stamps and stamp auctions. You don't. Besides, I intend to be there anyway."

"No," Davida said.

Jake couldn't see any problem in having Arthur along. Davida was more experienced. *Maybe she was right,* he thought. He'd go along with her decision.

"Kessler will think it's damn strange if I'm not there," Arthur said, firmly. "So accept my offer of a free ride, or not. Either way, I'm going to Israel."

Davida's lips were pursed, her brow creased. Jake clearly saw she was struggling, weighing the idea of Scanlon coming along, analyzing his objections. So far, Scanlon hadn't done anything to justify her negative feelings. So it was more a matter of . . . of what? Of his *not* doing anything? *Maybe,* she thought, *it was better to keep him close at hand.*

She took a deep breath and let the air out slowly. "Okay," Davida said, reluctantly. "I'll make the arrangements for airspace clearances and a location inside the Yad Vashem Museum grounds where Von Erbin and Dengler can view the stamp. The spot will have to be public enough not to scare them away, yet someplace where the Mossad can be in total control of security. When do you want to leave? Jake, did you hear me?"

Jake shook his head as if to clear it. "Sorry. I just was thinking about something Alan Carson said. My father told him that if, when he was gone, there was no one around to inherit the stamp, his letter and the photos—he wanted them all donated to the library at Yad Vashem Museum."

CHAPTER 66

"A QUARTER OF A MILLION?"

"It's a Dutch auction, *Mein General,*" Wilhelm Kessler replied, trying to keep his voice calm. "You know how that type of auction traditionally starts high."

The General made no effort to mask his irritation. "Well, they're certainly hewing closely to tradition. What if I refuse? The price will come down, no?"

"No," Kessler said. "An American is also bidding for the stamp and has agreed to the quarter million."

The General blanched. "Do you know who it is?"

"A man named Abrams. Reuben Abrams. I've never heard of him but Scanlon has assured me he has the means to meet the price."

"If he's a collector, shouldn't you know him?"

"Of course. But he's not a collector he's a philanthropist. He wants the museum at Yad Vashem to have the stamp for its collection of Holocaust items."

The General said nothing.

"Without question they're expecting a lot for the stamp," Kessler continued. "You must examine your heart and decide if it's worth the price. Because if the answer's no, you should walk away from it," The stamp dealer held his breath.

"If the stamp's as unique as I expect it to be, I'll buy it," the General said. "Yes, the price is high and sure to go higher. But you're a dealer; you know how these things work. Whatever I pay will set a price floor. If I decide to sell it in a few years, it'll probably bring more."

Kessler felt every nerve in his body relax. "Then proceed, by all means. Remember, your high bid allows you to examine the stamp but doesn't commit you to buy it."

"Do you think anyone beside the American will meet that quarter million?"

"I doubt it. But everything I've heard about the American says he'll be aggressive. The donation will give him a huge tax advantage. The price could go much higher."

The American, the General thought, was an irritant, not an impediment. "Very well, Herr Kessler, I agree to the $250,000. If I could change anything, it would be the auction's venue. You're sure it must take place in Israel?"

"It wasn't negotiable. The American wants the auction held where the stamp will reside when he buys it. He was the first to agree to the price and the arrangements for the viewing have already been made. Mr. Green assumed the sale would be made to the American. It was only my last-minute intervention that allowed your participation in the auction."

"Then maybe we can surprise all concerned and provide a different home for the stamp." The General's voice didn't reflect the depth of his anger. Jake Green—that *Jew*—would regret dictating to him like this.

Something didn't seem . . . quite right.

"There is one more thing," the General continued. "I

don't want you to use my name in your communications with the seller. Is that understood?"

"Of course."

"Tell them I'm . . . Hyman Calvillo." Calvillo was the name printed on a forged Argentinean passport counterfeited by Mendel Plassenburg and discarded years ago.

Kessler jotted the name on a pad. "Won't they learn your real identity when you make the financial arrangements?"

"No. I intend to bring the required amount in cash. If after examining the stamp I find it suitable, I intend to pay them on the spot."

"Understood," Kessler said, his voice tight from tension.

Scoville broke the connection.

It was time for his lunch appointment. He needed Joshua's help now more than ever.

It was time to apply more pressure on Mr. Green

CHAPTER 67

JAKE AND DAVIDA WERE WAITING IN THE HOTEL'S LOBBY.

Arthur arrived, spotted them and hustled over. "Kessler's got a buyer," he said in a low, breathless voice. "Name's Hyman Calvillo."

Jake glanced at Davida. "This guy's gotta be the one, right?"

"Should be," she said, wanting to believe, yet reining her enthusiasm. She was no stranger to well-paved roads that led to nowhere.

"According to Kessler, Calvillo was beside himself to see the stamp. Claimed the money was no problem."

"Do you know of this guy?"

"Nope," Arthur said. "Never heard the name before. But, then, I certainly don't know every collector."

"*Hyman . . . Calvillo!*" Davida said, no longer able to

mask her excitement. "So that's the name eluding us all these years!"

"Which one do you think he is, Von Erbin or Dengler?" Jake asked.

"My money's on Von Erbin," Davida responded, without hesitation. "From what we know, he was the brains of the trio. If he's alive, he'd be the one to show up."

"Was there any reaction to the competition from America?"

"Kessler claims it didn't faze Calvillo at all."

"What about going to Israel?"

"Doesn't seem to be a problem. It's all set. Calvillo will bring along cash. Enough, apparently, to blow away any offer our Mr. Reuben Abrams might make. If the stamp's right, the deal can be finalized on the spot."

Jake turned to Davida. "Maybe this is a silly question, but how will you be able to identify him? Are there fingerprints or photos?"

"It's not a silly question at all," Davida said. "Von Erbin had access to the files and cleaned them out. No fingerprints. Or official pictures. We've got one fairly decent newspaper photo of him, alongside Dengler and two others, standing with Hitler. But that was sixty years ago. It'll be hard to tell from a photograph that old. Even if he didn't have plastic surgery, he'll look completely different."

"So how will you know?" Jake asked.

Davida's right hand went up, palm down. "It's not much to go by, but Von Erbin and Dengler were both tall, over six feet. If Hyman Calvillo turns out to be short, he's either someone the Germans sent in their place, or he's what he claims, simply a very rich stamp collector."

"Once Mossad get their hands on him, I'm sure it will be sorted out," Arthur said. "After all . . ."

Jake interrupted. "First things first, Arthur. Did you and Kessler arrange a time for the viewing?"

"Calvillo can be there by tomorrow evening," Arthur

said. "I suggest we plan on taking off later today—say, around five. We can have a late dinner in Jerusalem and take tomorrow to get ready."

A young man crossed the lobby and approached the trio. "Excuse me," the man said, addressing Davida. "Are you Ms. Snyder?"

"Yes."

"Tony Beeching from the Israeli Embassy here in London. I wonder if I could have a word with you?"

"It's alright, you can speak in front of these gentlemen," Davida said. "I believe you have a package for me?"

"Yes. It arrived in the diplomatic pouch from Jerusalem a short time ago. It was marked 'urgent,' so I came right over. May I see your identification, please?"

Davida produced the desired documents. The young man studied them carefully. Once satisfied, he handed her a small package, then left.

"How did they know you were here?" asked Arthur, impressed.

"Because I told them." Davida tore off the paper. A small box emerged and she held it out, resting in the palm of her hand.

"What," Davida asked, "is the single most important fact we know for certain about the German stamp?"

The two men thought for a moment, finally Jake replied. "It's a red color . . . and we know its postage value 12.38 Reichmarks."

"No, we only believe it is. We're not entirely sure. Remember, Kunze never actually saw the stamp he described on the Internet. He just took Moe Green's word for it. But there's something very important that we do know, as an absolute fact."

Jake and Arthur wrestled with the question. Finally Jake said, "It's a fake! A *counterfeit.*"

"Exactly," Davida said, slowly removing the lid, then a

thick square of soft cotton batting. She held the opened box out to Jake and Arthur.

A whispered *'Holy shit!'* from Jake, as they peered into the box.

"Where on earth did you get this?" Arthur said, amazed.

Davida smiled. "Nice, isn't it?"

Nestled in one side of the box was a small, powerful magnifying loupe and next to it, pressed between two thin pieces of clear glass, was the German invert.

The paper was old and shopworn.

The red color was right.

The denomination was right.

And the head of Hitler was upside down.

"Not a bad job for two days," Davida said.

"But when Calvillo checks it under the loupe he'll know it's not the real stamp," Arthur said.

"Do you agree with that?" Davida asked Jake.

Jake thought for a moment before answering. "We've assumed there are instructions of some sort engraved on the stamp. Most likely coordinates, probably indicating the spot where the diamonds are hidden. I'd say that whoever examines the stamp better damned well see some numbers."

Davida handed Jake the stamp and the loupe. "Check it out."

He studied the stamp, turning it slowly, every which way. It didn't take long. "I see numbers! They're engraved . . . around the torch . . . and . . . the sword. Here, take a look." He handed the glass-encased stamp and loupe to Arthur.

Arthur located the numbers. "Amazing. But how could you be sure coordinates were engraved on the stamp and not, say, a map?"

"An educated guess."

"Meaning what?"

"Consider the alternatives. A map would be too complicated and there wasn't enough room for verbal instructions. Numbers seemed the most logical. The ones on the stamp show the location of the diamonds," Davida said smugly.

"And if you're wrong?" Arthur said.

Davida pursed her lips and shrugged.

"What coordinates did you use?"

"Since neither we nor they know the correct location, we picked the coordinates for a lake in the Potsdam area. The same spot where bodies of the German soldiers were found."

"I guess that makes sense," Arthur agreed.

Davida replaced the stamp back in the box.

Arthur stood. "Listen, I've got a hundred loose ends to tie up before we leave. I'll be out front with the car at 4 o'clock. I figure we should be wheels up by five."

Jake and Davida agreed, then watched in silence as Arthur left the hotel.

"I'm still not sure about Scanlon," Davida said, as she put the box containing the stamp into her bag.

"What can I say? So far, nothing he's done supports your bad feelings about him."

Davida shrugged. With no meaningful rebuttal beyond some vague intuition, she changed the subject.

"How are you holding up, Jake?"

Jake was surprised by the question, as well as the concern he saw on Davida's face. It was the only inquiry of a personal nature that she had ever ventured, and it pleased him. "I guess I'm doing okay. As long as I don't think too much about certain things. Like running away from New York, or that I'm most likely a suspect in Alan Carson's murder. If I stay away from thoughts like that, I'm almost fine."

He was silent for a moment, knowing he was about to open a door, and uncertain of what he'd find on the other side. "Do you mind if I ask you a personal question?"

Davida didn't answer right away. "I'll tell you if I mind after I hear the question."

"Fair enough. I was wondering . . . are you married?"

Davida sighed and nodded. "I was, once. He was killed years ago. Blown up in Jerusalem. Riding on the right bus at the wrong time."

"Kids?"

"No."

"What about now? Are you . . . involved . . . with anyone?"

Davida smiled and ran her hand through her hair. It was a habit he recognized as her way of playing for time. She employed it now, weighing his question. He had crossed a line that ran between them, and she knew his question, although oblique, carried complex implications.

"Why don't you just ask me what you really want to know?"

Jake laughed. "Touché. Okay, let me try again. When this is over I'd very much like to see you. How do you feel about that?"

"How do I feel about it?" she repeated. "Well, if you don't mind, I think I'll take the fifth, at least for now."

Then she stood up. Body language signaling an end to the conversation.

"You deserve an answer, Jake. And I'll give you one. But this isn't the time or place."

"And when and where might that be?"

"You'll be the first to know."

"I see," Jake mumbled, although it was clear that he didn't. Davida had given him such a confusing message. He felt he'd been neatly brushed off.

*   *   *

They stood facing each other in the hallway, outside their rooms. Not a word had been uttered on the way up in the elevator. Jake tried to decide exactly how he felt. It was somewhere between, pissed-off and petulant. And he was angry with himself for bringing up the subject. She was right. It was a stupid time to start anything. They were in the middle of a complicated and dangerous negotiation. Clearly, he had fucked up.

"I'll meet you in the lobby at four, okay?" Jake said, coldly. He turned, swiping his keycard through the lock and opening the door.

"Jake?"

He turned just as Davida stepped toward him, placing her hand on his chest, and gently pushing him into his room. She wrapped her arms around him.

"You have to agree, Jake, this would never do in the lobby, would it? Now . . . is the . . . time and this is the place," she whispered, her mouth close to his ear. Her smell was intoxicating and Jake's head swam. And then they were pressed against each other, hungrily kissing, pulling clothing, opening zippers, buttons, groping, clutching.

Later, on the crumpled bed, its coverlet pulled partially onto the floor, pillows scattered, their damp bodies spent, their breathing still heavy, they lay, fused to one another, impossibly close, mouth to mouth, exchanging each breath, both of them transformed, sated, content.

"You sure as hell gave me your answer," Jake whispered, his lips forming the words on Davida's mouth.

She pulled him more tightly to her body, her breasts crushed against his chest. "You deserved an honest answer."

At that moment Jake's love for Davida seemed to expand and exceed the confines of his being. And, to his amazement and relief, there was no guilt! No admonishing voice from his late wife. Without question, he was certain that Norma approved.

"I don't even know what to call what I'm feeling," he

said, emotionally. "Passion? Connection? Love? All of the above? Do you understand?"

"Me, too. Even before we actually met. Watching you come out of your apartment building, I knew."

"You're all I want."

Davida hugged him closer, tighter.

They lay that way for some time. Communicating without words, with kisses, hugs. Not wanting it to end. Each wishing for the impossible, that they might somehow remain isolated from everything outside of the confines of their room.

"Tell me what you really think is going to happen in Israel. Will you be in danger?"

Jake felt Davida's smile on his cheek. "Once Calvillo arrives in Israel, the Mossad will have him under control. Nothing bad will happen. We will get him. If we're lucky, he'll lead us to the other one. The case will be closed."

"I can't help it. I worry. I don't want to lose you."

"You won't, I promise."

Jake covered her mouth with his and held the kiss for a long time, reluctant to have it ever end.

He'd been dozing when Davida shook him awake. It was time to get ready.

At four o'clock they were both standing outside the hotel as Arthur's limousine pulled into the semi-circular driveway.

CHAPTER 68

THE ROYAL COACHMAN HOTEL SAT IN A SEEDY
AREA OF NORTHEAST London.

The "RC," as the regulars called it, was one of those
"hot-springs" operations where the only qualification for
renting a room, by the hour, day or week, was payment in
advance.

Theirs had two single beds; a desk, a chair, a dresser
and an ancient black and white television set equipped with
rabbit ears, draped optimistically with strips of aluminum
foil. The bathroom held an ancient tub, a cracked sink and a
toilet.

Adrian Green, her hands, feet and mouth secured with
duct tape and her eyes covered with a blindfold, lay in the
tub, which had been lined with a thin, dirty mattress, a few
pillows and a blanket. She dozed fitfully. When awake, she
wept and moaned from fear and confusion.

"Pizza!" The deliverer rapped three fast ones, paused, then added one, pause, and then another. The tall man with the bushy mustache cracked the door open to the length of its rusted chain, peeked out, and allowed entry.

Joshua crossed the room, tossed the pizza box onto the desk and looked around in disgust. It was stifling hot in the room, its two windows having long ago, been painted shut. Both men had stripped down to their boxer shorts and undershirts. The short man had removed his hairpiece; it lay on the dresser, like road kill.

"How is she?" Joshua asked.

"No trouble so far," the short one said.

"Have you spoken to her? About *anything?*"

"Just like you told us. Gotta go potty? Hungry? That sort of stuff," the tall one said.

"Good. There's been a change in plans. You're to take her on a little trip."

"Another god-damned trip? You said this job was supposed to be over last week. I got family . . . I got commitments, for Christ sake."

Joshua tried to be patient. "You're being well paid to do work that any brain-dead asshole could do, so stop complaining. All the details are in this envelope. I've arranged for a charter. You should be finished by tomorrow night and then you can do whatever the fuck you want. Meanwhile, your money is in the box. Please count it."

The two were each promised $10,000 for their work in London, in addition to the $10,000 they already got for following Jake Green from Florida to New York.

The tall man opened the box and took out two fat envelopes. Both men became absorbed in counting their cash.

The muffled report of a silenced pistol startled the tall man, and he jumped and wheeled toward the sound. A misty red spray splashed across his hands. Even as he watched his partner's body slide to the floor, he clung to the hope that he would not be next to die.

He spun back toward Joshua, horror contorting his face. Joshua lowered the silenced weapon. "Don't worry, I'm not going to shoot you. Just take a few deep breaths. You're going to be fine. I need you. Wash your face and get the woman dressed. Keep her blindfolded. Take the gag off. Do you owe any money for this dump of a room?"

"N-no . . . I . . . paid in advance."

"Good. Now go do what I said."

Joshua wet a pillowcase in the bathroom, ignoring the whimpering woman being helped from the tub, and wiped the blood off the money and the wall.

The dead man's money was packed into a second pillowcase, along with an additional $7,000 fished out of the corpse's trouser pockets.

The tall man helped the blindfolded Adrian out of the bathroom.

Joshua came close, spoke to her, softly.

"Listen to me. We've taken the tape off your mouth so you'll be more comfortable when you leave. Okay? But you must stay very quiet. If you do, you won't be hurt. We should be able to let you go by tomorrow. Between now and then—if you try to run away or to yell or call out to anyone I will kill you. Is that clear?"

Adrian had to pee something wicked. She nodded.

"Good," Joshua said.

The tall man guided the girl out of the bathroom, helped her into her coat, and led her out of the room.

Joshua waited five minutes, then left, placing the Do Not Disturb sign on the doorknob.

The blood-splattered surgical gloves Joshua had worn went into a trash receptacle a block away from the Royal Coachman.

CHAPTER 69

CRANE INDUSTRY'S CORPORATE JET LIFTED OFF THE RUNWAY, heading toward the Mediterranean and the Ben Gurion Airport in Jerusalem.

"The Mossad will meet us," Davida said. "Arrangements are set for the auction to take place in the library at Yad Vashem. They're working on the security details as we speak." She turned to Arthur. "Did you reach Kessler before we took off?"

"Yes. Kessler gave Calvillo all the information he needs. I don't anticipate any problems."

Jake poured three glasses of Burgundy. "I still don't know what I'm supposed to do."

"You don't have to do anything," Davida said. "The idea is simply to wait at Yad Vashem until they come to us. To tell the truth, unless you want to see them in person, you don't even have to be there."

"Oh, no! I'll be there."

"The minute they walk in, it will be all over," Davida said.

"If it's so predictable, why did you have the stamp made?" Arthur asked.

Davida shrugged. "Mainly because I could. Seeing what it looked like made it more real for me. Also it never hurts to be over-prepared. Like having some insurance."

The co-pilot came back to the main cabin. "Excuse me, Mr. Scanlon, a call just came through on SATCOM."

"Thanks, Kate. I'll take it back here."

"The call is for Mr. Green, sir."

Jake turned toward Davida. "Did you tell anyone how to reach us?"

"Just Mossad. But they'd ask for me, not you."

"Arthur?"

"No one. The pilot filed a flight plan, is all."

Apprehension and fear closed around Jake like a layer of fog.

He reached out for the phone.

CHAPTER 70

"MR. GREEN?"

"Yes. Who is this?"

"Hyman Calvillo."

Why would Calvillo call him now? Was he canceling the meeting? "Yes, Mr. Calvillo, what can I do for you?"

At the mention of Calvillo's name, Davida and Arthur turned toward Jake.

"I'm afraid I have to change the location for the auction."

"You *what?*"

"I've no intention of going to Israel. I've another location in mind."

Jake covered the phone's mouthpiece with his hand. "Calvillo," he whispered. "He refuses to go to Israel."

Davida threw her hands up. "Tell him Abrams is already there, waiting."

"The American bidder is already there," Jake said. "I've no way of contacting him."

Jake heard Calvillo take a breath and expel it. "Look, Green, I intend to buy the stamp. I don't give a damn about the American bidder, do you understand?"

"No, I don't."

"Well maybe this will clear things up."

The voice that followed was tentative.

"Daddy?"

"Adrian?"

"I don't know what's happening, daddy. I'm so scared!"

His daughter's panicked voice seared his brain. In that moment Jake felt certain he was dying. His chest constricted. He fought for breath. Ice, it seemed, replaced his bones, even as sweat broke out on he forehead and the receiver almost slipped from his hand.

"Adrian . . . Adrian . . . are you alright?" Jake tried in vain to keep his voice steady, knowing he would only add panic to his already terrified daughter.

"I'm all right, daddy. They didn't hurt me."

"Where . . . where are you?"

"I don't know. I'm scared. I've been blindfolded for days."

Jake covered the mouthpiece of the phone and, wild-eyed, yelled to Arthur and Davida. "*Christ!* Calvillo has Adrian!"

"*Oh God!*" Davida cried, and moved to Jake's side, pressing her face next to Jake's, her ear against the phone receiver.

"Adrian? Are you still there? Hello?" Jake cried.

Muffled sounds—Adrian's voice in the background, pleading with Calvillo to let her go on talking.

"Mr. Green, listen to me carefully. For the time being your daughter is safe. She will continue to be unharmed as long as you follow my instructions."

"What is it you want? Money?"

"I don't want your money. You have a stamp that belongs to me. I'm willing to pay a great deal for it. But to make that happen, to get your daughter back, there's going to be a change in the location of our meeting."

"What sort of change?"

"You will tell Mr. Scanlon to instruct his pilot to alter your route."

Jake felt Davida shake her head at the demand.

"We can't change our destination just like that. There's a flight plan. It's probably illegal."

"Of course you can change. I believe in the vernacular of pilots it's called a '*balk*.' Your new destination will be the Nice Cote d'Azur Airport in France."

"That's insane."

"No. The insanity would be to sacrifice your daughter for a little scrap of paper."

Davida clamped her hand over the phone's mouthpiece. "Tell him you don't have the stamp, that it's already in Jerusalem."

"The stamp is in Jerusalem," Jake said.

"You're lying, playing with her life and wasting my time."

Jake's hand clamped over mouthpiece again. "Where are we now, Arthur? Ask the pilot."

"Listen to me, dammit," Calvillo demanded, his anger palpable. "I will only say this one more time. Your pilot will know what to do. The location of your meeting has been changed. It's now in Nice. Your plane should be over Milan. That's about 260 kilometers from Nice. An hour should be more than enough time. If you haven't landed there, within that timeframe," Calvillo paused, "your daughter will be the one to suffer for your intransigence."

Scanlon rushed back from the cockpit. "We're over Milan."

Jake covered the mouthpiece again. "He already

knows. He wants us to be in Nice within an hour! What can I tell him?"

"Say we don't have enough fuel," Davida hissed.

Jake took a deep breath. "We don't have enough fuel to make it to Nice. Adrian knows nothing about the stamp. Please let her go."

"You're beginning to bore me, Mr. Green. I know where you are and I know the range of your aircraft. You've enough fuel to fly to Nice several times over. Why are you being so stubborn?" Calvillo's voice was menacing in its softness. "Come to Nice. Give me the stamp. Take the $250 thousand dollars and your daughter. That way each of us will have what we want. And please don't call the police or arrange to have anyone meet you when you land. We will know if you do. I'll leave the outcome to your imagination. Good-bye."

"Wait!" But the connection was already broken.

Jake, face ashen, voice husky with fear, turned to Scanlon. "Please, Arthur, tell the pilot. We have to go to Nice."

"I'll contact Mossad in Jerusalem," Davida said.

"No, for God's sake! Don't call *anyone*. If they even smell Mossad or police . . . anyone . . . they'll kill her. Three people are dead already. I'll give them the stamp. It's what they want. It will fool them long enough to get Adrian back. You said so yourself."

Davida removed the phone receiver from Jake's clenched hand.

She put her arms around him. "We'll go to Nice, Jake."

By her gesture, her tone, he knew, deep down, the chances of Calvillo trading Adrian for the stamp were non-existent.

The Nazis could never take the chance. But it was a fantasy that he needed to believe. And Davida was willing to let him believe it.

At least for the time being.

CHAPTER 71

WHEN THE FALCON TOUCHED DOWN AT THE NICE
AIRPORT, IT WAS dark.

The co-pilot popped the door. Air stairs unfolded to the
tarmac. A white van with darkened windows pulled within
twenty yards of the aircraft. A tall man exited and stood,
waiting.

Jake came through the door first. Followed by Davida
and Scanlon.

Jake spotted the tall man and stopped.

He clutched Davida's arm. "The driver—he's one of the
guys who followed me in New York."

The tall man approached. "Please, I am here to take
you to Mr. Calvillo. We will leave as soon as you clear customs." Then, without apologies, he carefully and thoroughly checked them for weapons.

Jake, Arthur, and Davida entered the van, sitting on

the seat behind the driver. To the tall man, Jake knew, they were nothing more than packages to be delivered.

Turning in his seat, the tall man pushed a cell phone toward Jake. "Mr. Calvillo for you," he said.

Jake took the phone. "Yes?"

"You'll be brought here by boat, Mr. Green. My yacht is equipped with sophisticated radar so I will know if any vessels follow you, on water or in the air. If that happens, your daughter . . . well, you know the result. Understood?"

"Listen, you fucking bastard, if you so much . . ."

The connection broke before he could finish the useless threat.

Jake handed the phone back to the driver. Davida and Arthur looked questioningly at Jake. "We're going on a boat ride," he answered.

*   *   *

In a matter of minutes customs was cleared and they drove from the airport.

"Jake, listen to me," Davida whispered, "It's going to be all right. The only reason they took Adrian was to force us onto Calvillo's turf."

Jake looked at her gratefully, recognizing the lie. It wasn't going to be all right, but at least the thought gave him a straw to grasp.

Ten minutes later they arrived at a marina.

The van stopped at a shack, blocked by a horizontal red and white striped barrier. A guard emerged, recognized the driver, raised the barrier and waved him through.

The van proceeded past big boats to an unlit section of the dock where a large black Zodiac outboard was moored. Bobbing. Waiting.

The driver gathered up the life vests stored in the Zodiac and handed them out.

"We'll have a short ride out to Mr. Calvillo's boat. It will take approximately fifteen minutes. Please stay seated. The water's choppy and you'll find rope hand-holds along the sides."

They motored slowly out of the harbor. Once past the sea wall, the Zodiac accelerated into the inky-blackness.

Jake felt Davida's hand searching for his. It was a small, but appreciated comfort.

CHAPTER 72

THE ZODIAC PLOWED OVER THE WASHBOARD OF SWELLS.

Finally a large black shape materialized into the outline of a yacht. The tall man maneuvered the Zodiac so that he approached aft, cutting his outboard engine and drifting up to a water-level platform where he secured the rubber craft and led his three passengers aboard.

Moments later, they stood in the center of the yacht's dimly lit salon. The tall man had disappeared.

The room was large. Windows on both port and starboard sides revealed nothing but pitch darkness and reflected back like mirrors. A bar ran along the port side. A door led out to the deck. Aft, were a couch, an oval coffee table and several upholstered chairs. More chairs were arranged under the window, along the starboard side.

The deck was carpeted, the pattern, a nautical montage.

Jake was pacing, so anxious he could hardly breathe. "If these sons of bitches hurt her . . . I swear . . ."

Davida put her hand on his arm. "I don't think they will. The only reason to take Adrian was for leverage. She's served her purpose—we're here."

Arthur, at the bar, poured a drink and stopped in mid-sip. "Wait! Did you hear that?"

Jake froze. "What?"

"A sound. *There! . . . that was it again.*"

They all turned at once, toward the sound. It seemed to be coming from the rear of the salon.

They approached cautiously. Muffled moans became louder.

Behind the couch, on the floor, they found Adrian. Hands, feet and mouth were taped and she was blindfold.

"Adrian!"

Jake fell to his knees and cradled his daughter. Then, with Davida's help they gently picked her up and placed her onto the couch. Ever so very carefully, Davida peeled the tape from Adrian's mouth and, once freed, she took large gulps of air. Then she threw her arms around her father and began to cry.

Jake held her shaking body, smoothed her hair, rocked her, kissed her face, tasted her tears, comforted her. "Thank God, thank God, thank God," he said.

"Here, Adrian, sip this . . . it will make you feel better," Scanlon said, handing her a glass of bourbon.

She sipped, coughed, sipped again, then handed it back to Scanlon.

They gathered around her.

"Can you tell us what happened?" Jake asked.

"I was working. A man came to the flat. He said he knew you, daddy. He said he owned an art gallery. He wanted to see my work. I let him in. It was so stupid of me. I'm not sure what happened next. I remember he pushed a cloth onto my face."

"Probably chloroform," Davida said.

"I must have passed out. Then I was in a car, blind-folded. They put something, that cloth, on my face again and the next thing I knew I was tied up in a bathtub."

No one had hurt her, Jake thought. She was just fright-ened out of her mind. His relief was so great he felt buoyant, almost giddy.

Someone coughed. All of them wheeled toward the sound.

A figure stood in the doorway of the salon. The hallway behind him was brightly lit, which made it impossible to make out his features.

"How do you do," the silhouette said and stepped into the salon.

Arthur Scanlon gasped and dropped his drink.

CHAPTER 73

PHILIPPE SCOVILLE WAS IMMACULATELY TURNED OUT, HIS DOUBLE-breasted suit perfectly tailored to his tall, slim body, his linen militarily starched.

"Philippe! *What the hell . . .*"

"Sorry to have deceived you, Arthur," he said. "I apologize for never mentioning that, like you, I'm an avid collector. How could I resist owning the Hitler error?"

Jake glanced back and forth between the two men. "Arthur, what's going on? Who is this?"

Arthur, ghost pale, raised his hand palm up to signal for time. Finally: "He's my partner. Philippe Scoville."

"What do you mean, *your partner?*" Jake tried. Nothing was computing. "Are you part of this?"

"Where are your manners?" Scoville interrupted. "Introduce me to your friends. I've already met Ms. Green. I assume, since Arthur referred to you as Jake, that you, sir, are the father. And who might this be?"

"Davida Snyder." Arthur managed. Jake saw her eyes narrow to slits; the hate that etched across her face was terrifying. Clearly, Scoville was one of the Germans. From the body type, most likely General Rutger Von Erbin.

"Ms. Snyder. How do you do? Your name sounds familiar. Something to do with Israel? Possibly Mossad? Don't tell me, I'll recall the context eventually."

Davida stared at Scoville without answering.

Jake moved a step toward him. "What's going on here? You owe us an explanation."

"Yes, I do. I asked you here because . . ."

"Asked us?" Jake said, incredulous. "You kidnapped my daughter. Put her in danger just to *force* us here . . . to *blackmail* us here."

"Yes, well, so be it. But as you can see for yourself, your daughter is fine. You will all be fine just as soon as I get my stamp. Now, if you would be so kind . . . as to let me see it,"

Davida pushed between the two men. "First, the money," she said. "You can have a look at the stamp as soon as we see that you've got the money to pay for it."

Scoville remained unruffled. "Of course, the money. You of the Hebrew persuasion always seem to eventually get down to that issue, don't you?"

Davida stared at the Nazi. "Come to think of it, why do you even bother with this money charade?" She said, her voice dripping with sarcasm. "You could just take the stamp from us—the same way you tried to get it from Moe Green, Carl Kunze, and Alan Carson."

"True. But a deal's a deal, is it not?"

"And we're supposed to trust you?"

Scoville smiled and walked to the intercom phone on the bar. "Joshua . . . would you please bring the bag into the main salon?"

Joshua! Davida stiffened at the mention of a name well known to Mossad. Well known but never seen. No one knew *who* Joshua actually was. No pictures of the legendary killer existed.

Moments later, Joshua, like Scoville, appeared as a silhouette in the salon's doorway, then stepped into the room, carrying a nylon sports bag.

Jake's legs gave out and he grabbed the edge of the bar to keep from falling.

CHAPTER 74

"NICE TO SEE YOU AGAIN, JAKE," JOSHUA SAID, WITHOUT EMOTION.

"Toby?"

"In the flesh. Ain't life a bitch?"

And then it all started to make sense. He'd been set up. Strung along from the first night at the Monkey Bar in Florida, to New York, then London and now, here in France. What a fool he'd been.

"You owe me some answers," Jake said, coldly. "How did you know how to find me in Florida?"

Joshua smirked. "Hell, middle-class white guys like you leave tracks easier to follow than a deer in fresh snow."

Scoville took a step toward Joshua. "We haven't time for this."

Joshua dropped the large bag on the carpet beside her. "Wait, please, Philippe, humor me. Yes, Jake. I've been in it from the beginning."

"And you murdered my father."

"That's a little melodramatic. He had a heart attack."

"But you caused it and, if he hadn't, you would have killed him, isn't that so?"

Toby's shrug and silence was answer enough.

"And Kunze? And Carson?"

"It's what I do," she sighed. "Like you design buildings."

More questions tumbled through Jake's mind. "When you called me about Kunze being murdered, it was about the same time Carson was killed. How could you have killed Carson and been at the Monkey Bar at the same time?"

"I wasn't. Remember, you were calling me on my cell phone. I was in New York having a bite to eat at P.J. Clarke's. Like I told you in Florida, all bars are pretty much alike. They sure as hell sound alike."

Scoville interrupted. "This has gone on long enough."

Jake ignored him. It was clear Toby was immune to his feelings—to any feelings. He remembered making love to this woman, this . . . killer. "What a fucking bitch you are!" He would have lunged toward the woman had Davida not blocked him with her arm.

"Enough!" Scoville's voice reported like a gunshot. "Let's get to the issue here." Now calm, in command, "I want to see the stamp," he said. "If it's right I'll give you the money that's over there." He indicated the bag at Joshua's feet. "A quarter of a million dollars in cash."

Jake turned. Arthur was standing next to Adrian, his arm across her shoulder. His daughter looked terrified. Then he glanced toward Davida. Her head dipped slightly. "Okay," he said, resigned. "But I want to see the money first." He walked toward Toby and the large nylon bag at her feet.

Her eyes were blank, without light. He no longer existed.

He placed the bag on the coffee table and opened it. Davida joined him. The bills were soft and worn. Davida riffled through several banded packets of cash, taking them from various depths within the bag, and studying several of the individual bills at random.

"All here," she said.

"Don't you want to count it?"

"It's fine. Just close it up and let's get on with this."

He zippered the bag and set it by Adrian's feet.

Once again Scoville took control. "You've seen the money, Mr. Green. Now let me see the stamp."

Davida removed the box from her pocket and handed it to Scoville.

His hands shook. He opened the box, removed the enclosed loupe and screwed it onto his right eye. Then proceeded to carefully examine the stamp.

Jake stopped breathing.

Finally, murmuring, almost cooing. "Yes. Oh, yes. Very nice. Very good. Perfect. A miracle!"

Davida reached into her pocket again, this time taking out a folded photocopy of a newspaper photograph. Jake saw that it pictured a knot of Nazi officers standing to the left and right of a beaming Adolf Hitler. Two of the soldiers' heads were circled with red marker.

General Rutger Von Erbin and Colonel Axel Dengler.

"Before you get too excited about the stamp, I wonder if you'd look at this," Davida said, handing him the photocopy.

Scoville studied the picture. "What about it?"

Davida shrugged. "Well, for starters, we already know you're not Hyman Calvillo. And I don't believe you're Phillipe Scoville."

"Really? I expect several people in this room would disagree with you—not the least of which is my partner and your friend, Mr. Scanlon."

"What is she talking about, Philippe?" Arthur asked.

"Your partner is a war criminal," Davida said. "A former General in the Wehrmacht. I believe his real name is Rutger Von Erbin," Davida answered. "And the gentleman in the picture standing to his left is Axel Dengler, isn't that so, General?"

He hesitated a moment, staring at Davida. "Yes, I am General Von Erbin," he sighed. "And now I remember why I know your name. You're part of *Golem!* You Jews never give up, do you?"

"No, we don't." Davida was implacable. Jake could see from her tightly clenched fists that she was barely restraining herself.

"This is one time when Golem's efforts haven't worked," Von Erbin said. "I'm going to leave you in the hands of Joshua. She'll make sure you're well cared for."

Joshua smiled. She had produced a pistol from one of the pockets in her jumpsuit.

Davida took a step forward. "Before you go. I'm curious. We know that Josef Hauptmann was killed in Berlin but what happened to your other friend, Dengler? Is he dead, as well?"

Von Erbin shrugged. "Yes, Dengler is dead. He was my partner, you know."

"What do you mean he was your partner?" Scanlon asked.

"Oh, my, Arthur. This is your day for revelations. You see, your dear father was . . . Colonel Axel Dengler."

Jake turned swiftly toward Davida; her look of amazement matched his own feelings of confusion and disbelief. Was Von Erbin's claim possible? Could Scanlon's father be the same man that Davida had described? The animal that supplied concentration camps with the Zyklon pellets used to exterminate millions of Jews? The same madman who was commended for devising a way to turn ordinary buses into mobile gas chambers?

Scanlon's voice dragged Jake back.

"You're insane! My father was a Jew. A Holocaust survivor."

Von Erbin held the photocopy out toward Arthur. "I'll

admit it was a brilliant deception. Posing as a Jew was a perfect disguise. Take a look. I think you'll easily recognize the man standing next to me in the picture. He didn't change very much over the years."

Arthur snatched the photo from Von Erbin's hand. The hatred in his eyes was eloquent. The hand holding the photocopy dropped to his side. "I don't understand."

"It was simple," Von Erbin went on. "We had the papers we needed to escape after the war. Sadly, our friend Hauptmann was blown up in Berlin. As far as we knew, the stamp was destroyed with him. Your father and I started in the oil business with a little money we borrowed. We were successful. Your father met a woman in Paris—an American—and he fell in love."

"My mother," Arthur whispered.

"That's right, your mother. They moved to America and he ran his part of Crane Industries from there. He liked living there."

"And the diamonds?" Jake asked.

"Ah, of course, you know about the diamonds. Yes, well, when poor Josef died, they became a lost cause."

"But you always dreamed that the stamp might somehow, someday turn up?"

"We were ninety-nine percent certain the stamp was destroyed along with Josef. The remaining little one percent chance that it survived became our—what would you call it? Our hobby. When it finally surfaced no one could have been more surprised."

"And my father?" Arthur asked.

"Well, you know most of the story. He worked hard. It was a good life for him until your mother's death. Actually, her dying was a blessing for the company. The inheritance Axel got was an infusion of cash we needed. It saved Crane."

"Tell me about his death," Arthur said. "Why was he cremated so quickly?"

"Ah, yes," Scoville chuckled. "The funeral. There was a

strong suspicion that your people, Ms. Snyder—The *Golem*—were close to identifying him . . . arresting him . . . isn't that so?"

Davida's voice was level. "We thought we were very close."

"On the outside chance that it might have been true, S.J., shall we say, participated in his own demise."

"He committed suicide?" Arthur was incredulous. "That's insane!"

Von Erbin laughed. "Not really. He simply peeled off one identity and assumed another. With, I might add, more than enough money to live comfortably. Our partnership agreement was clear on the succession of ownership. You inherited his half of the company, but only until your death, when it would revert back to me. I was willing to arrange for that occurrence but your father refused. The only time I'd ever seen him demonstrate any sentimentality whatsoever. As long as he was alive, I promised to abide by his wishes."

"Is he still alive?"

"He had a few good years of retirement, then he really did pass on . . . a heart attack. Very sudden. Very sad."

Davida had heard enough. "What do you intend to do with the diamonds? Is it to fund the ODESSA?"

Von Erbin stepped toward the outer doorway. "I couldn't care less about the ODESSA. Or the mythical Fourth Reich. The diamonds are for *me!* Taking them was my idea, my plan. I intend to have them. I'm afraid I've got to leave now."

"No!" Jake yelled as Arthur lunged toward Von Erbin.

Joshua whirled and in the same movement brought the butt of her revolver across the back of Arthur's head. He slumped to the floor, dazed but not unconscious, Jake saw.

"Now, Joshua, tape them up please. I'll hold your pistol."

It only took a few minutes for Joshua to secure Adrian, Jake, Arthur and Davida into chairs.

"Perfect," Von Erbin said, addressing Joshua. "When you're finished here take the $250,000 that's in the bag. Burn the boat and take the Zodiac. I'll wire the balance of the fee to your account as soon as I get to the mainland." He moved to the door. "Good-bye my friends. It was a pleasure—even though I had to wait a half-century for it to happen."

CHAPTER 75

JOSHUA PLACED HER PISTOL NEXT TO THE ICE BUCKET AND POURED herself a drink.

Then she picked up the phone and punched in two numbers. "Come into the salon, please?"

A moment later, the tall man entered the room.

"Would you be a darling and get more ice."

He approached to take the ice bucket. It slipped from Joshua's hand. When he stooped to pick it up she shot him in the back of the head.

Adrian screamed. Jake strained against his bindings. The others sat still, transfixed, helpless.

"Why are you doing this?" Jake asked. "Why did you kill those people? Why are you going to kill us?"

"I told you it's my job. I get paid. It's no more complex than that."

"Von Erbin's taking the helicopter, isn't he?" Davida said.

"Don't worry. He's an excellent pilot."

"I'm not worried about his skills with a helicopter," Davida said, "But I'm sure as hell worried." Her statement hung as a challenge in the air between them.

"Worried . . . ?" Joshua asked.

"Who packed the money into the bag? You didn't, did you?"

"Why should you give a damn *who* packed the bag?"

"It could be important."

"How's that?"

"I'd bet you're familiar with C-4 plastic explosives?"

"Yes. So what?" Joshua's voice was no longer completely confident.

"You've worked with it, you know how it smells, right?"

"Get to the point."

"Open the bag. Take a whiff."

Joshua only hesitated for a moment. She dropped to her knees next to the bag, unzipped it and dropped her face close to the opening.

"That fucking son of a bitch!"

The whine of the engine turning over on the helipad suddenly filled the salon.

In one swift movement, Joshua grabbed the bag and burst out of the salon toward the sound.

Davida struggled against the tape that held her wrists. "Jake, Arthur. We only have a few seconds. Try and move your chairs back to back so you can pull that tape off each other's hands. We've got to get out of here."

CHAPTER 76

JOSHUA SPRINTED AFT ALONG THE DECK.

As she approached the helicopter, the wash from the rotor blades blasted her back and she struggled to climb the ladder to the pad. The chopper was lifting off, rotating counter-clockwise, hovering above her.

Joshua reached up, grabbed the left landing skid and deftly looped the carry strap of the bag onto it. The craft began to lift away from the yacht.

She lay on the landing pad breathing hard. The helicopter moved higher. She could see Von Erbin clearly, illuminated by the panel lights. Right hand on the control stick, Von Erbin's left hand removed a small, black box, the size of a cigarette pack, from the inside pocket of his jacket. Using his teeth he pulled out six-inches of chrome antennae, then he looked down one last time. He didn't see Joshua lying there when he pressed the button.

The force of the C-4 exploding under the craft drove the helicopter another hundred feet in the air before it, too, exploded. Joshua was slammed off the pad and onto the deck below. Her eardrums were blown out by the concussion; blood poured from her nose and ears.

Two thousand pounds of the dead helicopter dropped onto the landing pad. A hundred gallon umbrella of burning fuel draped over the entire aft end of the boat, port to starboard. Hundred dollar bills fluttered everywhere. Teak began burning almost immediately. Brass fittings turned white hot before melting.

Joshua staggered forward, trying without success to move faster than the flames.

*   *   *

In the salon, Jake succeeded in freeing himself and Scanlon. He leaped across the room to Adrian and frantically pulled at the tape binding her hands and feet.

At the same time, Scanlon clawed the last of the tape from Davida's wrists, then fell to the carpet.

Joshua spilled in through the doorway. Her hair and black jump suit were in flames; every inch of skin on her exposed arms and face was melting from her body.

Jake moved to the bar where Joshua had left her pistol, then held it over the killer where she now lay. Her eyes pleaded with him.

Jake hesitated. Davida snatched the gun from him. She shot until the light in Joshua's eyes went out.

Jake ran back to Adrian. "It's okay, baby . . . I'm here . . . it's going to be okay . . . I'm here . . ."

Davida's shouts slapped at them.

"Get out! Get out!" Davida screamed and grabbed Adrian by the arm and shoved her toward the door.

Jake lifted Arthur to his feet, pulling him toward safety. His face was bloody.

At the railing, Davida took hold of Arthur and they leapt into the water.

Jake followed. "Davida," Jake cried out, as he struggled to stay afloat. "I'll try to find the Zodiac."

Jake swam aft, to where the small boat had been tied to the platform. It was nowhere in sight. He thrashed in circles; the Zodiac was either gone or outside the perimeter of light coming from the burning boat. The heat was intense, the water almost boiling.

Jake swam away from the heat into the dark, groping in the blackness for the Zodiac.

A blinding flash. The main fuel tanks exploded and within minutes there was nothing left of Von Erbin's ship except for a mass of debris floating in the water.

Jake clung to a piece of wood and shouted, frantically, for his daughter.

She was next to him and Davida was next to Adrian.

"I'm okay, daddy." She reached out and touched her father's face.

"Arthur?" Jake asked.

Davida just shook her head. "After we hit the water, I lost him."

The three of them clung onto each other, rafted together, bobbing up and down with the gentle motion of the sea. Davida leaned her head on Jake's shoulder and he kissed the top of her head.

"We've got to find the Zodiac," Jake said.

Then Adrian spotted it. Jake swam hard to catch it. He clutched at the mooring rope and swam the craft back toward them.

Minutes later—soaked and exhausted—they sprawled safely in the bottom of the Zodiac, about a hundred yards off the port side of the burning debris.

They shouted out for Arthur, over and over, until their voices gave out. It was futile. Arthur Scanlon was gone.

The motor wouldn't start but, Jake found wooden oars strapped onto the bottom of the Zodiac—little more than oversized ping-pong paddles, but they worked just fine.

EPILOGUE

It took almost a week before the Nice authorities were finally ordered to turn the case over to Interpol and release the prisoners.

After all, hadn't a boat and helicopter been blown up? Weren't several people dead? The story told by Jake, Davida and Adrian was bizarre, bordering on fantastical.

With their help, five murders were solved. In Florida the files were closed on the deaths of Moe Green, a stamp dealer named Kunze, and a bartender named Harry Lipshultz; in New York it was a lawyer named Carson; and in London, a "John Doe" found dead in the Royal Coachman Hotel.

Then there was the assassin, whose personal history had been buried so deep and for so long, that Joshua herself would have had a hard time tracing her true identity.

As for the tall man with the bushy mustache, his identity rested at the bottom of the Mediterranean, along with an unknown number of crew who also went down with Von Erbin's yacht.

After Davida submitted her report to *Golem,* Von Erbin and Dengler's records were officially closed by a clerk seated at a computer in Tel Aviv who keyed a notice into each of their files. The men, it said, were . . . *no longer at large.*

NEW YORK, A YEAR AND A HALF LATER.

Adrian Green, shaken by her ordeal, had returned to New York with Jake. She spent several months with her father before she felt secure enough to return to London.

Arthur Scanlon's estate was in legal quagmire, with the ownership of Crane Industries being fought over by lawyers on two continents.

Davida left Nice knowing that Jake's immediate priority was Adrian, and returned to Israel.

She and Jake spoke every few days and wrote endless e-mails.

Once Adrian went back to London, they met for long weekends. Once in Venice. Once in San Francisco. And once in Athens.

It wasn't long before a decision was reached and Jake began making space in his apartment for Davida's things in anticipation of her move to New York.

*   *   *

Jake enjoyed a performance of *La Traviata* at Lincoln Center, then ducked into Café Fiorello for a late snack.

His cell phone rang.

"How was the opera, darling?" Davida asked, from Jerusalem.

"Not as enjoyable, without you. Why are you out of bed so early?"

"Not as enjoyable, without you."

Jake laughed. "By the way, I've cleared out lots of space for you. Hope it's enough room. I can't wait."

"Me, too, darling. Me, too."

Later Jake strolled the short distance to his apartment. It was almost eleven o'clock by the time he arrived.

Stacks of boxes were sitting outside his front door, packed with things he was tossing to make room for Davida, and intended to be put out for collection.

Every night around 11:30 P.M. there was a garbage pick-up.

Hell, he thought, *this is a good a time as any to get rid of this stuff.*

It took several trips to get the boxes down the elevator and out to the curb.

Later, in bed, Jake heard the whine and grind of a hydraulic crushing mechanism as the Sanitation truck made its pick-up.

This particular night three men worked the truck. One man drove while two others hefted the bags and boxes from the sidewalk, throwing them into the steel trough at the rear of the truck, where they were smashed, mashed, and jammed into the body of the truck.

Jake's boxes filled an empty trough, but when the lever was thrown . . . *nothing* happened.

The three men conferred for a few minutes, jiggled the controls, and finally agreed to return to the sanitation garage for maintenance and repair.

Some time later, on its way back to the garage, the truck stopped for a traffic light. To the right was a vacant lot and on the sidewalk, a group of five people warming themselves around a fifty-gallon drum filled with burning debris.

One of the five was the neighborhood beat cop, bundled

head to foot in blue wool, his hands extended toward the warmth of the fire.

Two prostitutes hopped from one stiletto-heeled foot to the other, trying to keep warm.

The two others were homeless men, fairly comfortable thanks to the bonfire.

The man seated on the passenger side of the sanitation truck's cab rolled down his window and shouted out to the group.

"Hey, you guys use some more fuel to burn?"

"*Bettcha ass!* We was about to toss in old Jimmy here pretty soon," the cop yelled back.

"Help yourself to whatever's in the back."

The group ran to the back of the truck, pulled the boxes out from the trough, and hauled them back to the fire.

The light changed, the truck pulled away. Shouts of "*thank you*" floated out on the frozen air but were lost in the noise of the truck's acceleration.

The first few boxes contained magazines and periodicals and burned well.

By two A.M. the cop had gone and the remaining men and women unpacked the last box. It was filled with an assortment of old files and papers, which they slowly fed into the fire.

A manila envelope addressed to someone named Alan Carson was thrown into the drum. It bent and blistered in the intense heat.

On the upper right corner of the envelope was a block of common U.S. postage stamps. Nine stamps in all. Three across and three down. The heat melted the glue and the block of stamps curled slowly away from the envelope's surface. As the stamps twisted toward the flames, a single stamp, tucked beneath, was revealed. It was a German stamp.

Curiously, the head pictured on the stamp was upside down.

READ A PREVIEW OF
THE AUGUST STRANGERS
Another suspenseful and gripping novel from
MIKE SLOSBERG

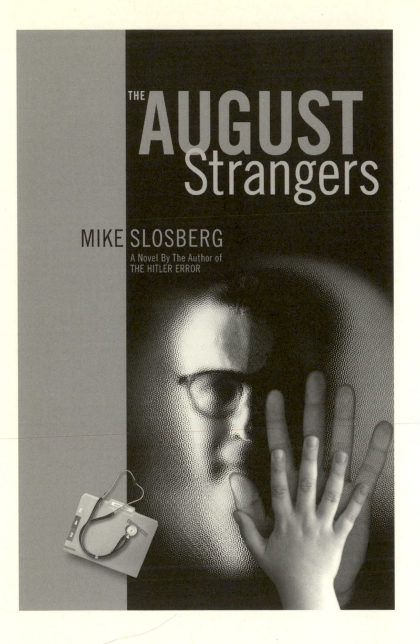

THE AUGUST Strangers

MIKE SLOSBERG

A Novel By The Author of
THE HITLER ERROR

"Mr. August, my name is Pomerantz, Dr. Seth Pomerantz," the slightly lisping voice said over the phone. "I wanted to discuss your son, David. Are you free?"

It was a pleasant voice. "I'm free. But who are you? What about David?"

"Let me assure you, Mr. August, everything is fine. You see, I run a large company that becomes deeply involved in complicated medical matters for . . . er, certain . . . " he hesitated and seemed to search his vocabulary for the right words, ". . . a certain stratum of the population."

"I'm not sure I follow."

"Oh my, my. I'm sorry, Mr. August, please let me apologize. I can never adequately explain my own company over the phone. I have long since stopped trying. Let it suffice to say," Pomerantz lisped, "that what we do will be of great interest to you and possibly be beneficial to your son, David.

"Would you do me a great service," he continued, "by meeting with one of my people? Then you can hear about the details of our service and . . ."

"Look, Doctor . . ."

"Pomerantz. Seth Pomerantz."

"Yes, well. I don't know what you have in mind, Dr. Pomerantz, but if this is some sort of insurance thing, I have an agent and all the insur . . ."

"Mr. August! Please! This is not insurance." Pomerantz's voice took on a much more serious and authoritative tone. "I promise you, this will be of vital interest to you. You have nothing to lose. Just name the time and place you'd like to meet and I'll arrange it."

Les Champs is one of the more popular East Side lunch restaurants in New York. I sat sipping vermouth, still puzzled by the call from Pomerantz but also curious and a slight bit apprehensive. I had told Mandy about the strange phone call, and she agreed that I should follow through with the meeting and see what it was all about.

I didn't even know whom I was supposed to meet or what he looked like. Well, Rodger at the door would keep an eye open and take care of that part of it.

"Your luncheon guest has arrived," Rodger, the owner, said as he stood over me.

I stood. "Thanks, Rodger." Then to the woman just behind me I said, "I'm Mike August."

Her tiny, gloved hand touched my arm as she sat down.

"Would you care for a drink?" I asked her.

"Sherry."

Rodger nodded and left.

"It's nice to meet you, Mr. August. You're much younger-looking than I'd expected. The busy life you executives lead tends to play havoc on the body. But then you jog, isn't that right?"

"Why, yes, I do, as a matter of fact. But excuse me, I don't know your name. . . ."

"How silly. I was so overwhelmed by the lovely restaurant that I simply forgot. Margaret Friday," she said.

If Seth Pomerantz was trying to sell anything he had certainly disarmed me by sending Margaret Friday. Who the hell could say no to a grandmother, for God's sake!

Margaret Friday was sixty-five years old if she was a month. Her hair was blue. She was wearing an expensive-looking, neatly cut tweed suit. Her cheerful face was tastefully made up and it was obvious that Miss Friday (no rings) was not trying to hide her age behind gaudy cosmetics.

"I don't mean to stare, Miss Friday, but I am not exactly used to dealing with salesmen who are, well, what I mean is . . ."

"You mean little old ladies?" Margaret Friday laughed. Her teeth were worn, but even and strong.

For the next few minutes we studied the menu and gave our orders to Rodger.

Miss Friday was a little old lady, but she certainly didn't eat like one. In fact, in the next forty-five minutes she put away enough food for a half-dozen little old ladies, and, between each forkful, she talked. And talked. It seems that Margaret was one of those people blessed with total recall and a lot of interesting things to remember.

During the linguine I heard about her early life growing up in Colorado. Over the chicken and broccoli it was the World War II years. It seems that Margaret was a nurse and also trilingual. These two facts, combined with a large portion of nerve, qualified her in 1943 to parachute behind the German lines and allow herself to be captured and interned, all in order to assess the medical conditions in the prison camps where American pilots were being held.

She was then secreted out of captivity and sent, via the French underground, back to England and her regular job with OSS.

By the time the table was cleared and the little silver pots of hot black coffee had been served, I was a total fan of Margaret Friday, age sixty-seven, and Seth Pomerantz's (literally) girl Friday.

"I'd like to compliment you on the choice of restaurant, the fine dishes you suggested, and the marvelous conversation."

"Margaret," I laughed, "I never got a word in edgewise. You are a fascinating woman, and I was captivated by your stories."

"Yes, I do have a habit of dominating a conversation," she said with a smile as she touched the tip of her right forefinger to her tongue and then to a crumb of pumpernickel that stood out on the otherwise immaculate tablecloth. "The wonderful talent you have as a conversationalist, Mr. August, is your ability to listen, and to learn. It's the mark of a good journalist. Did you ever think of being a member of the fourth estate?"

Her terminology was amusing, and I smiled as the back-and-forth movement of my head told her the answer.

"You're a perceptive and sensitive man," she continued, "and it is because of that, plus the problems you are now facing with your son, that your case was brought to the attention of Doctor Seth and our group."

"What exactly is your group, Miss Friday?"

"Let's say it fills a need. We have no name for our group, no official corporate offices, no stockholders. We just have an idea, and we provide a service, and we make a lot of money."

"That can't be all bad, Margaret."

"We make this money because we offer our unique services only to people who have a great deal of money, or who can get a great deal of money . . ."

I glanced at my watch. This thing was being strung out. I knew when I was being sold, and I could tell that Margaret was holding back, building a story. Frankly, I didn't have the time to do it that way.

"Look, Margaret. I don't know what you're selling. I was fascinated by Dr. Pomerantz's call, and frankly, anything even remotely connected to David grabs my interest. I love being in your company, but please do me a favor. Tell me what this is all about."

Margaret Friday looked at me over the rim of her coffee cup. Her expression, at first slightly puzzled, cleared into a broad smile. "Thank you. You've saved me from some very cumbersome and unnecessary dialogue. The details of our service are always awkward to explain. Even after all these years it is still difficult for me to find precisely the right words."

I leaned forward and covered her tiny, wrinkled hand with mine. "Please try."

"We would like to sell you a kidney for David."